THE HIDDEN MAN

A Q.C. DAVIS MYSTERY

LISA M. LILLY

1

———

I wasn't that late. It was only a few minutes after five. Yet the rolling chair behind the reception counter sat empty. One silver-gray trench coat hung on the coat rack next to it. Light shone through the glass block wall to my left but the conference room behind it was deserted. I paused for a second to admire the high-backed leather chairs around the polished wood table. So much nicer than the industrial looking furniture in the suite where I rent office space.

Open metal shelves housed reddish-brown legal case files at the far end of the space, and interior brick walls flanked a gunmetal gray staircase.

"Hello?" My low heels clanged on the metal steps.

My usual outfit for meeting a potential new client is a pantsuit or skirt suit. But this was a last-minute Friday evening meeting, which meant I was wearing my standard office uniform. Skinny, dark jeans and a fitted white T-shirt paired with the red pumps and charcoal blazer I kept in the office for just this type of emergency.

"Q.C.?" The woman's voice sounded tinny due to the open floor plan, but I recognized it.

I

"Maria?" I reached a wide landing and peered around a folding screen next to a concrete pillar. Behind it stood a desk and credenza, both dark wood and polished like the conference table below. Cardboard boxes stacked on an inner wall to one side.

Maria walked around the desk and gave me a quick hug. "Little Q.C. Davis. I barely recognized you all grown up. And you got pretty. So good to see you again."

Maria and I met when I was twelve and she played my mother in a storefront theatre production. I'd been going through an awkward phase where I was rail thin with dark hair springing out all around my face. Later I learned to wear it long and use the right products to pull the curls into loose waves.

Maria didn't look much different from what I remembered, though she must be in her fifties now. Her golden red hair still fell past her shoulders, her smooth, pale skin showed few fine lines, and her figure remained rounded on the edge of plump. She still wore tangerine-scented perfume.

"It's Quille now."

"Oh, right, sorry. Saw that on your website." Maria motioned me toward the padded visitor chair in front of her desk.

I dropped into it. "You said something about a lawsuit? And a crime? Not to rush you, but –"

"Right, right, you have another appointment. I appreciate your making time for me. For the firm."

My "appointment" was a Halloween party. Within a year of starting my own law practice I discovered I needed to schedule in personal time the same way I did court dates or client meetings. If I didn't, my life became nothing but work.

"How can I help?"

"Let's start with the lawyer part first. Another firm sued us over how to split attorney fees in class action cases we handled together."

"When was the suit filed?" I took out a legal pad and pen. In early meetings I like to write notes by hand instead of typing on a phone or tablet. Otherwise, some people think I'm multi-tasking and not paying attention to them.

"Two years ago. The senior partner was handling it. Kurt King. But, well, he died recently." Maria rubbed her hands over her forearms.

"I'm so sorry. Is that the crime you mentioned on the phone?"

After Maria called that morning, I'd done a quick internet search. King and Stillwell had two partners and two employees, Maria, who was the office manager and paralegal, and a receptionist. The website said nothing about Kurt King's death.

"Yes. It happened two weeks ago. He was handling the lawsuit himself – I know, I know, probably not the best idea. We need someone to step in and take over."

"I don't know much about class actions, but I can get up to speed quickly."

"I figured. With all the businesses you've represented." Maria straightened a stack of manila folders on her desk, aligning the edges. "But the crime, Kurt's death, it's the main reason we called." The wheels on her chair squeaked as she shifted position. "When Joe referred us to you, he said you've looked into crimes. Kurt was – he was murdered."

Joe and I have known each other since I was a kid acting in Chicago theatre productions. He's older than me and always looked out for me, even after we both left the profession. I was surprised he recommended me for this case, though, knowing murder was involved. While he helped me look into suspicious deaths in the past, it was only because they involved people I cared deeply about. And he made it clear that he worried about the risks I took doing it.

I let my notepad drop onto my lap. "How do you know Joe?"

"I don't. But he's been on the Goodman Theatre board for years with Tobias – that's Kurt's son."

"Aren't the police investigating the death?"

Maria nodded. "They are. Of course they are. But Tobias says there are circumstances – reasons – the police might not be able to do a good enough job."

"What reasons?"

"I don't know exactly. But Joe thought you could help."

"I'm not a licensed private investigator," I said.

"Joe said that. But he spoke so highly of you. And I remember you as a kid. So serious and hardworking, doing your homework in between scenes. Learning lines right away. I'm guessing that's paid off well in life."

I tucked my hair behind one ear. "The thing is, the murders I've looked into before were for people close to me. But it's not something I do for pay. I feel for Tobias, but I can't afford any more unpaid work this year."

Especially because I was thinking of looking into a murder in my family's past. Though that was still up for debate.

Maria rested her elbows on the desk and leaned forward. "But you could, couldn't you? Investigate for pay?"

"In theory. But I can't promise results. And I don't know forensics. What I do is talk to people, listen, try to put things together."

She clasped her hands together. "But that's exactly what we need. We'd pay your same law firm rate, if Tobias decides to go with you."

"A licensed private investigator would be cheaper."

I'd looked into that recently and discovered "real" private detectives earned about a third as much as my hourly rate. My license to practice law already allowed me to investigate, so I hadn't seen a reason to seek a P.I. license as well.

"But the referral is key. And even then, well, Tobias wants to meet you himself. Feel sure he can trust you to be discreet."

"About what?"

"Apparently Kurt held some unusual views."

"Unusual how?"

Maria frowned, the fine lines on her forehead creasing. "Tobias wouldn't tell me. But nothing criminal, supposedly. Will you meet with Tobias? He would've been here now but he has his own law practice and today was booked for him."

"How was Kurt killed?"

"Shot. Two weeks ago. In his home."

"Is anyone thinking this attorney fee lawsuit relates to the murder?"

"There's a lot of money at stake. But I don't see how it helps the other side to get rid of Kurt. He makes – made – a lot in his practice, but he was more focused on the crusade and less on the money. If his partner hadn't kept pushing him, he probably would've agreed to the other side's demands."

"You're assuming I'll be tougher."

She smiled for a second, but it quickly faded. "Anyone would be when it comes to looking out for Kurt's bottom line. For his clients, that's another story."

I opened the calendar app on my phone. "I'm pretty open early next week."

"How about tonight?" she said.

2

————

"WHAT WERE YOU THINKING?" My friend Lauren's tiara slipped as she arranged French pastries on a tray. "You and Ty have been seriously busy lately and you set up a client meeting for his party?"

My boyfriend Ty owns a small boat he keeps in the harbor at River City, an apartment complex along the Chicago River's south branch. Nearly a year ago I faced off with a murderer there, which didn't leave me with good feelings about the place. But it's the only harbor in the Chicago area that uses a bubbler so that the boats can stay in the harbor all winter. So I'd learned to take a deep breath and ignore the uneasy way I felt with the gray concrete complex looming over me.

Tonight, though, everything looked cheerful. The boats sparkled with orange, yellow, and white lights and adults and kids in costumes drifted from one boat to another, soda or cocktails in hand. Ty was growing tired of how much work and cost boat owning required, and he planned to sell soon. This was likely my one and only Halloween party in the harbor, at least where Ty was one of the hosts.

"He'll be mixing business and fun, too. He's four boats down right now." I gestured in the direction of one of the yachts.

Ty's a commercial real estate developer. Meeting new people is basically part of his job, as is entertaining. In some ways, any social event, unless it's only a few close friends or family, counts as business for him.

"Well, I'll be on the lookout for opportunity, too," Lauren said. She and I have been close since we met in law school, which she left to become a residential real estate agent. We live in the same condo building. "But that's not the same as setting up a meeting for it."

Lauren smoothed the front of her sheath-like red dress. She was meant to be the Queen of Hearts, thus the tiara. With her red dress, white-blond hair, and pale skin, she looked more suited to Valentine's Day than Halloween, though. As Queen of Clubs, I wore a black dress and used jeweled combs to tame my wavy black hair. I popped a tartlet in my mouth then pulled on elbow length black gloves.

"Tobias wants to get to know me," I said. "There might be a murder investigation along with the lawsuit."

Lauren's eyes lit up. She loves helping me sort through criminal investigations, and her tendency to make snap judgments about people balances my step-by-step approach. "Seriously? They want to hire you for that, too?"

"Maybe," I said. "But I'm not sure they should. It's not like I'm a professional investigator."

"But you're totally worth it."

"It feels wrong." The wind shifted, sending damp, chilly October air across the deck. I put my black leather jacket on but left it unzipped. "It's not like I can guarantee results."

"Did these people ask for guaranteed results?"

I spotted a woman who looked like Maria rounding the building to the pier, trailed by another person.

"No," I said.

"Then do it. You like investigating. And you can't keep doing it for free."

"There's also the risk. Did you know Joe recommended me?"

"Really? He never mentioned it." Lauren and Joe had only been seeing each other since summer, and I was still getting used to the idea of them as a couple. "Maybe he figures you're safer now with your training. Didn't you move on to boxing?"

In mid-summer I started working with a retired police instructor. At first, he mainly taught me how to spot and avoid conflict and pushed me to hone my reflexes and get in better shape. But we'd graduated to some self-defense.

"It's not what you think. I'm punching a bag that hangs in front of me. It can't hit back. Nothing like fighting a human."

"Hey there." Maria had reached the boat. She wore the same clothes as when I'd met her, dark jeans and a sweater, and carried her silver trench coat over her arm. "Sorry, no time for costumes."

I've been practicing law long enough to know there's no one way lawyers look, but my first impression of the man who boarded after Maria was that he didn't spend much time in courtrooms. His mustache needed trimming, his sandy brown hair grazed a wilted collar, and his shoulders rounded. When he shook my hand, he looked at the deck, though he met my eyes when I told him how sorry I was about his father.

We talked about how warm it was for late October — weather is always good for small talk in Chicago — I got him a glass of wine and grabbed a seltzer with lime for myself. Alcohol hits me pretty fast, and I wanted a clear head.

For about half an hour we wandered from boat to boat, crossing paths with Ty and later with Joe. Joe and Tobias fell into talking about the Goodman Theatre. Lauren rolled her eyes and went in search of anyone who might be looking to buy or sell a condo.

I learned that Tobias had two children, both under five,

and had been a chemist in Colorado for several years before deciding to go on to law school. He attended a part-time program at the University of Denver. Now he worked as a patent lawyer, preparing and filing chemical patents for clients.

When Ty started telling Joe about a potential new client, Tobias asked me if there was somewhere quieter to talk. I led him out of the harbor and up an outdoor stairway to a deck overlooking River City's main entrance. Lights strung out above the river, casting colorful reflections on the water. Tour boats filled with tourists dancing and waving glided by.

Tobias stood next to me holding his second plastic cup of wine, his free arm resting on the railing. His first question caught me by surprise.

"Are you religious, Quille?"

A general answer seemed best. "My Gram took me to church as a kid. But I haven't attended in a while."

"But how do you feel about people with strong beliefs?" The complex's floodlights washed out his skin, making his face paler than I guessed it looked in normal light.

"Religious beliefs?"

"Any beliefs."

Maybe his father belonged to an unconventional religion, but I didn't see why he'd hide it. Chicago skews Roman Catholic, more so than the rest of the country, but it's home to people who belong to all types of religions.

"I don't mind hearing about what a person believes. It can be fascinating. But I don't like anyone pushing me to think just like they do. Or telling me I'm wrong or my life will fall apart if I don't believe the same way."

I was thinking of a self-improvement company I briefly joined as part of an investigation for a friend. Its members made sales pitches in almost any situation. I hoped Tobias wasn't about to do something similar.

To my relief, though, he said, "I feel the same way. It caused problems with my dad."

"I'm sorry to hear that." I relaxed my grip on my cup of seltzer.

"Joe told me you've had some issues with your parents." Tobias's cheeks reddened and he stared at his feet. "He mentioned your sister who was killed. I hope that's all right. It's part of why I feel like I can trust you."

"I – it's not a secret." Q.C. – the original Q.C. Davis for whom I'd been named – was kidnapped and killed before I was born. "These unusual beliefs Maria mentioned – you don't need to tell me about them now if you don't want to. But if you hire me to look into this crime, not knowing all the facts makes it less likely I'll figure anything out."

Tobias studied the orange, green, and yellow lights strung along all the boats in the marina. "Dad and I didn't see eye to eye on much, but I want his reputation protected. Also, from what I picked up from my dad, the lawyers in class actions spend a lot of time fighting over who the court will let manage the case for the class. The other side uses anything and everything to show the lawyer's not a good choice."

"Do your dad's beliefs matter now that he's gone?"

"They might. Depending how the other side spins it."

The wind blew my long hair into my eyes. It also brought the faint smell of the river, a mix of fish, damp foliage, and minerals. "And you haven't told the police about your dad?"

"I told them what I felt safe saying. But I want someone I can trust who can really delve into it."

"It's hard for me to say if I'm that person when I don't know what the issue is."

"I know that. Here's what I propose," Tobias said. "The firm will hire you for the fee lawsuit. Send Maria a contract tomorrow. For the murder, I'll pay you to start looking into it. After I get to know you, see how you work, I'll decide. Either tell you everything and you can keep investigating or ask you to drop it and just handle the lawsuit."

"As long as you understand I'm deciding, too. I could choose not to keep investigating even if you ask me to go ahead."

One of the worst things in law is a client who won't tell you what you need to know to do a good job and then blames you for the result. I had a pretty good idea it would be the same with a murder investigation.

"Of course," Tobias said.

"Then I've got a lot of questions for you."

3

———————

"WHAT HAVE the police done so far?" I said. "Any suspects?"

We sat side-by-side on concrete steps leading down into River City's outdoor park. The park had closed for the night, and our view of Wells Street offered none of the harbor's beauty. But floodlights bathed the stairs. I'd told Tobias I wanted to sit for a while, but more than that, I'd wanted somewhere better lit so I could see his reactions.

"If there are, they haven't told me. They interviewed me. Maria. Dad's partner and other employees. Also my dad's girlfriend. And gathered evidence at the scene. He was killed in the coach house behind his home."

"Did they find anything useful?"

Tobias stared at the running path around the park as he spoke. "A detective warned me ahead of time it might be fruitless. Dad had a big party the night before. Which means fingerprints, fibers, and I guess DNA all over. And whoever did it took the gun with them. A bottle of wine sat on Dad's desk with a bottle opener, and there were two glasses out, but they were clean. The bottle wasn't opened."

"Do you know if he invited anyone to stop by that night?"

"No idea. But the police, from what I understand, think the killer was whoever Dad invited over for a glass of wine. Or at least that Dad wasn't unhappy to get a surprise visit from the killer."

That might be. But he also could have set out the wine for later and been surprised by the killer. I asked about signs of a break in or theft.

"No broken windows or locks. I didn't notice anything missing. And no one saw anyone entering or leaving." Tobias scratched the back of his head. "But I'm sure his neighbors had things to do other than watch his house on a Friday night."

"Security cameras?"

"Dad didn't have them. He had an alarm system, but it wasn't triggered. He forgot to put it on a lot of the time, though, so that doesn't mean much."

"Anyone upset at your dad for anything?"

Two motorcycles badly in need of mufflers roared around a corner below. One of the downsides of a warmer night. Tobias waited until the sound faded to answer.

"Isabel – that's Dr. Isabel Verde, my dad's girlfriend. She's a psychologist. She was supposed to stay the weekend. But I overheard her saying she needed to leave in the morning, she decided to go to the conference after all. When Dad asked why, she said 'You know why.'"

My legal pad was in my shoulder bag, which was locked in the cabin of Ty's boat. I noted Dr. Isabel Verde's name in my phone. "That could just mean she had a professional reason she already told him about."

"Could, yeah." Tobias picked up a twig that lay on the stair between us and rolled it between his thumb and finger. "But she straightened her back and poked her finger at him when she said it. And there was steel in her voice."

His shoulders sagged. I glanced at the time. It was after ten, and Maria had told me he usually started work at seven.

"That's enough to get me started," I said. "I assume I can get more information from Maria tomorrow?"

"And from Dad's partner. You should meet with him as soon as you can. About the fee lawsuit, too. I'll let him know."

"Great."

We stood. Tobias turned toward me. "One last thing – don't share what you learn with anyone but me."

"For the murder, you mean? Your dad's partner will need to know about the attorney fee dispute lawsuit. The firm's the client for that, not you."

"Right, yes." Tobias waved his hand. "But the murder, you can tell people you're looking into it. But report back only to me."

———

I'M NOT much of a late-night person, one of many reasons theatre wouldn't have been a great career choice for me. Fortunately, Ty's pretty flexible about that, so we left soon after Tobias did though the party raged on around us.

Ty linked his hand with mine as we waited for the light to change on Wells Street. His only attempt at a costume had been to unbutton an extra button on his collared shirt, claiming he was a commercial real estate developer on vacation. Though some developers dressed down, as the only Black man at his firm he felt he needed to appear more businesslike than anyone else.

"You couldn't just handle the lawsuit?" he said.

"I'm guessing I could. But the murder interests me. And they want to pay me to investigate."

"Fascinates you is more like it."

I squeezed his hand. "I'll be careful."

The Walk sign blinked on. We waited for a silver SUV that blew through the red light, then crossed the street.

"What happened last time shows it's not enough to be careful," Ty said. "Even if it was my fault."

Ty had agreed to back me up in a tricky situation in my last investigation but hadn't been able to come through.

We veered around sawhorses blocking an unfinished street excavation. "That was not your fault," I said.

"Yeah, it was. And I know this is kind of becoming your thing. But it's not like this is someone you love asking you to do this. And, by the way, if you go ahead with the investigation your parents want, that's two murders you're looking into. Double the risk."

"I don't think that one's dangerous anymore. It's over thirty-five years old."

"I can't believe I'm saying this, but anything can be dangerous."

"Is this my favorite eternal optimist talking?" I said. "I don't believe it."

He grinned. "I can be a realist now and then. Dessert?"

Ty waved toward Sociale, a neighborhood tapas restaurant across the street. It takes up the whole southwest corner of Clark and Polk. Rectangular firepits out front made it perfect for outdoor eating well into autumn, and despite all the food at the party I'd eaten almost nothing.

"Any leads at the party?" I asked once we'd been seated.

"For me? No. But I heard Lauren telling Maria about one-bedroom condos with garage parking."

We ordered wine and a plate of chocolate hazelnut donuts with vanilla gelato on the side. Ty ate a few bites and said the rest was for me. He'd been grazing all evening.

Then he reached around the glassed-enclosed flames to take my hand. "About this new investigation. I get it. I do. Your parents, your whole family, you've been in that limbo forever. It makes you want to help other people who might get stuck there. But you've got a lot on your plate. Can't your sister's death be your project?"

"And don't help anyone else?"

"I'm not saying don't ever. But isn't one murder at a time enough?"

I licked the last of the gelato off my spoon. "My legal clients matter to me. But these investigations – that's where I feel like I made a real difference in people's lives. And I figured out how to manage it time-wise. I'll stop doing taxes."

When I started my own practice, I included filing taxes for actor friends along with handling lawsuits for businesses. But the tax filings took a lot of time and paid very little.

"I thought you like staying in touch with your theatre friends. Also, taxes, very safe thing to handle."

"I can stay in touch by seeing more of their plays. Or getting together for fun. Which I'll have more time for. Including with you."

Ty smiled. "I'll never say No to that. But it's not just the time. I don't want to lose you if you cross paths with a killer. You might have noticed I've gotten pretty fond of you."

A horn blared from across the street for no reason I could see. Personally, I think about a third of the drivers in Chicago like to honk for the sheer joy of annoying others.

"I noticed. But you'll still back me up?"

Tobias had said I couldn't report to anyone but him about my investigation, and I wouldn't, but I still wanted Ty by my side. I learned early on that poking into the facts surrounding a murder puts you in danger and going it alone is a bad idea. If I didn't have friends to help, I doubted I'd keep investigating crimes.

"I will," he said. "And next time I'll be there."

"How about we aim for no next time? Hope that I'll figure it all out without confronting any killers?"

"You know, if you don't investigate murders in the first place
– "

I scooted my chair around and kissed him. His lips tasted of
the cinnamon from the donuts. "You really want to start this
whole conversation over?"

He laughed. "When you put it that way? No. Let's get the
check."

———

THE NEXT DAY I was only able to fit in a short phone call with
Maria to get more background. But I set a time to meet Monday
morning at 8 a.m. with Kurt's partner, Bryan Stillwell.

My instructor had recently insisted I work out twice a week
in a gym, but walking remained my daily exercise. I walked the
ten blocks to King and Stillwell in twenty minutes.

Bryan's office was directly above the landing where Maria had
her desk. He half-sat, half-reclined in his leather office chair, one
leg bent, his ankle resting on his opposite knee, reading something
on his phone. His collared shirt and dress pants looked tailored,
and his loafers had none of the scuffs or dimples that come from
striding through gravel and dust that the ever-present construction
sites in Chicago spread throughout the city. He must drive to work
and park in the garage on the lower floor of the building next door.

Bryan barely looked up when I introduced myself. I started
to offer condolences, but he interrupted me.

"Hope we can make this quick. Busy day." He waved toward
his visitor chair.

I placed my Chai tea latte on a coaster on the edge of his
polished wood desk and sat. "Lots to do with taking over Kurt's
cases?"

"You'd think. But Kurt's son – you met Tobias, right? He's
dragging his feet. Talking about bringing in an associate." Bryan

smirked. "As if some third-year lawyer will be a big help." He grabbed a file folder from the corner of his desk. A large Rolex watch on his wrist caught the light.

"Don't you need someone?" I said. "You can't handle all Kurt's matters yourself."

He flipped open the folder and glanced over the pages inside. "We don't need someone right away. The courts understand when something like this happens you need extra time."

"Were you and Kurt close?"

"Worked together for nine years. Since I got out of law school." His computer beeped and he glanced at the monitor and started typing. "Sorry, things are hectic."

His focus on the business issues might be a way of avoiding his feelings of grief, or he was someone who simply took a get-on-with-things approach. Or he didn't feel grief.

"So you were close with Kurt or you weren't?" I said.

"What difference does it make?"

"I'm not sure you know this, but Tobias asked me to look into the murder as well as handle the attorney fee lawsuit."

"He mentioned it." He pushed the keyboard aside and looked at me. One corner of his mouth turned up again. "I suppose your background as a former child actress qualifies you as a detective?"

"I've handled investigations before," I said. "I can give you my background, but being so busy I'm not sure it's worth taking the time."

He shrugged. "It's Tobias's dime. What I don't get is why he brought in someone from outside to handle the lawsuit."

It's rarely a good idea for lawyers to represent themselves. But it seemed Bryan didn't agree with the old adage about those who do it having fools for clients.

"Why do you think he did?" I said.

"Probably afraid I'll be like Kurt and just want to roll over, give the other side what they want."

"The case has been going on two years, though. Doesn't sound like Kurt caving in to the other side."

"Only because I kept pushing him."

The sounds of voices and footsteps drifted into the office. I guessed Maria and the firm's receptionist had arrived.

"Did you and he disagree a lot?"

"All the time," Bryan said. "That's part of why he made me a partner. He wanted a different view on things."

"Maria told me you became a partner two years ago. And that you thought it should have been sooner."

Based on the graduation dates in his website bio, Bryan was about thirty-three, so a little younger than me but he'd been practicing longer. He'd gone to law school right after college, while I worked for a couple years at an accounting firm first.

At large firms, lawyers sometimes become partners after six or seven years. But at a lot of small firms it takes a decade or so. Or it never happens because the lead attorney doesn't want partners. I wasn't sure I ever did.

"It should've," he said. "Kurt put off deciding until I threatened to leave."

"Why did he put it off?"

Bryan tapped his pen on the desk. "Tunnel vision. Focused only on his cases, not interested in running the firm."

"So who ran it?"

"Oh, Kurt did. He just wasn't that interested in that part of law. After my fifth or sixth year he started handing things off to me."

Since Bryan had dodged questions about how close he and Kurt were or weren't, I decided to try to get there another way. I asked how much he worked with Kurt on the fee lawsuit.

"Hardly at all. He said it wouldn't be helpful since I wasn't on the class actions it includes. Which is why a lot of them got nowhere."

Obviously Bryan didn't hesitate to sing his own praises. I

didn't know enough about him yet to guess if his view of himself was inflated.

"The class actions you're talking about are the ones the lawsuit calls the food cases?" I said.

Maria had created a secure website with literally thousands of pages in digital form to read. On the upside, I was getting paid by the hour to do it. On the downside, it was far from light reading so it'd be quite a while before I got through them.

"Right. Kurt handled almost all of those personally. Which is why it's insane for E. Drake Draper to claim he's entitled to half the attorney fees. He had less to do with those cases than I did."

Draper's firm often worked with Kurt's on class actions, and his lawsuit claimed he should get half the attorney fees earned in every class action Kurt's firm handled. Regarding the food cases, Kurt's firm had disagreed.

"Does Draper go by E. Drake? Not just Drake?" I said. When I met him, I wanted to call him by the name he preferred.

"Yeah, E. Drake. Probably thinks it makes him sound like he went to Harvard or comes from a good family."

Or maybe his parents called him that. I'd been Q.C. until college when I started going by Quille.

"And that's not so?" I said.

"His dad made his fortune running casinos in Vegas." Bryan snorted. "E. Drake paid his way through law school playing poker."

I found that last part impressive, but it sounded like Bryan would be more apt to admire someone lucky enough to be born to a family that could pay the tuition for him.

"It looks like Draper was involved in the earlier cases, the ones about French Fries."

Bryan shook his head. "His name's on the pleadings. But Kurt told me he didn't do the work."

"Kurt told you? You don't know firsthand?"

"Those cases started before I was at the firm, and Kurt finished them out himself."

In those cases, vegetarians and vegans sued fast food restaurants that didn't tell customers their fries were made on the same grill as the hamburgers or that they used beef stock to flavor the fries. They also didn't advertise the fries as vegetarian or vegan, and the defense lawyer in me thought that maybe the customers should have asked if it mattered that much. Though I supposed it wasn't unreasonable to assume that a french fry didn't have meat in it.

"And the later cases? About the coffee bars and ice cream makers? Was Draper involved?"

In those cases, plaintiffs sued because the products labeled vanilla flavored weren't made with actual vanilla beans.

"I came up with the idea of challenging artificial flavoring that gets called vanilla when there's no vanilla in it."

"And E. Drake Draper?"

"I guess he came up with the slogan about how vanilla is a bean. A plant. Not a flavor."

"You guess or he did?"

"He did."

"Doesn't that mean he should get some of the fees?"

Bryan's smartphone vibrated. He glanced at it, then turned it face down on the desk. "Now you sound like Kurt. Anyone can tweak someone else's idea. But Draper –'E. Drake' – didn't have the inspiration or do the hard work."

"If it was your idea to start with, why weren't you working on the cases?"

"Got busy with other things, and Kurt really liked those cases for some reason."

"And now will you take them over?"

"I'm the only one here so, yeah, for now I guess." Bryan folded his arms over his chest and frowned. "Until Tobias finds some class action whiz to step in."

"Are you worried he'll hire someone with more experience than you? Or less?"

"Either is bad. Less and it creates more work because I have to train someone. More and he might insist on running the cases and limiting my role."

"So purely on a professional level how does Kurt's death affect you?"

"Makes it harder. Obviously."

"And personally? Did the police suggest you might have a motive?"

"What? No. No motive."

"What about an alibi?"

He huffed. "Really? You insist on playing detective? Fine, my alibi sucks. I live in River North so I could've got to Kurt's house in Lincoln Park in twenty minutes or less. I didn't. But I could have. And I was home that Friday night reading a Stephen King novel."

"No one with you?"

"No people, no pets. Don't own so much as a goldfish." He glared across the desk as if challenging me to judge him.

"Neither do I," I said. "Any phone calls to a home landline that could show you were there?"

"Nothing. My bad. Didn't know I'd need an alibi."

"Were you at Kurt's party the night before?"

"For an hour or two. It was a cocktail party for Tobias's forti-eth. I had to go."

"Otherwise you wouldn't have?"

He smirked again. "Not big on firm social events. I work enough. My free time should be my time."

Part of me agreed. It narrows your life to create a social life only around your work. I had definitely felt that way when I'd worked at a large law firm where I averaged fifty-five hours or more a week. But once I started my own practice, I enjoyed getting to know other lawyers, and a lot of them had helped me sort out what I needed to do to be successful. Also, liking your coworkers usually makes work more fun.

"Did you hear anyone argue with Kurt that night?"

Bryan said he hadn't. He also had no idea who might be angry at Kurt or want to kill him.

"The lawyers on the other side of his cases don't love him," Bryan said. "But they don't – they didn't – hate him. If anything, he was too nice to them. Anyone asked for more time, he agreed. Got pissed at me once for saying No to a guy who'd had two extensions already."

Despite being a big city, the Chicago legal community feels fairly small. Which means you'll run into the same lawyers more than once. If you refuse to give someone extra time to get ready for a hearing or write a brief, word gets around and it's less likely anyone will extend that courtesy when you need it. I knew lawyers who didn't care, but I never noticed them winning more trials or appeals than the rest of us. Though they did make practicing law more stressful for everyone.

"What about Draper? This lawsuit is a lot like a partnership dispute, which can get pretty ugly." In a lot of my cases two or three partners, often in a family business, sue one another. It's great for my bottom line but makes me wonder why anyone related by blood wants to work together. Ever.

"I don't think it did. Get ugly. Kurt felt like Draper was trying to get more than he should on the food cases and he told him to file a lawsuit when they couldn't work it out. But they still worked together on all our other class actions."

"Why? What did Kurt think Draper brought to the table?"

Bryan spread his hands. "You got me. Yeah, I guess Draper's the one who got Kurt into class actions back in the day. Kurt represented individual consumers before that. Challenging mistakes in loan papers when someone got foreclosed on, suing if someone got sick from a restaurant. That kind of thing.

Draper figured out they could make a lot more money and change things more if they did class actions instead."

I asked Bryan a few more questions about the lawsuit and then about the party. He told me Kurt's ex-wife hadn't been there and that he'd met her only twice. Maria had told me the ex-wife remarried, but Kurt never did. I asked about Dr. Isabel Verde, the psychologist Kurt was involved with.

"Saw her at Tobias's fortieth," he said. "And every year at the firm's holiday party."

"What's your impression of her?"

"Little odd. Uses hypnosis in her practice."

"I'm not sure that's so odd," I said, but I made a note of it on my legal pad. Maybe it related to Tobias's comments about his dad's unusual beliefs.

"It is if you're using it to get at so-called repressed memories," Bryan said. "There's a reason the courts don't allow them into evidence anymore."

I vaguely remembered that from law school. "Did she and Kurt seem to be getting along at the party?"

"Sure."

His nonchalant tone suggested to me he hadn't noticed one way or another.

Before I left, Bryan offered to join me when I met E. Drake Draper, who was representing his own firm, about the fee lawsuit. I politely declined. Most attorneys feel freer to tell you what they think about the case when no clients are listening. I also wanted Draper's impression of Kurt.

And of Bryan. Though he'd worked with Kurt for eight years, nothing in his manner or words suggested sadness or grief over his partner's death. Still, a murder is so shocking it might take a long time to sink in.

Part of him might still be expecting his partner to walk through the door.

The walkway outside Bryan's office overlooked the staircase

and the first floor. An iron railing that felt cool to the touch bordered it. I ran my hand along it as I headed for Kurt's office. I had nearly an hour to kill before my 10 a.m. call with Dr. Isabel Verde, the person who seemed to have the closest personal relationship with Kurt.

If the police took their usual approach, she was also the main suspect.

4

———

I'D ASKED if I could use Kurt's office this morning partly because I share an office with a criminal defense attorney. She's out most days at one courthouse or another. But today she planned to be in returning phone calls, which meant Kurt's office would be far quieter.

I also wanted to get a feel for Kurt's professional life. His office smelled of paper and dust. His plain wood Shaker-style furniture featured what looked like decades of nicks and scratches. Files, legal pads, and printed pages were stacked all over the floor and on a rectangular table against the back wall. His desk, though, was clear. Not a pen, sticky note, or stray sheet of paper to be found. His computer's heavy, thick monitor and clunky keyboard sat on the right front corner.

The bookcase behind the desk held legal reference books, more file folders, and a half dozen painted plastic models of authentic-looking rockets and futuristic space ships. A silver-framed photo showed a recent picture of him with Tobias. Kurt was a heavier, older version of Tobias, with wavy grayish-white hair and bushier eyebrows. His long-sleeved polo shirt looked clean but wrinkled as did his khaki pants.

In one other photo Kurt stood behind a woman, his arms around her. She was laughing, her head tilted back a bit to look at him. The lines around her eyes made me guess her in her early sixties at least. Close to Kurt's age. Her skin's shade was similar to mine but with a warmer tone I liked much better than my olive complexion, which can tend toward sallow in the winter. Her hair was a brilliant white.

The photo matched the head shot on Isabel Verde's online biography other than that the professional photo showed dark hair streaked with white. She'd earned a B.A. at Yale and Ph.D at Columbia University, then worked at the National Institute of Mental Health. Her private practice and academic papers focused on addiction and suicide. She was a full professor at the University of Chicago.

I reviewed the questions I'd put together the evening before to ask Dr. Verde, then emailed an attorney at my old firm who defended a lot of class actions. I asked if I could buy her lunch or dinner and pick her brain about her practice.

Though old, Kurt's computer allowed me to sign into the website with the lawsuit documents. I found the phone number of the plaintiff in what looked like the most important food case. Her voicemail picked up, and I explained that I was handling a related case for the firm following Kurt's death and hoped to talk with her about Kurt and the class actions. Tobias had suggested that might be a quick way to get familiar with the ins and outs of the food cases.

Dr. Verde called at exactly 10 a.m.

"I'm sorry for your loss," I said. "I understand you were seeing Kurt for a long time."

"Over twenty years." Her voice was pitched low and she spoke quickly. "I still can't take it in. My phone beeps and I grab it, thinking it's him texting me. I had to start leaving it on silent all the time because I can't stand that moment where I forget for a second he's gone and then it hits me all over again."

"This may be the last thing you want to talk about. But Tobias told you I'm looking into the circumstances of Kurt's death?"

She sighed. "He did. And I'll answer your questions, but I wish he'd listened to my advice."

"What advice was that?"

"That it makes no sense bringing in someone to look into a murder the police are already investigating."

"Is there a particular reason you think that?"

"Nothing against you personally. I'm sure you're very competent. But what if you inadvertently confuse things or complicate the investigation? Tell the killer something the police don't want them to know? Also, Tobias is opening Kurt's entire personal life and possibly his confidences to another stranger."

Another person concerned about Kurt's secrets.

"Those are important concerns," I said. "And I'll keep them in mind. But sometimes there are good reasons people want someone on their side. Someone who's not police but can work with them."

"You're working with the police?"

"Not now as to Kurt. But I have worked on investigations with police in the past."

Saying that was a bit of a stretch, but not by too much. This past summer a Chicago Detective Sergeant, whom I first met when he investigated my then-boyfriend's death, had gone beyond tolerating my help to asking for it.

"What can you do that the police can't?" Dr. Verde said.

"The police have multiple crimes to investigate. I only have this one. Also, they pass cases, including homicides, from one detective to another as shifts change. I follow one crime all the way through. And some people don't trust police and won't tell them things, or they get nervous and clam up. But they might talk to me."

"Well, I did talk to the police. But I told Tobias I would talk to you, too, so ask away."

Restless from sitting so long, I threaded a path through stacks of paper and boxes to the window. The office looked down on the Greyhound bus station, which probably kept the rent low.

"Any idea why someone would want to kill Kurt?"

"Kurt was scatterbrained." Her voice grew softer. "The absent-minded professor type."

Seeing his office, that didn't surprise me. "And you think that relates to his murder?"

"No, the opposite. I can't imagine anyone killing him. Outside of his law practice, I can't see him being at odds with anyone."

"Anyone he was angry at?"

"Angry? Large corporations, I suppose. He thought they were always scamming and hiding things. But I can't think of any person he said that about."

"How was his relationship with his ex-wife?"

From the criminal defense attorney I share an office with I know most murders that don't involve a criminal activity like drug trafficking are domestic.

"Does it matter? They've been divorced for decades."

"Right now, anything might matter. I'm starting from zero."

"He told me it was a drawn out divorce. But by the time I started seeing him she'd moved to Colorado and remarried. Once Tobias became an adult, they had little contact."

Tobias had told me his mom and stepfather still lived in Denver. He and his wife and kids had flown there for his birthday weekend, leaving the day after Kurt's party in the afternoon.

"Do you know why they got divorced?"

"As if there's one single reason?" she said. "Life's never that simple."

Her tone remained pleasant and her voice steady, but I wondered why she shied away from direct answers. It might just be her conversational style. Or she was buying time to think through her answers.

"I agree. But sometimes there's a key issue the spouses can't work out."

"That really wasn't my business."

Another question without a direct answer.

"Your business or not, was there anything Kurt told you about?"

"I don't have anything to say about that. Tobias and his mother are the ones who will know about Kurt's marriage."

"Did you and he ever talk about getting married?"

I'm not someone who thinks a relationship can't be serious if the people aren't married to one another. But most people I've met in their sixties do think that, so I wondered if that might signal some friction or unresolved issue.

"We didn't see any reason to. Our kids were grown. We both liked living alone better than we'd liked being married and sharing space. It worked well."

"How often did you see each other?"

"Nearly every weekend. We alternated staying at one another's home."

"But not the weekend of Kurt's death?"

"No. I had a professional conference to attend."

No mention that Kurt might have been surprised or unhappy about that.

I nearly knocked over a leaning stack of papers as I returned to the desk. "How was your relationship overall?"

"Good."

"You weren't arguing over anything?"

"All couples argue."

"Did you argue the night of the party?"

"Not that I remember."

I debated pushing more, but I wanted to see her face and body language.

"Do you remember anyone there who seemed unhappy with Kurt?"

"I've thought about that and no. Overall, it was a lovely party."

"What conference did you go to that weekend?"

"A University of Wisconsin at Madison symposium on neuroscience and emotion."

"If you don't mind telling me exactly where you were Friday night, it'd be helpful."

"Narrowing your pool of suspects?"

Dr. Verde said "pool of suspects" as if it were in air quotes. I didn't mind. People speak more freely about both lawsuits and murder investigations when they think you don't know what you're doing. "I met some colleagues for cocktails around four and was in my room for the night by seven. The conference started with breakfast at nine the next morning. Plenty of people saw me there."

It didn't exactly rule her out. She could have driven from Madison to Chicago at seven, killed Kurt, and driven back in time to get a little sleep and appear for breakfast in the morning. I made a note to see if I could learn from the police whether they'd collected security camera footage at the conference hotel or the University.

I asked how she and Kurt met and she told me at a conference for a shared interest. When I asked what it was, she said something that sounded like moof-on or muffin.

"Sorry. A muffin conference?"

"Moo-fon. M-U-F-O-N. The Mutual UFO Network. It's a non-profit civilian UFO research and investigation organization. We're both UFO enthusiasts."

I glanced at the model spaceships on Kurt's bookshelves. This interest might be the unusual belief Tobias mentioned.

Yet Dr. Verde, who evaded a lot of other questions, volunteered it.

"What does being a UFO enthusiast mean?"

"Some members investigate known places for UFO sightings. Others help the government track sightings in databases or advocate to make the information public. MUFON was a big reason the FBI finally released that report about unidentified flying objects."

"Did Kurt do any of those things?"

"Hold on," Dr. Verde said. The line went dead for a few minutes, then she returned. "I need to go. My student's here early for her 10:30 conference."

"Can I meet with you in person? I want to learn more about Kurt's life and it sounds like you knew him best."

"You really think you can help find his killer?" she said.

"I do."

She agreed to email me some times she could meet during the next couple days. Before we hung up she said, "Quille? I do hope you'll respect Kurt's privacy."

"The only person I report to is Tobias. You're not worried about him, are you?"

"Oh, no. He knows all his father's secrets."

I doubted that was true of any child of any parent.

———

I RETURNED to my own office that afternoon to catch up on several of my cases and attend a phone conference with a lawyer about a chocolate chip brownie advertising lawsuit. I felt pretty sure my client, who owned the bakery that sold the brownies, could win in the long run. But she'd spend a lot on my fees doing it. At my urging, she had offered an amount equal to an hour or two of my time just to be rid of the case early on.

The associate who represented the plaintiff was a nice guy. He was a newer attorney but he never strutted around acting tough to prove he knew what he was doing. But today only the partner talked. He blustered for fifteen minutes about how great his case was.

"So far, the judge hasn't agreed," I said.

"That's because I haven't been personally involved. This version of the Complaint will stand."

Shades of Bryan Stillwell. But the judge had already dismissed the case three times based only on the written documents.

"We'll see," I said. "But if you make a counter-offer that's reasonable in the meantime, I'll listen."

After we hung up, I emailed the client an update, left Tobias a voicemail asking when we could meet, then spent the early evening researching and writing a brief. Ty was working late, too, but Lauren texted to see if I wanted to meet for dinner. I turned her down, but I did take a break. I headed down to Café des Livres, a French bakery and café on the ground floor of the building. While I ate a ham and brie croissant and sipped dark *chocolat chaud* I researched MUFON on my laptop.

After adding what I learned into my notes on Kurt's murder I texted Tobias, who hadn't returned my call yet. He called ten minutes later.

"Is it MUFON?" I moved to a quiet corner at the far end of the café opposite the bookshelves. "Is that what you don't want anyone to know?"

"No, no. Dad was into that, but it didn't concern me."

I settled into an overstuffed armchair and set my mug on the side table. "A lot of the articles and member posts talk about UFOs they think are piloted by aliens."

"Sure, but 60 Minutes had a whole episode on UFOs and how the government's tracking reports. And the Chicago Tribune, back when it was a real paper, did a story and talked to my dad about it because he helped collect oral histories of people who saw UFOs."

"Are those published somewhere?"

"I'll send you a link. You won't be able to tell which ones Dad wrote, though. The focus is on the reports, not the people who took and edited them, so they all did it anonymously."

I wondered if that was the reason or if Kurt preferred to downplay his interest in UFOs. But Dr. Verde, who worried about keeping Kurt's personal life private, talked about it freely, so I might be reading too much into the anonymity.

"Bryan told me your dad didn't like to write."

According to Bryan, he was the brains and the worker bee behind all the written briefs in the class actions he worked on with Kurt. And from what little I'd seen so far, that type of legal work required a lot of writing, lending some weight to Bryan's view that he was a big part of any victories.

"Dad didn't mind writing. But he didn't like sitting still. Without Draper pushing him into it I doubt he'd have ever gotten into class actions. The briefs can be fifty pages long and need tons of research. Dad didn't have the patience for either of those things."

"And E. Drake Draper does?"

"Him or someone on his team. So does Bryan I guess."

"Maybe that's why Bryan sounded so anti-Draper. He feels competitive with him."

"Really?" Tobias said. "To hear my dad tell it, Draper's the one who taught Bryan most of what he knows."

That didn't rule out feeling competitive.

"So the two firms did work together very closely?" I said.

"From what Dad said, all the time. Very collaborative."

"Huh."

Articles about the Millennial generation – I'm about five years too young to qualify as Gen X – say we love collaborative working. But in college and law school I discovered that often meant two thirds of the group members drink beer, kick around a few wild ideas, and wait for the couple students who cared the most about their grades to do the work.

If the same pattern applied with legal teams, that might cause a lot of bad feelings. Whether it was enough to motivate a murder was another question. But worth thinking about.

My email buzzed with a message from the partner at my old firm. She'd be happy to talk to me next week but was tied up in depositions for the next few days. After two polite emails with E. Drake Draper's assistant and a call where I empathized with the difficulty of working for lawyers, I'd gotten on E. Drake's schedule for the end of the day tomorrow. Ready or not, with few other leads to follow and a lawsuit to defend, I didn't feel I could put that meeting off.

I'd just have to talk to him with less background information than I'd hoped.

5

———————

"LET ME GET THIS STRAIGHT. You're taking over the fee lawsuit –
which I'm happy to hear, by the way – and you're looking into
Kurt's murder? Never heard of that mix of specialties."

E. Drake Draper leaned back in his mesh wire chair. The
floor to ceiling window behind him made it look like he was
about to topple into the air. Or into Lake Michigan, which
sparkled silver-blue in the early evening sun. Other than the
view, his office lacked any décor. And no files, cabinets, or
papers cluttered the room. A striking contrast to Kurt's
workspace.

The only personal touch was a shifting photo collage on the
flat gray desktop. Photos of a young man playing electric guitar
at an outdoor party faded into the same young man with E.
Drake on a sailboat and then a series of shots of a black and
white Border Collie.

"It's a long story how that happened," I said. "Let's talk about
the fee lawsuit first. Why are you happy I'm taking over?"

"Not happy it's you instead of Kurt. We had our differences.
Obviously. But Bryan – you met Bryan?"

Based on his website biography E. Drake must be at least

sixty-three, but he looked ten years younger. Clean shaven, he wore a starched collared shirt that reminded me of Bryan's, dark jeans, polished loafers with small tassels, and a Rolex. Unlike Bryan's, his was on his right wrist.

"Once," I said.

"Typical young male lawyer. Knows better than everyone. Thinks he can do better than everyone."

"Including you?"

"Heh." The sound he made was a cross between a thoughtful Huh and a chuckle. "Especially me."

"Since you feel that way, will you keep working with King and Stillwell on cases?"

E. Drake swiveled his chair from side to side. "I'm in wait-and-see mode. Never know what'll happen with a firm in these types of circumstances."

"These types of circumstances? Does a senior partner often get murdered?"

He smiled. "Let's hope not or I'm in trouble. I meant any time a senior partner leaves. Sometimes the firm reorganizes and is better than ever. Other times it falls apart. If Bryan Stillwell takes over, my bet is it falls apart."

"You must have felt differently when he started out. I heard you taught him everything he knows about class actions."

E. Drake arched one eyebrow. "Bryan said that? Surprised he gave me any credit for what I'm sure he sees as his massive successes."

I saw no reason to tell him that information hadn't come from Bryan. "So you did teach him a lot?"

"Bryan shadowed me for two years. More or less. But he won a few motions on his own, started thinking he already learned all he needs to know."

I made a note to ask Bryan for his side. I knew young lawyers, male or otherwise, like what E. Drake described, but I suspected there was more to the story.

"So that's your issue with Bryan? He doesn't listen to you anymore?"

E. Drake waved a hand. "Not listening is not so bad. Sometimes a new lawyer has a fresh take. Reminds me I've been doing this too long, gotten too stuck in my own view. But Bryan goes beyond that. If I say black, he says white. To spite me. Does it to lawyers on the other side, too. After a while I noticed – Kurt noticed too – that every time he took an active part in a case, it stretched out twice as long."

"Then why did Kurt make him a partner?"

"He said Bryan balanced him out. Kurt loved spotting wrongdoing and making speeches about the injustice of it all in the courtroom. But he didn't want to wrangle with the other side over getting the facts or sort out complex legal arguments. Or try the cases."

"Maybe I'm not familiar enough with class actions, but didn't you just rule out pretty much all the work?"

E. Drake shook his head. "These cases have lots of layers. Lots of stages. Kurt was great at finding clients. Getting judges to let the case go forward even where we were let's say pushing the envelope on a new type of claim. There's room for everyone on the team to do what they like best."

"And what do you like best?"

"Making money." He laughed, but I thought he might mean that. Not wrong, so long as he did a good job for his clients, too. But very different from what people said about Kurt. "No, seriously, I love trying cases. Personal injury, medical malpractice, class actions. I try the cases. And do the class cert hearings. Some of those are a lot like trials. I like those."

His office phone rang. He frowned but answered. "Did I or did I not say don't interrupt?" His fingers whitened as he squeezed the receiver. "No. No. I'll call them later." His lips stretched into a grimace. "I don't know when. Later."

He banged the receiver into the cradle. "Sorry. My secretary retired last month. After thirty years. You just can't find good legal secretaries anymore. The smart ones, the hard workers, go to law school themselves."

I wasn't sure what to say to that. It sounded like he felt sorry that more women now became lawyers rather than legal secretaries.

"You can manage a lot through technology these days," I said.

"*You* can. I can't. Old dog, new tricks. It's the only thing that makes me consider retiring."

I asked, but E. Drake claimed to have no idea who could want to kill Kurt.

"He was a bit of crusader," I said. "Could that have gotten him on someone's bad side?"

"Heh. We're all crusaders on the plaintiffs' side. Fighting for the little guy."

"And earning millions and millions of dollars in fees while they each get a couple bucks."

I'd read a lot of the case materials the day before and been shocked at the amounts attorneys earned by bringing class actions.

E. Drake's smile showed bleached white teeth. "Sure, we can earn a lot. But some cases go on for years, cost us money, and earn us nothing. Or average out to two or three dollars an hour. And those giant fees are split among multiple firms. In the last one, eight firms represented the class."

"Why so many?"

Most of the ones I'd looked at involved three or four firms total.

"In that case? One firm filed a similar case in Texas, I filed here in Illinois, and another firm the same type of case in federal court in California. They all got put together into one. So that's three firms right there. Plus the lawyers who started the Texas and California cases filed individual lawsuits. Then realized these could be class actions so they brought in class action lawyers."

"They couldn't do it themselves?"

"It's a specialized type of law. Not something to dabble in. You'll go broke."

"But Kurt's firm didn't start out doing class actions. Why partner with them?"

"Kurt had an eye for cases, and clients, that were perfect for class actions, he just didn't recognize it until I came along." E. Drake glanced at his phone. "I do need to return a call. Anything else about the fee lawsuit?"

"Did Kurt ever answer your last settlement demand?"

"Other than to laugh in my face? No."

"He laughed?" That didn't fit with Bryan's claim that Kurt was ready to give away the store.

"Kidding again." E. Drake gestured as if flicking a fly away. His fingers, long and slim, looked as if they belonged to someone else. A piano player maybe. "Kurt told me it was high but he'd look at it. That was only a few days before he died, so he probably hadn't looked yet."

"Did you talk to him about it at the party?"

"Nope. Said hello. Had a couple drinks, made the rounds, and left."

"Did the police ask where you were Friday night?"

"You want my alibi?"

"It could be helpful."

"Not sure about that." E. Drake's eyes shifted to the phone and back to me. "But if it'll get you out of here, I was home drinking a glass of Scotch. Surrounded by boxes and watching back episodes of *Elementary* on Amazon."

"Big weekend," I said. It sounded a lot like Bryan's, though he had read rather than watched a television show.

He shrugged. "Just moved into a new condo. I was exhausted."

"How did the fee lawsuit start? From what I saw, for ten years you and Kurt split fees on your cases with no issues."

The first document in a lawsuit, the Complaint, tells you the plaintiff's version of what happened. If you read between the lines you can usually see clues about the other side's story, too. But this one had very few facts and lots of legal jargon.

"I blame Bryan," E. Drake said. "Kurt and I agreed that whatever class actions the firms both worked on we'd split the fees fifty-fifty. Made it easier than sorting out how many hours we spent on each separate case and who contributed more."

"Don't you track that anyway?"

"Sure. The court wants that info. But we didn't need to decide who contributed more or less to each result. Say I get a key witness for the defendant to admit damaging facts in an hour-long deposition. That matters more than if a first-year lawyer reads the defendant's routine emails for eight hours. But the reading needs to be done, too. So instead of wasting time valuing all the work we decided to split all the fees evenly."

"And for ten years, you both felt it was fair?"

"Fair enough. Some cases I did the lion's share of the work or my firm did, in others Kurt did, but it balanced. Then Bryan pokes around. Decides since Kurt does all the food cases mainly on his own and brought in those clients, those cases fall outside the fifty-fifty agreement."

Bryan hadn't said he started the dispute. But he had said Kurt was being too agreeable.

"So Kurt was easier to deal with?"

"He was more reasonable."

"Crusaders aren't typically known for being reasonable."

"He crusaded against corporations. Like playing David and Goliath. This was different. Two guys who disagreed on a business deal."

"Eighty percent of the cases I handle are about business

deals between two guys who disagree. And they are not happy with each other."

"That's not how it was between Kurt and me." E. Drake stood. "I do need to wrap this up. Happy to talk another time."

I closed my legal pad and stood. "One last thing. Someone mentioned Kurt had some unusual beliefs, but not what they were. Any ideas?"

Tobias had said to ask people whatever I wanted. I wasn't sure he meant this, but I couldn't get anywhere if I didn't ask.

"Unusual?" Still standing, E. Drake tapped his index finger on his desk. His nail made a clicking sound against the top. "Well, there was his UFO obsession."

"I heard a little about that. Did it affect the cases?"

"Not that I saw. One judge downstate found it fascinating. He and Kurt talked for an hour in his chambers about whether the UFOs belonged to countries with advanced technology versus aliens."

On the way out I stopped to thank E. Drake's assistant, a young man with black framed glasses, for helping arrange the meeting and to ask about his day. Ten minutes later I emerged onto Michigan Avenue feeling no more enlightened than when I entered.

So far almost no one had a solid alibi for Kurt's murder, but it also seemed no one had a motive.

Time to call the police.

6

I ALMOST THINK of Detective Sergeant Beckwell, a fiftyish man whose suits always look a bit too large on him, as a friend. Almost. We met when he was the lead detective looking into the death of Marco, my then-boyfriend. After that we crossed paths a few times. Most recently I solved a crime outside Beckwell's jurisdiction that involved his son. As a thank you, he paid for me to train with the retired ex-cop and police academy instructor.

Also, in an odd twist, somewhere along the line he started dating Marco's ex-wife. Something I would have teased him about if I didn't suspect I'd need favors down the line.

None of these connections made him especially talkative, though, about the Kurt King murder when I called.

"Not my case," he said.

I stood in the middle of the Lurie Gardens in Millennium Park, heavy leather jacket zipped but my hands bare. Despite the early November chill in the air, when I exited E. Drake's office building across the street I couldn't resist the pull of the prairie plants and garden paths. Between Michigan Avenue and DuSable Lake Shore Drive, the gardens are set apart enough that the foliage mutes the traffic sounds, plus few people walk through on weekdays, so it's a peaceful place.

"But you can tell me, can't you, off the record, if they've zeroed in on anyone?" I said.

"It's all off the record, Quille. You're not a reporter."

"I heard forensic evidence isn't likely to help a lot because so many people were in the house the night before. True?"

A monarch butterfly zipped past me, its yellow and brown wings fluttering.

"Too many people can cause problems. Hair, fingerprints, DNA from too many sources. Any good defense attorney would claim the killer was just there for the party, not the next night to murder someone."

I heard keys clicking in the background and hoped it meant he was looking up the file.

"Unless the killer wasn't at the party," I said.

"Unless," Beckwell said. "But if I were planning to kill someone on a Friday night and he had a party on Thursday you bet I'd be there. Best way to shield yourself."

"Thanks for that look into your psyche."

"It's my job. It's your hobby, so who's stranger?"

"I'm getting paid for this one."

"You're getting paid to do my job now?" Beckwell said. "It is time for me to retire."

"I think you're a little young for that." Beckwell was in good shape for a man in his fifties, though his salt and pepper hair added the years his physique took off.

"And a little poor."

I paused near the artificial stream that bordered the east edge of the gardens. Pennies and dimes people had thrown in reflected light through the water. "Plus you'd miss helping me."

"You've got a great sense of humor for a lawyer."

"Seriously, Wayne, anything you can tell me?"

He'd invited me to call him by his first name after I helped out his son. I hoped doing it might remind him that our arrangement had mutual benefits.

He sighed. "Nothing suggests a stranger broke in and killed this man. So it's probably personal, putting it in your wheelhouse."

He confirmed that witnesses saw Dr. Isabel Verde at the conference hotel in Madison, Wisconsin, during the early evening the night Kurt died. But there was no video footage available, and no one saw her after seven p.m. that night or before ten a.m. the next morning. So she could have returned to Chicago during the night. Tobias, too, might have killed his father, as he'd caught a later flight to Denver than his wife and children did. But he had been on a plane by seven p.m. He worked as the killer only if the time of death was two hours outside the medical examiner's window.

"And the gun? Was it found?" I said.

"Nope. Bullet was a nine millimeter. That's a medium-sized pistol. Lots of civilians buy them for self-defense but police use them, too."

"You said something about if you planned to murder someone. Does some evidence suggest this was planned?"

"Nope. Just my attempt at wit. No facts scream planned or heat of the moment. Other than it looks like the victim let the killer in."

"Any signs of a fight?"

"Nothing knocked over. No defense wounds. Straight shot through the heart."

"Did Kurt King own a gun?"

"Not one that was registered. And none were found in his home."

"If the killer brought a gun does that suggest it was planned?"

"Maybe yes, maybe no. Applications for concealed carry permits soared last year. Lot of people worried about self-defense. Or they think they'll foil the next mass shooting with their quick reflexes and a fancy firearm. You found anyone mad at the victim?"

The smell of caramel corn drifted my way as a teenager carrying a large bag of Garrett's popcorn strolled past. "Nothing that seems likely to lead to murder."

"Don't count anything out," Beckwell said. "Last month I arrested a man who killed his brother for eating the last donut."

"Really?"

"Humans are complicated. Sometimes in a dangerous way. Promise me you'll be careful."

My phone dinged with a reminder about a video chat tomorrow morning.

"I will," I said.

But I was already thinking ahead to tomorrow's video meeting. It was with my most difficult client. My mother.

7

TY PERSUADED me to stay overnight at his condo. We normally didn't spend a lot of time there. It was less like an apartment and more like a medium-sized bedroom with a row of kitchen appliances along the wall and a breakfast counter. And it wasn't like the new luxury high rises that have been going up near downtown where the apartments are tiny but there are floors of common area rooms and amenities and vast outdoor spaces. He lived in a converted warehouse in the West Loop. The only common space was a bike room and a lobby. But the rent was reasonable, which allowed him to afford to maintain and dock his boat.

Staying at his place, though, meant I could do my video call with my mom there in the morning and hang out with Ty for a while afterward.

"This way if you feel upset or angry after the call, when you come back home at night you won't associate sitting at your dining table with those feelings," he said to me as we got off the bus two blocks from his apartment. "Or with the call."

"I'll just associate your place with it?"

He pulled me close to him and kissed my cheek. "Ah, but I'm so much fun you'll forget all about that by your next visit."

I laughed but he was right. If the call upset me, I'd rather come home at the end of the day to somewhere where I hadn't spent a frustrating hour or so talking to my mom.

In the morning he made me bacon and eggs. Before he left for the Peet's Coffee across the street he poured me a large glass of water and set it next to my iPad. "You know what my mom always says."

"Rough day? Don't get dehydrated, too. It'll make it worse."

"Yep. I'll give you some privacy. See you when you're done."

He headed out. I took a long drink of water and started the video meeting.

But my mom didn't answer. My dad did. He'd grown a beard since I last saw him. Gray threaded his hair for years, but the beard came in with almost no hint of his natural color, which was dark, almost black, like mine. It reminded me he was in his early sixties. An age I didn't associate with my laid-back, guitar-playing father.

"Sorry, Quille. Mom can't talk this morning."

"Is she – where is she?"

We'd planned this call a week ago, but I wasn't surprised. My mother typically showed up only a third of the times she said she would. I expected Dad to tell me she was still asleep or lying on the couch staring at the TV. Or doing one of the other things she did when depressed or especially anxious.

"Out for coffee."

"Out." I shifted on the counter stool. "The new medication's working that well?"

Normally, my mother's anxiety kept her from going anywhere unless she was with my dad and sometimes not even then. But a few months back she'd started a new mix of anti-anxiety medicine and anti-depressants. That had led, on my last visit, to her angrily asking why I never looked into the original Q.C.'s murder. She did an about-face the next morning. It planted a seed with me, though, and in our next phone call I said I wanted to look into the crime anyway. She'd agreed to talk with me.

Dad held up crossed fingers. "So far still so good. She's out with your Aunt Cathy. Second time this month."

"Did she remember we had a call?"

"She wasn't up to it, sweetheart. I hope you didn't spend too much time putting things together."

"Not too much."

I clicked a key so the video chat screen expanded, blocking the outline I created, at my mother's request, so I could explain how I might go about investigating. As I did for court arguments, I had spent hours researching, then writing out key points so I could speak clearly. My mother tended to interrupt more and be more combative than most judges.

"Does this mean she doesn't want me to investigate?" I wanted to go forward regardless, but it'd be hard without her cooperation. Also, I didn't want to threaten her mental health.

"No, no. She thinks it'll be good for all of us if you can get some answers. And she's said that for the last two weeks so I think she means it."

"But she didn't want to talk to me." I twisted a long strand of hair around my fingers, a habit I was trying with mixed success to break.

"It's not you. She's just not ready to talk about all of it yet. She asked me to tell you whatever I can first." Dad took off his wire-rimmed glasses and adjusted his screen so his face loomed large. "Before I do, though, you're sure you want to do this? After all these years, the odds of finding anything the authorities missed must be near zero. And you'll need to spend so much time on it. It's not fair to you."

My fingers, still wound into my hair, stilled. "You're concerned about the effect on me?"

My dad showed more interest in my life than my mom did when I was growing up, but my Gram was the one who really raised me and my sister Kendra. Dad took care of my mother.

"I just don't want you to feel you need to do this for your mother or for me. You've spent enough of your life in Q.C.'s shadow."

I cleared my throat. "I – thanks, Dad. But I want to do this. I think it'll be good for me, too."

"You know if you start, your mom will never let it go."

I nodded. "But you both understand, I hope you do, that if a stranger took her there's no chance I'll find answers. My only shot is if it was personal. That's the kinds of crimes I've solved. Where it's about how people interacted with each other, the ways they felt, what they did that led to one of them doing something awful."

"We know. The police always thought it was someone Q.C. knew, and we did, too."

"You did? Why?"

"She knew not to walk off or get in a car with a stranger. And she wasn't shy or quiet. She would have screamed her head off if anyone grabbed her."

"Unless they surprised her and it happened too fast."

My dad's Adam's apple bobbed as he swallowed. "I suppose it's possible in the sense that anything is. But either it happened inside the pizza parlor, which means someone should have noticed a stranger there. Or someone lured her outside and took her, and to do it she'd have to have known that person."

I didn't feel as sure as my dad did about that. People of any age, including five-year-olds, sometimes do surprising things.

"And the police thought the same?"

"Yes. Where we differed is they thought it was us – me, specifically."

I set my pen down. "You specifically? Why?"

No one ever told me that. I knew the police focused on my

parents for months, quite possibly missing or ignoring evidence that pointed to anyone else, but not that they targeted my dad.

"I left the party to get more balloons and pick up her cake. I was gone an hour."

"Wait – her cake? I thought it was a cousin's birthday party."

Dad looked puzzled. "What? No. Why did you think that? It was Q.C.'s birthday."

I tried to think who told me it was someone else's party. But my whole life everyone in my family talked about how wonderful Q.C. was but said nothing about the crimes. I'd done a paper on kidnapping in college and researched some information about Q.C.'s abduction. Maybe one of the articles I read had the information wrong.

"Okay," I said. "So you were gone the same hour Q.C. disappeared?"

"Most likely. Though no one knows exactly when it happened. But she was in the ball game – you know, one of those net cages with all the plastic balls and the kids jump around inside? We waved good-bye. One of her friend's mothers saw her there, too, a little after two o'clock. When I got back to the party a little after three, we looked for her to cut the cake and no one could find her."

"Wasn't the bakery right across the street?"

While no one had told me about that day, my sister Kendra mentioned getting birthday cakes there when she was little.

"It was. But first I went to the drugstore for the balloons. That was eight or nine blocks away. Plus it took time for them to fill the balloons. They had one of those machines in the back."

"So about twenty minutes each way and some waiting time. That could be close to an hour. Why did the police find that suspicious?"

"Because I admitted to taking my time coming back. To not rushing."

"You talked to them without a lawyer."

If sharing space with a criminal defense attorney taught me anything, it was that the police are not your friends. Innocent or guilty, if they're questioning you about a crime, you're in danger of being arrested. Something I already knew because of my parents' experience.

"Of course I did, Quille. My daughter was missing. I wanted them to find her. I spilled everything whether I thought it might help or not."

"And they didn't understand why you didn't rush back to her party."

"No. Especially because I'm a musician. A performer. They didn't believe me that I don't like crowds or parties."

My dad's an introvert. A lot of people think anyone who performs or acts or does public speaking must love people and attention. But I knew plenty of introverted actors, musicians, and courtroom lawyers, including me. There's a big difference between performing on a stage or in front of a group and making small talk or telling stories to a group of people. The first you plan and prepare for and, a lot of the time, control. The second not so much.

"So they thought you were at the very least a terrible person for not racing back to your daughter's birthday party?"

"Their questions gave me that impression. And it didn't help that I felt guilty." He looked to one side at something off camera. Maybe one of the many photos of Q.C. that hung throughout the house. "I've replayed that day so many times. If I'd come back sooner, maybe only a few minutes sooner, I might have stopped it. Or seen whoever it was taking Q.C. away."

I drank more water. If I meant to do this, I couldn't shy away from uncomfortable questions.

"You said you took your time," I said. "Meaning what?"

"I meandered around a few blocks. Including to our house and back. Killing time." He winced as he said the last words.

"Dad – none of it – it's not your fault."

"Maybe it is, Q."

The use of his childhood nickname for me told me how far into the past he had gone in our short conversation. It was the compromise name. My mother insisted on calling me Q.C. and my dad felt I needed my own name, but didn't want to upset my mother by calling me something too different. So, Q. Until I reached high school and began going by Quille. He was the first in the family to adopt it.

"It's the fault of the killer. No one else."

"But if that's someone we knew, someone we brought into our lives?" Dad said. "That's our fault."

"You can't see into anyone's heart or soul. I've learned that from the murders I've looked into."

"That doesn't change that she was my daughter. And I didn't protect her. And I didn't save her."

Somewhere outside brakes squealed and what sounded like a foghorn blared. I looked toward the windows, away from my dad's face. My whole life I had heard about how Q.C.'s death affected my mother. I'd never thought half as much about how it affected my father.

"Is this going to make it worse, Dad? If I look into this?"

"Nothing can make it –" He stopped, swallowed, shook his head. "Nothing can make it worse. If you find answers, even if it was someone we knew, at least we can stop wondering. That'll help. Me. Your mother. Your sister. Gram."

"You're sure that's how you feel?"

"It's better to know than not to know."

I hoped he was right.

8

————

AFTER WALKING Ty to his office, I met Tobias on the corner of Wacker Drive and Madison Street outside the Civic Opera House. His law firm had an office there ten floors above the auditorium where Chicago's Lyric Opera performs.

I'd layered a black zippered fleece with a hood under my long black leather jacket and added fingerless gloves. Perfect for a sunny but chilly day with no wind. As Tobias and I headed south his brisk pace matched mine.

After a couple blocks, we started across Wacker Drive.

"I didn't realize until Bryan told me that the party your dad hosted was for your birthday," I said as we reached the first concrete island on Wacker. Two islands and a ramp divided the northbound and southbound lanes. The ramp led down to lower Wacker Drive. Though we still had the Walk signal, we stopped because a cab darted from the northbound lane, pulled a U-turn, and careened down the ramp.

Tobias eyed the traffic. "Yeah. At least it's a good last memory. We were getting along."

"Did you not usually?"

He glanced sideways at me. "Mom says we were too much

alike. Both sure we were right and bent on convincing the other."

"Right about what?"

His pale cheeks reddened. "Cubs versus Sox. Whether the Senate should end the filibuster. Home ownership versus renting. Pick an issue."

It sounded a little like how E. Drake Draper described his conflicts with Bryan. If Kurt also clashed with Bryan, he might have inadvertently repeated his family dynamic in his workplace.

"Sounds stressful," I said. "Though I kind of envy you. My mother's not interested enough in what I think for us to argue about any of those types of issues."

The Walk signal returned. After waiting for a Toyota whose driver subscribed to the "it's only a little red" theory of traffic lights, we finished crossing Wacker.

"We had plenty of personal arguments, too," Tobias said.

"And your dad and your mother? What caused their split?"

Kurt's ex had been across the country when he was killed, and nothing Tobias had told me suggested she had anything to do with it. But learning about Kurt meant learning about his relationships. Unfortunately, the ex wasn't willing to talk with me. And Tobias wasn't exactly dishing out a lot of information.

"Me. Mostly. They disagreed on how to raise me."

There must be more to it than that, but we'd reached the Starbucks on the ground level of the Willis Tower, the tallest skyscraper in Chicago. Tobias pushed the revolving door to get it moving, then stepped back so I could go through. An old-fashioned gesture I'd never seen any man under seventy make.

We'd both ordered on our phones while waiting at one of the intersections. The mobile pick-up line was two-deep. I switched the conversation to his law practice. Tobias told me starting next week he was taking a leave of absence to sort out his father's estate and law practice.

"And then what?" I said.

"In theory, go back to my practice. But I'd like to do something more meaningful. Maybe in the non-profit world. As a chemist I worked mostly on creating better diapers and soaps. Now I handle patents, and an awful lot of them are still for diapers and soaps. Does it make the world that much of a better place?"

"If you're a parent of a new baby, probably. But I get what you're saying."

Tobias wore only a lightweight denim jacket over khakis and a long-sleeved shirt. Out on the street I'd noticed him shivering. So though I'd planned to suggest sitting in one of the nearby office plazas to get away from the other customers, I pointed instead to an open table sandwiched in a back corner away from the windows and other people.

"Is that something you can afford to do?" I said. "Work in a non-profit?"

"Now I could. Dad didn't leave me enough to retire and never work again. Which I couldn't see doing anyway. But if I find something with health insurance almost any salary will be enough."

I sipped my Chai latte, enjoying the foam and the cinnamon taste. It was too much caffeine for me this late in the morning, but I needed a treat after my talk with my dad. And the lack of a talk with my mother.

"Anyone else who benefitted from your father's death financially?"

"No. I inherited everything."

"What about your dad's firm?" I said.

"I inherited his shares – eighty percent."

"Anything look off to you in the finances?"

He fiddled with the plastic top on his coffee. "I'm better at math than most lawyers. Obviously. But not great on business. I'm hoping you can tell me."

In the United States you can major in anything in college and go on to law school, which is a graduate degree program. Except that patent lawyers like Tobias need to earn a science degree first, which I guessed required a fair amount of math. A lot of other lawyers, though, go into law partly because they dislike numbers. That creates a lot of opportunity for me. I majored in business in college, concentrating in accounting, thinking at first it would help me manage my acting career. I discovered I liked it. I worked at an accounting firm for a couple years, and then decided on law school.

"I can't analyze the firm's books the way a forensic accountant could," I said. "But I can tell you if I spot something that looks off."

"Great. One less stress. Thank you."

"It almost sounded earlier like you think you were the cause of your parents' divorce."

He looked at a group of tourists fanning out across the wide sidewalk. Behind them a woman with a briefcase swerved in a failed attempt to get around. "Not that I caused it. I mean, as a kid I thought that. But there were issues – it's related to my dad's beliefs. My mom was protecting me. Maybe she could have lived with it otherwise."

"Is that what she says?"

The cappuccino machine behind the counter ground and whirred. Tobias waited until the noise stopped. "No. She says they would have split up anyway."

"What can you tell me about Dr. Verde?"

"Isabel? I was around twenty when they started seeing each other. I first met her when I was nearly done with college."

"Did you see her very often?"

He frowned. "Dad and I only visited a few times a year even after I moved here. She came with him once or twice when we met for dinner. It made it easier, really. He was more relaxed when she was around."

"Most murder victims, if it's not gang or business related, are killed by someone close to them. Often a romantic or sexual partner. Any gut feeling about that?" I said.

Tobias shifted so he looked at the coffee bar rather than outside or at me. "I can't imagine her as a murderer. But I don't know her that well. And I didn't see her enough to know what their relationship was like."

"Your dad was found in the coach house. Are you surprised he was there instead of in the main house?"

The police hadn't released the crime scene yet, but I'd pulled up photos and information on Zillow and other real estate sites about Kurt's home, which was in Lincoln Park, an upscale neighborhood about three miles north of downtown. His main house had two stories and three bedrooms. The previous owner had rented the coach house in back to a tenant.

"He used the upper floor as a sort of study or home office. It's all one big loft space. I could see him sitting there at night, looking up through the skylight. Having a drink with someone there."

"Did he use the rest of the coach house, too?"

"Not for himself I don't think. But for guests. Downstairs was a kitchen, bath, living room, and bedroom. When he had a party, he put the food out there in the kitchen. And the yard had a hot tub so people could change in the bedroom or use the shower. Not have to go in the house."

"He liked the house neat?" I thought of the stacks of papers and files all over his law firm office.

Tobias gave a half-hearted chuckle. "The opposite. The house was always clean – he had a cleaning service. But never neat. My wife said it always looked like a toddler just threw a tantrum. Books, papers, junk every which way. But the coach house was only used for parties. So it stayed neat."

"Your dad ever say anything about problems with Isabel? Or anyone else?"

"We didn't talk about those kinds of things. It was all work or sports or politics."

"The things you disagreed on."

"Yeah. My mom says that's how my dad keeps people at bay."

"Did he need to keep people at bay?"

"Mom told me he had a hard childhood. His father, a doctor, worked all hours. Something was off with his mom, I don't know what, but his older sister basically raised him. And resented him. Maybe hated is a better word. She used to lock him in a closet as soon as he got home from school to keep him out of her way. He still had this thing about it. My whole childhood our closet doors always stood open. I never saw him shut one my whole life."

"Is his sister still alive?"

"Died of a heart attack five years ago."

I already knew from my research that Kurt's parents had died over three decades ago a couple months apart.

"My Gram mostly raised me. But she made it seem like a pleasure, not a chore." I swirled the latte left in my cup. "It must have been a huge life change, though."

I shifted in my chair, embarrassed that I hadn't thought much about it before. Knowing Gram, she might very well have had plans to try a new career path or travel the world in her late fifties and early sixties rather than raise kids.

"Lucky," Tobias said.

"I was. Am." My oldest sister and I aren't terribly close, but I don't think she resents me though I got more attention from Gram, being the youngest. I love hanging out with my niece and nephew. And however challenging my relationship with my mom, she and my dad are still part of my life.

I pushed my tea to one side. "Are you ready to tell me about your dad's beliefs?"

Tobias flipped the green coffee stirrer between his fingers.

"Soon. Or I'll let you off the hook for investigating the murder. I don't know which yet."

I nodded, suppressing a sigh. In my regular law practice clients sometimes don't tell me things I need to know, but I don't discover that until it's too late. At least here I was aware I wasn't getting all the information.

And knowing that, maybe I could find a way around it.

"I'd like to talk to Maria more. About the fee lawsuit and the firm. You don't have a problem with that, I take it?"

"No, no problem."

In a three-way text, we arranged for Maria to talk with me at six.

When I got back to my office my landline was ringing. It was the client from the food cases.

"What do you mean Kurt's dead?" she said. "Why didn't anyone tell me?"

9

———

MY MOUTH DROPPED OPEN. At my old firm, if a partner died, someone called the clients within a day or two to reassure them their cases were in good hands. My officemate and I had agreed to do that for one another so no case or client fell through the cracks. Yet Kurt died nearly three weeks ago and it was news to this woman.

"I am so sorry," I said. "I didn't realize no one had told you. Is – do you – I can ask Kurt's son or Kurt's partner, Bryan Stillwell, to call you."

"You're taking over the cases?"

I shut my office door. The suite's new receptionist had sprayed a Eucalyptus and peppermint scent she said promoted calm around the common area. Some smells trigger migraines for me. Peppermint is usually fine, but the jabbing pain behind my eyes strongly suggested Eucalyptus was not.

"No. I am a lawyer, but not one working for the firm. That is, I represent the firm." I paused. I needed to pull it together and reassure this client. "Let me start over. Did anyone tell you that two of the firms that represented you – King and Stillwell and

E. Drake Draper and Associates – are involved in a lawsuit against one another?"

I dug my bottle of Advil out of my purse and shook out three as I spoke. The lawsuit was in the public record, but I still felt odd telling her about it if neither Kurt nor Bryan had done so. In the same situation, I wouldn't want someone else explaining that type of issue to my client. But I didn't see another way to explain my role.

"No one told me that, either," the client said. "This is my fourth case with Kurt. Why wouldn't he tell me that?"

"Probably because it won't change anything for you. It's only about how the attorneys get paid."

The class actions the lawsuit covered were done, and all the clients had been paid whatever they were owed.

"Well, what happens with the cases that are left?"

I swallowed the first two Advil together, then downed the third with the dregs of my Chai latte.

"Kurt's partner, Bryan, will get in touch, or Kurt's son." I'd make sure one of them called her. "I'm sorry if this is a shock. You probably knew Kurt well – "

"No. I only talked to him three or four times. I just can't believe no one told me."

"Three or four times?" I tried, and failed, to keep the shock out of my voice. Kurt represented this woman in four different cases over eight years. "So you were dealing with his partner, Bryan?"

"No, no. I talk to a girl. Margie? Melissa?"

"Maria?"

"Yes, Maria. She calls me. Or emails about dates if we need to schedule something."

I knew firms where paralegals took very active roles, and as long as a lawyer ran the case and the paralegal didn't give legal advice that was fine. But I couldn't imagine a lawyer talking so little with a client.

"If you have a few minutes, could you tell me how you first met Kurt?" I said. "I'm trying to better understand the cases."

"I answered an ad saying if you had gone to this one coffee chain – it's out of business now – and ordered a latte you might be entitled to money. I had, so I called."

I massaged my forehead with my free hand. Despite the closed door, the Eucalyptus smell permeated the air. "Did all four of the cases involve lattes?"

"Lattes. Ice cream. Milk shakes. That kind of thing. Wherever I went, basically, whatever I bought, I saved receipts. Then if it was advertised as vanilla I checked to see if the ingredients listed vanilla bean."

It had nothing to do with my work, but I had to ask. "Did you taste a difference? Was it better with vanilla bean?"

"Well, sure. The cheap ice cream and such is never as good as premium right? And that's usually what's got the real vanilla. Lattes and that, I don't know. I mean, I don't really taste the vanilla in them, it's more the general latte taste, right?"

"How often did you talk with Maria?"

"Once a year? Maybe twice if something important happened. Except when I was deposed. That was in three of the cases."

"What about when they were filing something with the court?"

"Like what?"

I didn't know all the phases of a class action, so I didn't know what example to give. "A motion maybe. Or interrogatories."

Interrogatories are questions clients answer in writing early in the case. They sign their answers swearing they're telling the truth.

"Yes, I saw those."

"They didn't interview you or talk to you about your answers?"

"No, just sent me this document to read and sign. Should they have talked to me?"

In my opinion the answer was Yes, but I couldn't speak badly of a firm that was now my client. "If it all made sense and you had no questions it sounds like they didn't need to."

She hadn't spoken to Kurt in over nine months, so I didn't see any point in asking anything else. The whole conversation left me feeling we were talking different languages. When anything happens in a case, I email or call my clients right away. Plus I have a calendar system that reminds me once a month to check in. If nothing's happened, I send a standard email that says what I'm working or waiting on and expected next steps. I couldn't imagine going for months or years without sending an update.

To get farther from the scent, which was now making me feel sick to my stomach, I called Tobias from the conference room landline. Though I couldn't have known how uninformed the client was, I still felt I'd stepped out of line in telling her about Kurt's death.

I sat in the corner and twisted the black phone cord around my fingers. "I hope I didn't cause any problems for the firm. The client had no idea your father died."

He was as shocked as I was and conferenced Bryan in. Bryan, though, was unfazed. "There was probably nothing for her to do. Hold on." Keys clicked in the background. "Yeah, she doesn't need to do anything unless we get close to trial and there's a settlement conference. Or a trial. But that hardly ever happens."

Most lawsuits of any kind never get to the trial stage. But I'd learned through research that it was even less likely with class actions because so much money was at stake.

"But don't they still want to know what's going on?" I said as Tobias said, "But he was her lawyer."

"Look, Maria or I will call the clients today if it'll make you feel better. But I don't think you should worry about it."

"No one called any clients yet?" Tobias said.

"We've been a little busy," Bryan said. "But we'll get it done."

I called Maria separately to be sure she could still meet tonight given the extra work.

"It'll be fine," she said. "I got in early today to catch up. Now I'll just be the regular amount of behind anyway. But I hope you don't mind – I emailed Joe and asked him to join us tonight. Tobias thinks he'd be a good contact for me. Theatre-wise."

"He would be. But I thought we were going to talk about the lawsuit. And Kurt."

"We can do both. Oh, and I told Joe to bring his girlfriend."

"His girlfriend? Oh, Lauren."

I'd known Joe much longer than Lauren, but I couldn't imagine ever thinking of her mainly as his girlfriend rather than my best friend.

"And you should invite Ty. They can all chat over drinks while you and I deal with business, then we can all have some dinner together. On the firm."

"Is this still about getting to know my friends?"

"No, no. It's more – I know this is silly but – I've been working a lot lately. I could use the chance to have a little fun along with work. I bet you could too."

"I can. And I know Ty can. All right, I'll see if he's free."

"Great, see you tonight."

I stared at the phone for a few minutes after ending the call, rubbing the back of my neck. It ached, but between the Advil and the change of location my head no longer throbbed. Maria had said she wanted to have fun tonight. But she also invited Joe as a potential theatre contact. Those two didn't need to be mutually exclusive, but I didn't quite buy it. Also, the lawyer typically buys for the client, not the other way around.

Something else was going on.

10

———

The text was the fourth one from Maria about being stuck at work and running late. I sipped my wine and scrolled to the bottom of the screen on my iPad, corrected a typo in my electronic signature, and closed the document. While waiting I had finished revising a motion I needed to file tomorrow, so at least I didn't need to be in the office quite so early. On the downside, my wine glass was half empty and I hadn't eaten yet, leaving me feeling a little buzzed. And the half hour I'd hoped to spend with Maria before my friends arrived was nearly gone.

Maria rushed in as I closed my iPad. "So sorry. That client just would not get off the phone. Let me get a glass of wine and I'm all yours."

She draped her peacoat across a chair and darted away before I could tell her the server would come to us. I'd scored a quiet corner in the lobby bar at the Chicago Athletic Association Hotel. My coat and shoulder bag rested on the love seat across from me to reserve it for Joe and Lauren, and my legal pad on the armchair to my right for Ty.

Maria returned a moment later. "Oh, sorry, didn't realize

there's no bar. I'm a mess today. Things have just been crazy." She dropped into the high-backed armchair on my left and twisted sideways to face me. "How're you?"

"Good. I've got a couple questions before anyone else gets here. Whose idea was it to cut E. Drake Draper out of the food cases?"

"Straight to the point, huh? Hmm. Never thought about it. Maybe three years ago Kurt started talking about how those cases weren't really part of our agreement."

"Kurt? That wasn't Bryan's idea?"

"Bryan?" Maria glanced over the paper menu. "Could've been, I guess. He's always saying Kurt doesn't, or didn't, pay enough attention to the bottom line."

"Is that true?"

"Kurt wasn't, let's say, detail focused when it came to the books. Or the cases really. So Bryan might be right."

A server appeared with ice water for Maria and to take our orders. Maria asked for another glass of wine for me, debated between two cocktails, and asked a few questions about the appetizers before settling on the cheese and crackers plate and the white cheddar kettle corn for the table.

Once the server left I asked, "Anything Bryan was unhappy about at the firm?"

"Oh, he always thought he ought to get to take the lead more often. He's got way too high an opinion of himself. Thought he was behind every success and completely discounted all Kurt's work."

"Bryan told me he came up with the vanilla idea."

Maria rolled her eyes. "I doubt it. Kurt told me he and E. Drake brainstormed that together."

"Yet he didn't think E. Drake should get half the fees?"

"He thought E. Drake should get some, just not half. Kurt was the one who brought in the clients and did most of the work."

Before I could ask anything else, Joe and Lauren arrived.

After hugs and introductions, the conversation turned to theatre. Ty arrived a few minutes later. When the drinks and appetizers arrived, Ty scooched his chair closer to Lauren and Joe and got Lauren talking about her latest real estate showings.

I asked Maria more questions about King and Stillwell as I spread soft herbed goat cheese on crackers, figuring it didn't hurt if my friends overheard the answers. Nothing she said struck me as key for the murder investigation. She explained a little more of what she knew about class actions and said she thought E. Drake and Kurt had gotten along well.

Maria ate a handful of white cheddar popcorn. "What about you? Learned anything that might help with the murder?"

I ate some popcorn too. It tasted wonderful. Buttery, slightly burnt, and cheesy. "Just getting a feel for everyone involved." Tobias had told me to report only to him, so I wasn't about to share with Maria. "Have you thought more about who might be angry at Kurt? Or had an argument that led to a shooting?"

Her lips pressed together and her whole body sagged. "I think about that all the time. I just have no idea. I wish I did. The idea of his killer being out there, getting away with it, it's awful."

"Do you know anything about his relationship with Dr. Verde?"

"Isabel? They were seeing each other for a long time. And I think she was his therapist at one point."

"When?"

"Maybe when they first met, but I'm not sure."

"What makes you think they had that type of relationship?"

"I walked into his office about a month ago when he was on the phone with her. And he said it was her hypnotherapy that started things. He sounded angry about it."

"Started what things?"

"No idea."

The server returned with each of our entrees. This part of the lobby bar had pub food only, so I'd gotten a thick burger topped with sliced black olives.

"What made you think he was angry?" I asked after I'd taken a few bites.

She shut her eyes for a moment. "The way he said 'your.' Like 'it was *your* hypnotherapy that started me on this path.' As if she'd complained about something and he was putting it back on her."

"Started him on this path? Or started things?"

She waggled her hand. "Could be either. It was the hypnotherapy that stuck with me."

The conversation between Lauren, Ty, and Joe hit a lull as Maria spoke.

"Hypnotherapy?" Lauren said. "I've seriously always wanted to try it. See if I had any past lives where I was a princess."

"I feel like you would have been a queen," I said.

"Or king," Lauren said. "You don't know."

"Could be," I said.

"Is this about your new case?" Joe said.

"Just something Maria overheard in her office," I said. "I don't think it was about past lives."

I made a mental note to ask Dr. Verde how she used hypnotherapy in her practice. And if she had treated Kurt.

"I'm filling Quille in on what might help her solve my boss's murder." Maria pointed a skinny French fry at me. "But she won't tell me what she found out so far. Even though she knows I have an alibi. My sister was with me all weekend."

An alibi from a sister is better than none. But it wasn't airtight. Juries recognize that family members might lie for one another.

"Ask Tobias. He can fill you in if he wants to," I said.

Later, after I finished my burger, I spotted a couple vacate the two armchairs near the fireplace in the far room. I turned to

Maria. "There's something else I need to ask you. Let's step over there for a few minutes."

"Oh fine," Lauren said. "Just leave us out of everything when you know we could help. At least, I could. We'll get you back by ordering fabulous dessert and eating it all ourselves."

I led Maria across the marble floor and into the alcove with the fireplace. The only light came from a few banker's lamps with amber shades and a small Tiffany floor lamp, so I wouldn't be able to see her face well. But it gave us some privacy. Our other option was the game room past the elevators. It was far better lit so people could see their pool cues and ping pong paddles. I'd be better able to read Maria's expression there. But from experience I knew I'd barely hear anything she said.

"Lauren really wants to hear about the murder investigation," Maria said as we sat across from each other. "Don't you think she could help?"

"Probably. She's got good insights into people and I like bouncing things off her. But Tobias said to keep everything to myself, so I am."

"She seems a little mad about it."

"She's pretending. She gets that I can't tell her anything."

Maria glanced at the table. Lauren was gesturing toward the menu. "She might be serious about that dessert threat."

"She might. Listen, Tobias still won't tell me about these unusual views or beliefs Kurt had, so there's no way for me to tell if they have anything to do with his murder. Any idea at all what they were? A guess?"

Maria and I sat across from each other in two armchairs, our drinks on side tables. She rested her hands on her thighs. "No. I've tried to think what a judge or client might find odd. He liked to build those model rocket ships. But who would care about that?"

"Just model rockets?"

"That's all I can think of."

"Is there anything you know about that you feel you can't tell me? It would help to know if you're aware of something whether you can tell me what it is or not."

She shook her head. "No. Really. Nothing."

I debated asking directly about UFOs. After all, E. Drake Draper mentioned them. But despite Tobias's claim that it wasn't a big deal if people knew, if Kurt hadn't mentioned that to Maria I wasn't going to. At least not until I got a better sense of who Kurt was and what secrets he kept.

"Nothing about religion or politics or, I don't know, New Agey?"

Maria tilted her head. "He talked politics sometimes, but he was independent. Maybe that's unusual. He didn't think either major party had it right about everything. Or sometimes anything. He wasn't terribly religious. Or if he was he didn't talk about it. And I've known him – I knew him for nearly eleven years."

I felt more and more puzzled.

"Any idea why he and Tobias didn't get along?"

"He said his ex-wife turned Tobias against him."

"Did he say why or how?"

She shook her head. "I never asked. It seemed to upset him to talk about."

We returned to the table where Lauren had, as promised, ordered dessert. But it was to share. One flourless chocolate cake drizzled with raspberry sauce and a gooey butter cake.

Lauren and I live in the same building, so after Maria's Uber picked her up the four of us strolled south on Michigan Avenue.

"Is it my imagination or was that mostly a waste of your time?" Ty said. "Not that Maria's not fun to be around, but what was the point?"

Lauren linked her arm with mine. "Seriously. I hope you got

some information from her before we got there because she seemed more intent on picking your brain."

"I thought so, too," I said. "And it felt like she was purposely late."

"When you visited the restroom, she grilled us majorly about what we knew about your investigation. Which I told her was nothing. No lies there." Lauren pouted in mock frustration.

"She also asked us about your other murder investigations," Joe said. "We told her she needed to ask you. I figured you didn't want us to share details with anyone else."

"You're right," I said. "But I didn't think I was gone that long."

"It is a maze to get to the restrooms," Ty said. "I got lost twice."

There are a couple ways to get to the restrooms from the lobby bar, none of them easy. I'd gone past the main elevators, through the game room, down a flight of stairs near the hotel's fancier restaurant, and along a catwalk that fronted yet another hotel bar, this one with a 1920s speakeasy vibe.

"She definitely made good use of the time you were gone," Lauren said.

"I may have to tell Tobias I can't do this. I feel for him, but fumbling around in the dark is pointless."

I'd learned with one of the first cases I took on when I started my practice that if a client makes it impossible for you to do your job, it's time to get out.

"Isn't the money the point?" Lauren said.

"In some ways it makes me feel worse," I said. "Like I'm scamming Tobias out of money when I know I can't help him. It's because he won't let me, but that doesn't make it okay to take his money."

"I think it does," Lauren said.

Ty tapped her on her shoulder from behind. "Shh. Less money, less risk. Sounds like a good deal to me."

Joe groaned. "You had to say that. Now you're going to make her want to continue."

My phone buzzed. Normally I don't talk on my cell phone or text while walking on Chicago streets. It's like a giant sign telling criminals you're not paying attention. But we'd reached my block, and with my friends around me I decided it was safe enough and took out the phone. Tobias had texted me.

Can we talk? Ready to tell you Dad's secrets.

———

"You were testing me?"

Tobias and I sat across from each other at a high top table in the front window of Sociale, overlooking the patio where Ty and I had sat after the Halloween party. A large bar took up one corner of the restaurant. Ty, Lauren, and Joe perched on stools on the far side of it drinking more wine and observing, though well out of earshot.

I didn't think Tobias meant me any harm. But the late evening invitation to meet alone made me wary. Also, investigating crimes had taught me that you never know for sure what's going on in someone else's head or what they're likely to do. And you can't have too many back-ups.

Tobias had just told me Maria filled him in on the evening as soon as we parted ways. The fact that I didn't reveal anything to her about what I learned in the investigation so far, and that it was clear my friends didn't know anything, reassured him he could trust me.

"I know it's odd, Quille. But this isn't a normal case. I needed to be sure. Plus I've known Joe a long time but not Lauren or Ty."

I rubbed the back of my neck, trying to loosen the knotted muscles. "And that matters why?"

"Joe told me he and your other friends helped with your

investigations. And that you sometimes sort through things partly by talking with them."

"You could have told me not to do that."

"I want you to do whatever works best for you. These other crimes you resolved, you always had some input from friends, didn't you?"

"At some point." I took a few sips of water, then pressed the cool glass against my forehead. I didn't want to take more Advil, but the tightness in my head and neck suggested maybe I should. "It's not that different from law. You handle the case yourself, but bouncing things off another lawyer who isn't involved helps refine your thoughts. They ask questions you might not because they have different experience. They spot where you're assuming something you shouldn't."

"I guessed that might be the case," Tobias said. "And I decided right off if I was hiring someone unconventional for the job I needed to let her do things her way. Which meant learning more not just about you but your friends. Besides Joe, who I already trust."

The waiter appeared with a glass of Merlot for Tobias and a glass of Coke for me. Two glasses of wine is my limit, and I'd already had that. And sometimes caffeine helps stave off a migraine. Other times it makes it worse, but since I didn't feel any actual pounding yet I was hoping for the positive effect.

"And now you're good with my friends?"

Tobias traced a circle on the table with his index finger. "Between Maria's impressions and mine, yes. So long as any information you share stops with them."

"It will," I said.

"Okay. You were on the right track about my dad. His beliefs relate to the UFOs. Have you heard of people who think they were abducted by aliens?"

I was about to pick up my Coke glass, but I let my hand curl around it instead, feeling its chill. "Your dad thought he was abducted by aliens? I didn't – I thought people who believed that..."

I stopped. Nothing good could come at the end of that sentence. What little I knew about people who claimed that aliens abducted them came from comedy sketches or tongue-in-cheek news reports, plus reruns of the X-Files.

I drank some Coke. "I'm sorry. I know almost nothing about that."

Tobias's lips twitched upward. "It's all right. I know what people think. The stereotypes. That's why I wasn't in a hurry for anyone to know. But according to my Dad – and Isabel – all kinds of people are abducted. It's not just people driving around drinking beer on woodsy country roads."

"Isabel – Doctor Verde – says she was abducted, too?" I said.

"No, but she helps people who say they were. She referred my dad to a support group. But the abductions, that's not the key thing."

"There's something more unusual?"

Tobias pressed his hand flat on the table. "My dad thought he was a hybrid. Part alien, part human. And he believed I am, too."

11

———————

"OH." I used the neutral tone I adopt when something unexpected comes out in court and I want to hide that I'm surprised. And a little worried. "So that's – so when did your dad start to believe these things?"

"Mom was about seven months pregnant with me. Dad told her he believed aliens were abducting him. She says she listened and tried to keep an open mind, but she never believed it was happening. Never saw evidence of it. She finally persuaded him to see a psychiatrist."

"Isabel? No, she's a psychologist."

"Right, not her. He saw her for treatment years later, I'm pretty sure, for a year or so."

I ran my fingers over the condensation on my glass of Coke. So many questions ran through my mind I wasn't sure where to start. "What happened with the psychiatrist?"

"Dad didn't like the first one he saw. Or the second. But the third one hypnotized him, and Dad claimed to remember he'd been abducted throughout his life, not just recently. Later he started saying the aliens told him, through some sort of telepathy, that his mother had been abducted, too. But it had a rare side effect on her. She was supposed to forget the way most people do, but instead she remembered and it messed her up. And that was why she was never quite right."

"Was your dad angry about that?"

I couldn't imagine believing aliens abducted my mother, but if they had I'd feel mad that they'd changed her. Turned her into someone who couldn't take care of me.

"I got the sense he was relieved. That it explained things. Made him feel better. Like it wasn't his fault."

"Not his fault that his mother couldn't love him the way he needed?"

That made a lot of sense, too. Minus the alien part.

"Yeah. That. And it snowballed from there because then he learned, supposedly, that the aliens impregnated her. His mother. Making my dad a human-alien hybrid."

I swished my glass and watched the ice swirl. "His psychiatrist never suggested these beliefs might be a way of dealing with parents who let his sister abuse him?"

"No, but my mom did."

"That must have been a lot for her to take in."

"It was. But if it ended there, she could've lived with it. That's what she told me. Agreed to disagree. But then he said —" Tobias winced. "I never talk about all of this."

"Take your time."

He clasped his hands together and stared at his entwined fingers. "By the time I was eight my dad insisted the aliens had regularly abducted my mom. Resulting in her pregnancy with me."

I'd almost forgotten that Tobias said his father believed he was an alien-human hybrid too.

"Did he tell you that when you were eight?"

"Yeah. Before he told my mom." His pale skin turned a mottled red. "He said his role as my caretaker father on earth was very important. Someone who knew what I was going through because it happened to him, too. But to me, it sounded like – I felt like – I mean, what's a kid supposed to do with that?"

"You felt like he was saying he wasn't really your father."

He nodded and kept staring at the table. Cleared his throat. "When I got older, I wondered if it was some weird way of accusing my mother of having an affair. My mom doesn't think so. It was just something in his head, something that went wrong."

The hum of conversation around us had quieted. I glanced around. The tables closest to ours were empty. And other than Joe, Lauren, and Ty only one other person sat at the bar, a man wearing an I Love Chicago ball cap on his head that made me think he was from out of town.

"Is this what you meant when you said your parents disagreed about raising you?"

"Mostly. I remember them fighting. Mom calling him delusional. Dad saying his doctor had run all these tests and he was perfectly sane and Mom saying he doctor shopped and found one who was as crazy as he was. Not great. The last straw was my dad trying to convince me that I was being abducted regularly."

"Generations of alien abductions?"

"Dad said that was common. That just like aliens come back a lot to the same places they return to the same families." Tobias's shoulders hunched and drew together making him look like he was folding in on himself. "Something about studying human genetics."

I wanted to squeeze his hand in reassurance, but we didn't know each other that well. I settled for sliding my hand halfway across the table toward him. "I'm so sorry. That must have been really hard for you. Especially at eight years old."

"Yeah. But Mom did her best." He glanced at me from under his eyelids, gave me a half smile. "And at least he agreed with her about one thing. That he shouldn't tell all the world because they wouldn't understand. And maybe clients would drop him."

"Did you tell the police any of this?" I said.

If not and if the murder related to Kurt's views, Tobias might have doomed the investigation.

"I told them about his alien abduction beliefs and that he attended a support group. And that Isabel knew about all of it. Not the hybrid part. I was afraid it would make them try less hard. That they'd just see him as this crazy guy."

My friend of sorts Detective Sergeant Beckwell wouldn't let that sway him, at least not consciously. But police are human, and I couldn't swear that none of them would see Kurt that way or that it wouldn't cloud their judgment.

"What did you say about this support group?"

"That it exists. And I gave them the name of the one person I met from it. He's a dentist who doesn't mind people knowing about that part of his life. Doesn't advertise it, but doesn't mind. He's willing to talk to you if you think it'll help."

"I think it'll help," I said.

12

"Can you think of anything about your dad's beliefs that might cause someone to want to kill him?" I said. "For example, if he were going to expose someone in his support group?"

Tobias took out his credit card and waved to the waiter for the check. I'd never had a client foot so many bills before.

"Can't see my dad doing that. Other than the one member, he never told me anything about the other group members. Though he did beg me to come with."

"Maria heard your dad saying something to Isabel about how her hypnotherapy started it all. What does that mean?"

"Wish I knew. It doesn't make sense if he was talking about himself. He recalled all these things under hypnosis before he met her. You think you'll be able to talk to Art Feffor soon?" Art Feffor was the dentist in the alien support group. "I think we should move quickly."

Because he was clearly struggling, I didn't point out that we could have saved almost a week if he'd told me all of this on Day One. To be fair, if it were me, I'm not sure I would have.

"I'll do my best to reach him tomorrow. You're all right with me talking with my friends about all of this and possibly involving them?"

"Involving them how?"

"Not sure yet," I said, though I had an idea. "But when I talk to people and tell them I'm investigating the murder they'll be on guard. My friends might be able to get to know people another way."

The waiter interrupted with a card reader and Tobias inserted his card and tapped out his information.

"Do whatever you think is right." He put his credit card back in his wallet. "But you'll run it by me before they do anything that might expose my dad's secrets?"

"Definitely." I slipped on my leather jacket and fingerless gloves. "What's your gut feeling? Do your dad's abduction beliefs relate to his murder?"

Tobias stood. "I don't have a gut feeling about any of this. But I also think how could it not be related? It's the only thing unusual about him."

"There doesn't need to be something out of the ordinary about a person to become a crime victim."

I've learned through my law practice, and when investigating murders, that something unusual going on doesn't always relate to the main issue, whether it's a crime or a falling out between business partners. On the other hand, Kurt's beliefs about hybrids and aliens were part of his life. And a victim's life always matters.

"No, I guess not. But it's like this thread I have to pull on." Tobias pushed his chair into the table and we headed for the bar where Joe, Lauren, and Ty were gathering their things together.

"We should definitely pull on it," I said. "Let me think about the best way."

———

I HAD two conference calls with clients in the morning. Before the first one I emailed the dentist who belonged to the support group. We set a time to video chat late in the day. After my second conference call I researched alien abductions online. Each article I read led me to another website or topic. After two hours I took a break to catch up on other work, then grabbed a gourmet root beer from the office kitchen – the only real perk the suite's landlord provided – and signed into my video conference with Dr. Art Feffor.

Rather than a white dentist's coat Art wore a lightweight olive-colored turtleneck over jeans. Balding in front, he'd drawn his long whitish-gray hair into a ponytail, a look I've never loved but that a lot of Baby Boomer men in Chicago favor. Though I shouldn't be too hard on Boomers since I also didn't love my generation's fondness for man buns.

"Sorry." He gestured to the vinyl patient's chair and metal tray of instruments off to the side. "I close at four on Thursdays and my bookkeeper comes in. She's in my office. So here I am in an exam room." He laughed. "I promise not to examine your teeth."

A giant fish tank took up the entire wall behind him. It reminded me of the one in my orthodontist's office as a kid.

I adjusted my webcam so that when I looked at Art's image on screen, it looked as if I were meeting his eyes rather than staring above his head. "Thanks. Tobias told me he'd emailed you about my investigation. Before I start, anything you want to ask me?"

"Probably, but you first. I'm done for the day, and if I know lawyers you've got hours of work ahead of you."

"I hope not too much or my boyfriend'll be unhappy."

Ty and I had plans for dinner at a new wine and cheese bar, then a walk through a park-like neighborhood a few blocks south of my condo.

I covered basics first. Art told me he joined the support

group five years before and met Kurt the first night. He also freely shared that he'd been at an office event the evening Kurt was killed and home with his wife the rest of the night and the next morning.

"How did you find the support group?"

"Through my internist. She referred me to a therapist after I started having what I thought might be recurring nightmares."

"Might be? Something made you think you weren't dreaming?"

He shifted on his stool and it rolled sideways. Art gripped the counter to his left. "My eyes were open. I saw my bedroom and my wife sleeping next to me. But I also saw these beings around me. I couldn't move or speak. That's how it started."

"Something like sleep paralysis?" I said.

My research had led me to articles on sleep paralysis, which about twenty percent of people experience at one time or another in their lives. Our bodies become paralyzed when we sleep. It's normal so that you don't act out your dreams. If it wears off too soon, you'll sleepwalk. But sometimes while still paralyzed you start to wake up. It frightens most people because they can't move and their dreams and reality mix. According to one article's authors, a neurologist and psychologist, people interested in aliens and UFOs might attribute their paralysis and nightmare images to that. Someone with a fear of ghosts or vampires could see those. And other people might feel frightened in the moment but realize they'd been dreaming once they were fully awake and could move again.

"She thought it might be some type of sleep disturbance, yes," Art said. "But a sleep study didn't show anything. Eventually she suggested a therapist."

"For something specific?" I said.

Art shrugged and smiled. "Stress. The catch all when a doctor can't explain something. Which I admit I envy. I never get to blame dental problems I can't solve on stress."

"Are there a lot that you can't solve?"

He laughed again. "No. Most are pretty clear. Though some relate to stress for sure. Like teeth grinding."

"What happened with the therapist?"

"She thought I had sleep paralysis that just didn't happen to occur during the sleep study." His head turned the slightest bit side to side as he spoke.

"You didn't agree?"

"I knew it was more. And if I could just remember it all, I'd understand. I asked for a referral to someone who handled repressed memories. That brought me to a psychiatrist who said he had a client who saw similar things and underwent hypnosis. It turned out she was an alien experiencer."

"Experiencer?"

"Experiencer is what most of us who've been abducted by aliens prefer to be called."

I typed a quick note about that so I could use the right term if I talked with anyone else. People tend to relax more and feel safer if you use their language.

"And did you try hypnosis?"

"I did. It made a huge difference in my life. Before it when I woke up paralyzed with these beings all around me, I felt so helpless. And fearful."

The video froze for a second. When it came back, I asked if he felt the aliens wanted to hurt him.

"I didn't think they wished me well," Art said. "Why else would they paralyze me?"

Art told me that during a series of ten sessions he remembered many times that aliens visited him. They floated him out his window and into their spaceship. He was put in a chair much like his dentist's chair. They paralyzed him and fed a tube up his nose. Once he felt it all the way in his brain.

"It felt like something broke in my head when they did that." His hands rose to the sides of his head. "So painful."

"Did your doctor find anything wrong with you?"

"I felt fine in the morning, so I didn't go to see her."

Unlike Tobias, Art's body language was open and relaxed for the most part. Still, I chose my words carefully.

"I'm sure Tobias told you this is all new to me. At trial, there needs to be proof. Most courts won't allow testimony of memories retrieved through hypnosis because studies have shown therapists' suggestions can cause people to imagine and believe things that didn't happen."

"I've read that, too." He rocked back on his dentist's stool, hands on his knees, but his expression stayed relaxed. "And it doesn't apply to me. The therapist didn't suggest anything."

"But before you were hypnotized, she told you about a patient who discovered she'd been abd – she was an experiencer."

"Right. But she didn't tell me what the aliens looked like or what might have happened specifically."

"How did they look?"

He described beings with wide heads, large eyes, spindly fingers, and grayish skin. It conjured up images from X-Files episodes I'd watched as a kid on Friday nights with my sister.

"Experiencers call them the Grays," he said. "But I didn't think about any of that when the therapist counted me down into a trance state. I had a completely open mind."

We had different ideas about what an open mind meant, but my purpose here wasn't to argue with him.

"Why do you think the aliens do this to you?"

He leaned toward the camera, making his forehead and the bald area on his head appear larger. "That's how therapy helped me. Despite that sometimes it was painful when they took me, I let myself relax and listen to what they had to say."

"They spoke to you?"

"More like conveyed knowledge without speaking. And I learned they were taking people, studying us, for the good of humanity. To help us evolve. Now when it happens, I awaken in the morning with a strong feeling of peace."

"Did Kurt think that, too?"

"Oh, yes. We talked about it a lot, especially when I first joined the group."

"And did he tell you he believed he was a hybrid and Tobias was, too?"

Tobias had told me I could share this with Art, though it had taken a little cajoling on my part during our walk home. Despite that Kurt and Art met in a support group, Tobias thought his dad might have kept the hybrid part of his beliefs to himself.

Art didn't look surprised. "It was one of the first things he told me."

"What did you think about that?"

"It's not for me to judge anyone else's experience. That's the point of the group. We're all free to say what we need to say."

"You said it's not for you to judge. Were you tempted to?"

He rocked back on his stool again. "It was a little hard for me to accept. Which probably sounds strange, I know, after what I told you about myself. But my experiences are less – how do I put it? They're more limited. Some people report the aliens harvesting their eggs or sperm to create hybrids. Or what sound like sexual encounters with aliens. And that's not – I never had that. It's a little outside my experience."

I shifted my chair and bumped the edge of my desk, making the camera on top of my monitor bounce. I readjusted it. "And that makes you doubt it's real?"

"You're probably thinking pot meet kettle. And you're right. Who am I to question it? But these reports feel a little too much like adolescent sci-fi fantasies." He spun sideways on his stool and back to face the camera. "Never thought that about Kurt, though."

"Why not?"

"Hard to say. But he was so matter of fact about what happened."

I glanced at my bullet point outline at the bottom of the screen. "And the support group? How did you find it?"

"The therapist knew Isabel – Dr. Verde. Isabel had told her about a support group. So I went. And felt like I'd found my home."

"And your wife? How does she feel about all of this?"

"She believes I'm telling her what she calls my truth. But does she think this truly happens to me? I don't ask because I know she doesn't want to tell me No." He put a hand to the side of his mouth as if telling me a secret. "But she'd say No."

"And you're okay with that?"

He tilted his head. "I wish she could accept that it's real. But a lot of spouses and partners have trouble supporting alien experiencers. That's why they're allowed to come to the support group. To help them understand."

"Has she ever seen the aliens? Or noticed you missing from bed?"

"Nope. She's out like a light when it happens. But she's the soundest sleeper I ever met."

He told me he had no idea who might have killed Kurt.

"Anyone who was angry at him?"

"Only one person I can think of. Isabel."

13

————

Art told me the group met every other week. Two weeks before Kurt's death they met at Art's lake house in Indiana. He was swimming in the pool alone when Isabel and Kurt arrived, but they didn't see him because a stone fence surrounded the pool area. They were having a heated argument, one he felt sure they'd had before.

"What about?" I said.

"She kept saying he needed to listen to her, and he kept saying he'd listened and listened and listened. And weighed all the pluses and minuses. She said he clearly hadn't or he'd understand what she was saying. And it started over. I got out of the pool and called out to them. It felt wrong to keep listening."

An email notification popped up from the partner at my old firm who handled class actions. I excused myself for a moment to read it. She said she could meet me the following evening if I could come to her office. I sent a quick yes and clicked back to the video chat screen.

"Any idea what the fight was about?" I said.

"None."

"You've known Isabel and Kurt for years. If you had to take a wild guess?"

He scratched the side of his nose. "Sometimes they sniped at each other about retirement. Kurt was sixty-five and Isabel sixty-two. She has family in Ecuador and owns some property near a beach there, but she hardly ever visits. Kurt told me he'd love to retire, spend half a year here, split the rest between Florida, Aruba, and Ecuador."

"Isabel didn't want to do that?"

"She never meant to retire."

I didn't know if that would cause a running series of fights. But maybe. Ty worked a lot but he was much better at relaxing and setting work aside than I was. I could imagine some conflict on that front down the road.

More interesting, though, was that Kurt wanted to retire. No one else had suggested that.

"I don't know if he was determined to do it," Art said. "But he was getting tired of the court battles. Said he wanted a little more peace in his life."

"Hard to argue with that," I said, though perhaps Isabel had.

I asked if Art thought other support group members would talk to me about Kurt's murder or about their alien abduction experiences.

"Everyone cared about Kurt, so I'm sure they'd talk to you, at least on the phone, about anything that might help solve his murder. But I don't know if many of them would tell you their last names. Or share their experiences. It's a little like AA. Some people have no issue telling others they belong but others stay completely anonymous."

"Really? I had the impression that – that is, based on the articles and videos of interviews that I saw –"

"That experiencers are publicity hounds?"

"Not hounds. But that some of them may like the attention."

"Very few of us want attention. That's why the anonymity."

"If you meet at each other's houses, it's not exactly anonymous," I said.

"I'm the only one who offers a place I own. Otherwise, we
meet in private rooms at restaurants."

"Why aren't you concerned about anyone knowing?"

"My patients have been coming to me for years. I've got one
who moved six hundred miles away and coordinates her six-
month check ups with her visits to her parents. If she found out
about my alien experiences she might think it was odd, but
she'd keep seeing me."

"What's your secret?"

"I strive to make everything as pain free as possible. Always
have. I was an early adopter of those swabs to numb your gums
before the Novocaine shot. And to give my patients headphones
to listen to music during long procedures. If you're a dentist
people feel calm seeing, word gets around."

I wondered if his concerns about not causing pain to
patients might play into his nightmares, if that's what they
were.

We talked a while longer, but Art had no ideas about
anyone else who might have a grudge against Kurt. He also
didn't know much about Kurt's law practice other than to say
he never complained about his clients. In my view, that made
him the rarest of lawyers.

"It sounds like there's no chance I could attend the support
group?" I said.

"Sorry." He chuckled. "Got someone you can send in under
cover?"

"Actually...."

———

Lauren clapped her hands together. "I knew you'd need me
eventually. And by the way, I'd never go to a dentist who thinks

aliens are abducting him. No matter how good he is at his job. There's a lot of other dentists in the world."

We stood in the reception area outside my office. She and Joe had stopped by before heading to dinner and then a play at The Goodman. I still needed to do a couple more hours of work for a new client. I'd planned to do it in the morning, but Maria called to say the police finally released the crime scene, so I was touring Kurt's house first thing.

"But are you willing to pretend you've been abducted?" I said.

Joe, who was leaning on one elbow against the reception counter, raised an eyebrow. "Which one of us?"

"You've got acting experience." I buttoned my blazer. The building's heat is set lower in the evenings. It wasn't freezing inside, but it wasn't particularly warm.

"So do you," Joe said.

"But Isabel Verde already knows about me. Knows I'm investigating. And so does Art Feffor. So even if they let me attend, and Art doesn't think they would, they'd know why I was there."

"You said you need both of us?" Lauren said.

"Yes. One to be an experiencer, one to be the girlfriend or boyfriend."

"You seriously think Tobias will agree to this?" Lauren said.

"He said he was leaving it up to me what to tell you guys and how to involve you."

"But you're not specifically telling him we'll be infiltrating the group?"

"I prefer to think of it as actively observing. But no, I'm not. Either he trusts me or he doesn't, and he says he does. Are you both okay with this? It's a step beyond backing me up."

Lauren frowned. "Which none of us did great at last time. So whatever you need. I'll put on a tin foil hat if I have to."

"No tin foil hats. But this group might include whoever

murdered Kurt. There are risks, which is why I'm not that excited about sending you in."

Joe shot me a look. "Not so fun when your friends are thinking about doing risky things, is it?"

Joe had always been the most vocal about me taking too many risks.

"This is no time for sarcasm," I said. "I just want to be sure you're both careful."

"I am absolutely the most careful person you will ever meet," Lauren said.

"Your self-delusion knows no bounds," I said and glanced at Joe.

"We'll be careful," he said.

"But I should be the experiencer," Lauren said. "I don't care if he used to be an actor. Joe will find it impossible not to roll his eyes."

14

Early the next morning, half an hour before I needed to leave to meet Maria at Kurt's house, I dialed the number for my former therapist. I wrote out what to say ahead of time, but I got her voicemail.

"Rachel, hi, it's Quille Davis. I saw you about fifteen years ago when I was in college, back when I went by Q.C. Davis. I'm hoping I can tap into your expertise. One of my cases – I'm a lawyer now – involves repressed memories. I'm not looking for an expert, just to be able to talk some things through. If you can help, please let me know by text or calling. I'll pay you for your time of course." I left my number and hung up.

Therapy with Rachel hadn't ended well. She pushed me to accept that on some level I felt my dad abandoned me when he quit his full-time job two years before I started college. He and my mother moved back to Edwardsville, where they were from. I kept living with my Gram in LaGrange, a near west Chicago suburb.

I had already spent a couple years in therapy talking about my childhood and my mother. I knew I felt angry at her. And disappointed. She was the one, not my dad, who noticed me only when I stood on stage acting or singing or rehearsed with her.

Some of my actor friends envied me. They had to pay for voice lessons. I had a built-in teacher. But I never felt my mother was all that interested in me. I was named for the original Q.C. Davis, who started dancing and singing as a toddler. When my mother bragged to family members about "my Q.C." she never meant me.

My dad, on the other hand, listened when I told him about school, or what I did for fun with my best friend, or boys I liked. He came to see the plays and choir concerts I was in, but he made it clear it was for me, not because he missed Q.C. so much.

They moved because my mother wanted to be near the original Q.C.'s grave and her sister, my Aunt Cathy. But Edwardsville also was a much cheaper place to live than Chicago. I felt sure Dad also wanted to go back there because he longed to play music with his old friends again and work in the music store he had once owned rather than full-time in downtown Chicago as a copier repairman.

I felt my dad deserved some joy in his work again. It left me to pay for college on my own, but Gram had a room for me in her apartment and all the meals I needed free. The money I saved from working as an actress paid for my books and some of my tuition and I applied for every grant and loan under the sun, plus worked through college.

When my parents moved back to Edwardsville, I refused to talk to them on the phone for weeks. But within a month or so, I felt freer to make my own choices. I started figuring out what I wanted rather than how to get my mother's attention or please her. Dad listened to my doubts about pursuing singing or acting as a career, though he struggled to understand why I wanted to switch from artistic work to accounting, and later law, when I didn't have to.

Rachel helped me make that shift, too. Helped me identify what I loved about the business classes I took and see why I longed for work where I had more control over my professional life.

Years later when I went to law school, I was shocked at how many middle-class parents supported their kids well into graduate school. It dawned on me that Rachel hadn't been completely off base in saying my dad as well as my mother let me down. My mother was unable to work due to her severe anxiety and depression, but my dad chose not to keep his full-time job. I didn't feel entitled to anyone putting me through college. But support past the age of fifteen didn't seem like too much to ask.

Ty opened my eyes, too. His sister texted with him nearly every day. He and his parents talked once or twice a week and they asked about his life. His work. Me. Whether he was taking enough time off. They all did a video call once a month with extended family in Jamaica. It showed me how close families could be. And how much parents can be there even if they don't live nearby.

If I talked to Rachel again, I meant to tell her all of that. Well, not all of it since it would take a long time and I didn't plan to go back into therapy. But I meant to thank her for her help. And tell her I now got a lot of what she'd been urging me to see. I couldn't do that, though, if she didn't call back.

Part of me hoped that's what would happen. It'd be simpler.

––––––––

"The police really didn't clean up after themselves," I said as Maria and I exited Kurt's bedroom and headed downstairs. Piles of books and papers had been shoved against the wall on the landing and had crowded the corners of every room I'd seen, including the two spare bedrooms.

"No, but to be fair it pretty much looked like this before they got here. Minus the fingerprint dust. This way to the coach house."

We crossed the living room and kitchen, then walked through an enclosed porch on the back of Kurt's house.

"Normally all available surfaces were covered," Maria said as we stepped onto the stone patio. "We pushed his work out of the way for the party."

Overnight the wind had shifted and the temperature dropped so that it suddenly felt like November. The air bit into my cheeks. I raised the collar of my wool coat.

Padded chaise lounges and a wrought iron table and chairs with striped cushions covered one half of the patio. The other, which fronted a large above-ground hot tub, stood bare. No clutter here.

"He kept everything in the main house," Maria said. "The patio and coach house were for entertaining. Other than his study upstairs."

"Didn't he worry about people reading client files in the house? I saw court papers there," I said. In my own office suite, which was shared between over a dozen people, I kept all my files in my own office. I knew my officemate never went through my things, and I never read her documents.

"But that's all they are. Court documents anyone could get online and read. Kurt dictated his thoughts into his phone and emailed them to me later if he thought they were important. So nothing confidential there."

Kurt's home stood on a corner. Seven-foot wooden privacy fences blocked any view of the sidewalk, street, or his neighbor's patios, back yard area, or first floor. Anyone on the second or third floor next door could see into the yard, though.

"Is there any indoor passageway between the house and the coach house?" I said.

"Nope. The only way to get in is from the alley in back or across the patio like we're doing."

Maria took out keys and unlocked the door to the coach house.

"Beautiful." I pointed to the miniature crystal swan with ruby red eyes on her key ring.

Maria held it up. "Gift from an ex-boyfriend. Current at the time. I was in a play that was a feminist take on the Greek myth Leda and the Swan. He gave it to me opening night. Best thing about that relationship."

The coach house's kitchen was also neat except for the fingerprint dust everywhere. It smelled of lemon dish soap and looked like it was last updated in the 1990s, with white appliances and black Corian countertops. The ceramic tile floor in the family room looked perfect for wet feet from the hot tub. A basket of movie DVDs sat underneath a large flat screen TV and DVD player. The guest bedroom looked like it belonged in a beach house, all blues and beiges and framed photos of sea shells and sea shores. L train rumbles and squeals from two blocks away undercut that illusion, though.

The lofted second level was Kurt's study plus a three-quarter bath. Dark wood bookshelves stuffed with books and papers lined the back wall but there were no court files or papers anywhere. A large desk stood in the center of the hardwood floor directly below a skylight.

Maria pointed up. "He once told me he loved to sit here and look at the sky at night. Said he imagined he could see the stars."

I wondered if it also made him think of the aliens he believed visited him.

A large telescope stood in the corner of the study. "Was he interested in astronomy?"

According to Tobias, Maria didn't know about Kurt's alien

experiences. But she might simply never have mentioned it, thinking Kurt kept it secret from his son.

"Space flight fascinated him," Maria said. "And UFOs. Earlier this year he pulled everyone into the conference room to watch a recording of that 60 Minutes episode on them. The one where the military pilots said they saw aircraft do maneuvers that were impossible."

"I saw that, too." I'd watched the segment as part of my research yesterday.

The photos on the bookshelf included several of Kurt with two boys who looked like miniature versions of Tobias but none of Tobias himself. There were two others of him with Isabel Verde.

I picked one with a heavy pewter frame and turned to Maria. "Other than that phone call you heard did they seem to be getting along?"

"Sure." She smoothed her hair. "Well, no. I got the sense they might be on the verge of splitting up."

"Really? Why?"

"Hard to say." She wound her long hair around her fingers, a habit I share and have been trying to break. It might mean she was nervous or it might just be habit. "But it was like the magic was gone."

"After twenty years, that doesn't seem unusual."

"No, I know. But the last few months when he left for the weekend – he spent most weekends with her – he seemed, how do I say it? Flat. No excitement. No bounce to his step."

"Just the last few months?"

"Maybe a little longer than that." She trailed her hand over the desktop. "I started noticing around Easter."

It fit with Art's impression that Isabel and Kurt had been fighting regularly.

"Nothing Kurt mentioned being upset about?"

"No. But he didn't tell me everything. No reason he would."

———

"It still boggles my mind that someone shot Vanilla Man," Calista Zopp said.

My old firm has several floors in the Willis Tower, which was known as the Sears Tower when I worked there. It's the second tallest building in the United States. Tenants have access to a lounge on the 66th and 67th floor. It's filled with couches and chairs with sleek lines, bowl-shaped copper-colored coffee tables, and art deco style brass and glass light fixtures. Calista and I sat along the west window with a view of the expressways heading into and out of the city. The cars and trucks driving on them looked like strings of white holiday lights.

I'd gotten a glass of Pinot Noir at the bar. It was dry but with some cherry undertones. It was Monday evening, and Calista still had to head back to her office. She drank a cappuccino.

"You called Kurt Vanilla Man?" I said.

"Everyone did. At least on the defense side. It's for all those class actions where he claimed it was fraud to label anything vanilla flavored or strawberry flavored or what have you if it didn't contain vanilla beans or bits of real strawberries."

Calista started her career at the Cook County State's Attorney's office. After two decades prosecuting criminal cases she came in as a partner and gradually moved into class actions. She was the only part-Asian, part-Black partner at the firm and one of the only women on its powerful ten-person management committee. But when she started out, we were on a women's business development committee together, and she'd cheered me on from afar when I opened my own practice.

"Wish I could sue over all the Neapolitan ice cream I ate growing up," I said, thinking of many bowls of the pink, white, and brown ice cream my dad and I had shared. I was pretty sure the flavors were labeled vanilla, strawberry, and chocolate.

And equally sure, because they were the cheapest store brand versions, that their ingredients included no real fruit, beans, or plants.

Calista nodded. "Never ate that. But plenty of soft-serve vanilla cones. Back when I was growing up and chemicals in food were the latest and greatest thing."

"What was Kurt like to deal with on cases?"

She sipped her cappuccino and wiped the foam from her lips with a cocktail napkin. "To use the most apt words in my extensive vocabulary, a pain in the butt."

"A jerk?"

"Worse. A true believer. Which is harder to deal with in a class action than in regular cases."

"Why?"

True believers are lawyers who wholeheartedly believe everything their clients say, can't see a single problem with their cases, and can't imagine the other side making any valid points. Sometimes they trip themselves up because they miss the flaws in their claims. But they almost always make lawsuits take far longer and cost much more because they refuse to compromise on anything.

"A lot of class action plaintiff attorneys comb through regulations, find something that violates the fine print or say an act that's perfectly legal violates the spirit of the law. I always love that. Then they sue on behalf of everyone in the entire United States in the same spot. It can be over ridiculous things, like these vanilla cases, but it takes years to work out. One of mine took a decade. And a fortune to defend. The clients want the bleeding to stop, so they settle whether or not they did anything wrong."

"But sometimes they did do something wrong?"

"Sure." She twirled a cocktail straw in her fingers. "It's about the same as other types of cases. I'd say about fifteen percent of the time my client's absolutely wrong."

I nodded. "Same here. Then about fifteen percent of the time the client's absolutely right and the rest are in the gray area."

"Except in class actions there are a lot more completely bogus cases."

"You really think so? Or is it just that you've been doing it so long?"

If you're almost always working for the same types of clients, you risk losing perspective. You don't become a true believer necessarily, but you don't see the facts as clearly as when you walked out of law school.

"No. I noticed it from my first year here. The payoffs are so high the attorneys will spend more time on iffier cases. And the clients aren't paying by the hour, or paying attention, so the attorneys do whatever they want. Thus cases about vanilla beans. I want to say thirty different courts have thrown those kinds of suits out. But you only need a single court to let one go ahead and some group of plaintiff's attorneys will make hundreds of thousands or millions of dollars. Inspiring copy-cats everywhere."

I thought of Bryan's cavalier attitude about failing to tell the client that Kurt died. "Why don't clients pay attention?"

Clouds had drifted over from the lake and now I saw nothing out the windows but gray.

"They don't have much of a dog in the fight," Calista said.

"Ever?"

"Oh, now and then. A consumer who got roped into some cable TV deal and can't ever cancel it and is justifiably angry about it. But usually it's like these flavoring cases. The client knew what they were buying and would never have complained without an attorney suggesting they could make some money off it."

"Okay, but the client cares about the money, right?"

"Not the way the lawyers do. When I say money, I mean the

client, the plaintiff, might get five thousand dollars. Not nothing, but not the millions the attorneys can get. And the class members –"

"They get a few bucks each."

I wondered if there might be a disgruntled client or class member out there who figured out it was a bad deal.

"Sometimes not even that. They get a postcard in the mail that tells them how to make a claim. But most people throw it out. In other cases, everyone gets a check, but it's rare that it's for more than five or ten dollars."

"But there's a reason for these kinds of cases, right? The person overcharged for cable isn't going to sue for twenty dollars. No lawyer will take it. Without class actions big companies could overcharge a million people five dollars each and never have to pay that back."

"You're not wrong. But most of the cases I defend aren't like that. They're a cottage industry that pays lawyers on both sides to no good end." She sighed. "And maybe I *have* been doing it too long."

"Would it be unusual for an attorney not to tell the client about something important? Let's say one of the lawyers who represented the class left the firm?"

I didn't want to reveal anything about how Bryan or his firm did things, but I needed to know if his way of handling the clients was unusual.

"Well, they'd need to tell the court. But it wouldn't surprise me if it took a long time to get around to telling the client. Most of the fights in class actions are about complex legal issues that people who aren't lawyers don't know or care about."

I couldn't ask Calista about Kurt's alien beliefs, but I could ask around it. "What if an attorney for the class has some very odd religious beliefs or, say, belonged to a cult? Would the court care?"

"If the defendant showed the beliefs interfered with the ability to do a good job."

That didn't seem to go anywhere in terms of Kurt's beliefs about abductions. But I could see where Tobias felt some concern. A judge might think there was something mentally wrong with an attorney who claimed to be a human-alien hybrid.

I scrolled through the notes I'd taken on my iPad. "You said true believers are worse in class actions than other cases. Why?"

Maybe a lawyer who ran up against Kurt got fed up. I'd interviewed several by phone and all sounded sorry about his death, but perhaps one of them was hiding a grudge.

"When the attorneys on the other side only care about how much money they'll make, most of the time you work out a number everyone can live with. But a true believer will ask for changes a company just can't make."

"Can't? Or won't?"

"Okay, I didn't work on those vanilla cases. But as an example, maybe the plaintiff wants the company to label its ice cream Fake Vanilla Flavor. Or Dangerous Chemical Vanilla Flavor. Or stop using the word Vanilla at all and call it White ice cream. I can't do anything with that."

"Couldn't the defendant just start using vanilla beans?"

"Sounds good until you look at the cost difference. Suppose I make a fortune selling dollar-a-cone soft serve made with artificial vanilla flavoring to tired, broke moms who want a cheap icy treat for themselves and their kids. Those moms aren't following me over to Whole Foods to pay four or five times that much for a vanilla bean ice cream sandwich. Especially if they've got three or four kids. It's a whole different business."

"So someone like Kurt might have a lot of enemies because of his practice?"

"Enemies? No. He was frustrating, but also basically a full-employment act for everyone like me on the defense side."

"How about at the corporations he sues?"

"They weren't thrilled with him. But it's part of the cost of doing business. Get rid of Kurt and someone else steps in. You want to know who was mad at Vanilla Man talk to people on his side."

"Why?"

"On the plaintiff's side whoever controls the case earns the biggest fee, and we're talking huge amounts. You know the salaries here." I had been earning well over six figures when I left, something I didn't feel I was likely to replicate on my own for a long time, if ever. I guessed Calista earned somewhere around a million dollars a year. "But guys like Kurt and that E. Drake Draper – they're the ones who can afford the yachts and private jets and homes on Martha's Vineyard."

"E. Drake told me he has cases where he earns nothing."

"True. We have our share of success on the defense side. And there are class action plaintiff's attorneys barely scraping by. Mostly the ones who try to dabble, which is like playing the lottery and calling it a business plan. But E. Drake's figured it out. He's good at choosing what horse to bet on."

"Was there tension between Kurt and E. Drake?"

"Not that I noticed. They were a good team." She finished the last of her cappuccino. "Kurt had a lot of passion, knew the law inside and out. But he came to court and settlement conferences wearing suits it looked like he crumpled on the closet floor and stamped on. E. Drake Draper, he tells a good story, looks polished but not too slick. I'm not convinced he always understands what he's saying, but he makes it sound terrific."

"And Kurt's partner?"

"Bryan? Waves his arms too much for my taste. But he doesn't crumple his suits. And I suspect he's the one who does all the grunt work and analysis Kurt relied on."

"What do you think will happen to King and Stillwell with Kurt gone?"

"They'll probably recruit a new attorney. Or two. But it'll take a while. They'll lose momentum."

That suggested E. Drake and Bryan both had more reason to keep Kurt alive than kill him off.

"If I want to know more about all of them – Draper, Bryan, Kurt – who should I talk to?"

Calista looped her purse strap over her shoulder. "Try Fred Varnes. He has a lot of cases with King and Stillwell and Draper but he's no fan of either. No fan of anyone as far as I can tell. He'll tell you exactly what he thinks."

The rain had stopped, but the Loop empties out not long after six, especially in the chillier months. I didn't want to walk home in the dark though it was only a mile. I took one of the two cabs in line across from the Tower.

On the ride home, I typed in an entry for the time I talked with Calista about topics related to the murder investigation so I could bill Tobias. I left out the time spent asking questions to help me understand class actions. It was too general for me to feel right charging the time to the fee lawsuit. When I got home, though, I scanned the receipt for my wine and sent it to a separate app that tracked business expenses.

As I closed the app, I had the nagging feeling I'd missed something about the evening. But I couldn't think what it might be. Ty texted to ask if it was too late to come over. I told him it wasn't and read through my notes as I waited for him, hoping some brilliant insight might pop into my mind. It didn't.

But I was meeting Dr. Isabel Verde tomorrow, and I had plenty of questions for her. And if I could squeeze it in, I'd call Fred Varnes, the attorney Calista mentioned.

15

____

My morning court appearance took less time than I expected, so I researched Fred Varnes. He didn't have a website, but I found an online listing in a lawyer directory. He answered his phone on the third ring. I introduced myself as an attorney defending King and Stillwell in a fee lawsuit E. Drake Draper brought.

"Good luck to you." His voice was low and raspy. "That pr – excuse me. I can't say what he is to a lady. But he chiseled me on fees. I'm sure he's doing it to King and Stillwell."

"You've worked with him on a lot of cases?" I said.

"Hah. Worked. No one works with E. Drake. E. Drake, who goes around being called that? Pick a name. First, middle, don't care, just pick one. Not all this initial crap."

"But you've got a number of cases with him?"

"If you call five a number. Five's enough. Screwed me over every time."

"He didn't pay the amounts he agreed to?"

"He weaseled out every which way from Sunday."

I wasn't exactly sure what the phrase referred to but I could guess. "Sorry to hear that. But why keep sending him cases?"

"Never sent him a thing. Talked to Kurt King when I heard he was starting class actions, brought him a case. King worked with E. Drake. On the other cases E. Drake horned in. Had his own client, then took over."

"That happens a lot in class actions?"

"Someone's got to run the case. Won't be me. Not my area. But godda – excuse me again. Don't know why it has to be him."

I typed a few notes. "You got along with Kurt better?"

"Got along? Not sure that's the word. But he was a straight shooter. Damn shame – pardon me – he got killed."

His language was hardly the worst I'd ever heard. Including in an email an opposing counsel sent me by mistake. I found it almost charming in an old school way that Varnes felt he needed to apologize.

"Any ideas about who might have wanted to kill Kurt?" I said.

"His ex-wife or girlfriend probably."

"By girlfriend, you mean Isabel Verde?"

"Who's that now?" Varnes said.

"The woman he was seeing."

"No idea who he was seeing. Though he looked pretty chummy with that secretary of his. What's her name? But all I meant is it's always a woman. Gets jealous, gets angry, shoots the guy."

The charm faded abruptly. Also, what he said wasn't true. Women are more often murdered by people they know, while men are more likely to be killed by strangers.

"The office manager, Maria?" I said. "Is that who you mean?"

I couldn't imagine who else. Bryan was the only lawyer. The firm had two employees. Maria and the receptionist, who was a male night student at one of the city colleges.

"Don't know her name. Pretty girl, long hair, on the heavy side. Lost twenty pounds she'd be a real looker. Shame when a woman lets herself go."

Fred Varnes's online photos showed a seventyish man with fringes of curly dull gray hair springing out from the sides of his head, a belly that hung inches over his beltline, and a double chin. Maria would be distraught that he thought she'd let herself go.

But his comment made me wonder. Maybe Maria claimed Kurt no longer seemed excited about Isabel because Kurt said that and started seeing Maria. Off-putting as he was, Varnes could be right about jealousy as a motive. But who was jealous of whom?

I asked Varnes a few more questions, but he had nothing to add about Kurt or the fee lawsuit. After hanging up I quickly filled in my notes about Varnes. I started to review what I'd discussed with Maria, then glanced at the clock. There was no time to call her. I needed to finish revising a brief and file it today before meeting Isabel Verde at six p.m. I sent a quick text to Tobias.

Ever think your dad and Maria might be interested in one another?

He answered right away.

Romantically? No. He was with Isabel forever.

I wasn't sure why he thought that answered the question.

———

DR. ISABEL VERDE was meeting me after she finished teaching for the afternoon at University of Chicago in Hyde Park. I borrowed Lauren's Volvo. She doesn't own a parking spot and I do, so she parks in mine. In exchange, she lets me use her car whenever she doesn't need it. It's a few years old now but handles well, which I especially like because I don't drive that much. I walk or take public transportation. In Chicago that's far less expensive than paying to park wherever you go. Plus I get exercise and avoid driving in heavy traffic.

There are buses that stop near my condo and take me within a few blocks of the University of Chicago campus. But the restaurant Isabel suggested was six blocks from the nearest bus stop, and it wasn't the safest area to walk in during the evening.

It did, though, feature free parking for patrons, something that's non-existent in my neighborhood. I arrived early and sat at the bar drinking a seltzer with lime while I reread the outline I wrote for the interview. I didn't plan to look at it during dinner or to take notes. Better to have a conversation. That might help Isabel relax and let down her guard. Plus I wanted to observe her reactions.

Through the glass entryway I had a view of the stores outside the restaurant and of the street. About ten minutes to six a shiny black SUV pulled to the curb. A woman with bobbed white hair stepped out of the back. Her slim build matched the woman in Kurt's photos.

I walked toward her as she entered.

"Doctor Verde? Quille Davis." I held out my hand.

"Good to meet you, Quille." Her handshake was firm and her fingers cool. "And please, call me Isabel. My friends do."

I wanted to take that as a sign that she meant us to become friends.

"What do your clients call you?" I asked as we stepped over to the host stand.

"It varies." She unwound a gold silk scarf from her neck. "But eventually most of them call me Isabel."

We sat along the windows, also with a view of the parking lot. Inside, the restaurant featured lush plants in wooden planters overflowing with thick vines and purple flowers, iridescent blue plates that matched the hanging light fixtures, and interior brick walls, giving the place a gleaming, urban feel.

"So sorry I didn't get back to you sooner about getting together." Isabel folded her long wool coat over the chair back next to her and set her leather briefcase on the seat. She slipped off her suit jacket. "Busy week. I'm on several committees at the University, plus doing intake on two new clients. All while trying to process my own grief."

It was a long explanation I hadn't asked for. I wondered if she felt guilty about not making time sooner. Or maybe about something else.

We agreed on a mushroom, goat cheese, and arugula flatbread to start. Isabel ordered an Anjou pear martini. I stuck with seltzer since I was driving.

Isabel unwrapped her black cloth napkin. "This probably isn't what you want to hear, but I won't be able to tell you much of what Kurt said to me."

"Why not?"

"Therapist-client privilege."

"He was your client and you were involved with him?"

It's a bad idea for lawyers to date their clients, and I was pretty sure doing the same could cost Isabel her practice. Or her position at the University of Chicago.

"He wasn't my client per se. But I conducted a few sessions with him over the years, so the privilege applies."

"But privilege ends with death," I said.

"Legal authorities differ about that."

The scent of braised short rib filled the air as a waiter walked by carrying two plates with small servings of it.

"Were they hypnotic sessions?" I asked, thinking of the phone call Maria overheard and Bryan's reference to hypnosis.

"As I said, privileged."

"Your website says you use hypnotherapy. For weight loss, smoking, other kinds of addictions."

"I do. It can be very helpful."

"Not asking about Kurt, but do you use it to help clients recover memories?"

"To get in touch with their memories, yes."

Our drinks arrived. Isabel took a swallow of hers and kept her hand on the stem after setting the martini glass on the table.

"I take it you can tell me about what Kurt said outside of therapy?"

"Quite possibly. But I'm simply letting you know up front that I consider anything related to what came out during our sessions confidential."

That isn't how the law on privilege works, but I didn't want to argue. Finding points you can agree on and working from there makes most interviews more productive.

"If Kurt talked to Tobias about something, you could talk about it, right? Because Kurt wasn't keeping it secret."

"True."

I squeezed my lime slice into my glass. "I'd like to hear about Kurt's belief that aliens abducted him."

"Not his belief. His experiences."

Despite contradicting me, Isabel's tone remained pleasant. Her elbows rested lightly on the table as she sipped her martini.

"Did you ever see one of these experiences happen?"

Between the accounts I'd read online of abductions, my other research, and my call with Art Feffor I didn't expect Isabel to say she'd seen aliens abduct Kurt. But it pays to keep an open mind and ask rather than guess.

She set down her glass and shook her head. "It doesn't work that way."

"How does it work?"

"Typically, if the experiencer has a spouse or partner who's in the room or the house, that person remains unaware. In a deep sleep. Almost a trance."

"That's something the aliens do to them?"

That was a question I'd never thought I'd ask in the course of my legal work life.

"As far as anyone knows, yes. Some experiencers try to wake up their partners to show them what's happening and can't."

"Is the other person hurt in any way?"

"No. At least I've never heard of that."

I wanted to know if Isabel believed these things herself or took what her clients told her at face value so that she could treat them. But no matter how I tried to appear neutral, my skepticism might show through. I needed other questions answered before I risked that.

"What makes you think a person who reports this kind of experience wasn't dreaming?" I said.

The server set down the flatbread. It smelled of baked bread, olive oil, and oregano and was topped with goat cheese crumbles and mushroom chunks sprinkled among tiny leafy greens.

Isabel used a butter knife to slide a quarter of it onto her plate. "The fact that I hear so many of these experiences that are so similar. There's no reason a twenty-five-year-old man in Chicago and a sixty-eight-year-old woman in Charleston would dream about an encounter on the same type of spaceship with aliens that have grayish skin and large eyes. Or have night-mares about the same types of experiments being done on them."

I bit into the flatbread as she talked, enjoying the mix of spices, greens, and mild, creamy cheese.

"But don't most people who say aliens visited them live in the United States? Or other countries where the public's familiar with alien abduction stories through novels or other media?"

"What's your point?"

"I read that in countries where UFOs and aliens aren't part of popular culture, no one reports alien abductions. Instead, when they report similar experiences they believe the gods spoke to them or angels took them flying through the heavens."

"That's not surprising." Isabel waved to the server and pointed to her empty glass. "We all filter new experiences through the lens of what we know about the world."

"Agreed. So what convinces you that your clients are being abducted by aliens rather than being visited by gods or angels?"

She set down her fork. "I believe my clients. I haven't seen them confabulate in any other area of their lives. They don't show symptoms of schizophrenia or psychosis. And as a psychologist I have good insight into whether people are telling the truth. I believe they are. Don't you believe your clients?"

"Not always."

"Well, our professions differ," Isabel said.

Unless I knew for a fact a client was lying, it was my job to accept their story and present it to the court in the best possible light. The other side did the same thing for their client and a judge or jury decided what was true. While I sympathized with most of my clients, I didn't believe they always told me the truth.

"I read an abstract of a study that seemed to show people who report experiences are more likely to form false memories, particularly if they hear suggestions while under hypnosis," I said.

"Well, I don't try to trick my clients into believing things that aren't true, including under hypnosis, so I can't speak to that."

"But you must have read the literature on suggestibility. What do you think about it?"

Isabel ate the last of her flatbread as the server set another pear martini on the table. "All it means to me is that experiencers are more open to possibilities outside of the rigid world of Western thought. And I personally think that's healthy."

Stripping away the commentary, it sounded to me like Isabel agreed that experiencers were more suggestible than average, yet it didn't change her views.

"What about the spaceships? Tobias tells me the neighbors never saw one though Kurt said he'd been abducted from each place where they lived."

"People don't see what's unimportant to them," Isabel said. "If you're walking down the street absorbed in your smartphone, you won't see a bus that drives right past you. Also, I'm certain aliens advanced enough to reach our galaxy and planet have ships that operate without lights or sound, allowing them to be unobserved."

"But didn't Kurt see the spaceships from outside? Tobias told me that's what some of his models are based on."

"My theory? I believe the experiencers are chosen. Special. Particularly the ones who remember what happened. The aliens trust them and are fine with them, but not anyone else, seeing the ships inside and out."

Art Feffor said experiencers weren't seeking attention. But the longing to feel special or chosen might sway a person to see themselves as being part of a larger purpose rather than having a sleep disorder.

"Do you treat a lot of experiencers?"

Isabel smiled. "You're wondering if I buy into all this, or pretend to, because it's a lucrative practice area for me?"

"I'm just curious how many clients you're basing your views on."

"I've treated thirty or forty experiencers over the last three decades."

"Yet you haven't authored any articles on it. Do you think it would hurt your career if you did?"

"Wouldn't it hurt yours? I don't need to guess how the establishment will react. An established psychiatrist at Harvard was subjected to tenure review when he started talking about treating patients who were experiencers."

"John Mack? The psychiatrist? But he retained his tenure."

Mack's name came up early in my research. He went

beyond talking about treatment and said he believed his patients who claimed to have been abducted.

"After a long fight. Also, he was a man and a medical doctor. As a woman psychologist I've no confidence I'd get the same result."

"I thought academia might be different from law. On the gender front. It seems like there's more openness there."

Her eyebrows raised. "Funny. I assumed law might be better given that lawyers ought to understand the law about equality."

I shook my head. Women had been fifty percent of law school graduates in the U.S. for over twenty years. Yet, the most recent Glass Ceiling report found women made up only a quarter of law firm partners.

Isabel sighed. "I don't know why I'm surprised. As to Mack, it worked out for him as far as staying in his position at Harvard. But he became a laughingstock."

"How do experiencer clients find you?"

"From other experiencers. Or a doctor or therapist who thinks that might be an issue for a client refers them to me."

"Did you tell the police that's part of your practice?"

"I did. In case it might be relevant. But I hope you'll do me the courtesy of not telling anyone else."

"I'll do my best," I said. "But how do these other therapists know to refer people to you?"

"Like Kurt, I don't hide my interest in UFOs. If another therapist knows me well enough to know about that, they'll send over a client thinking I'll have a bit more insight. Not that they believe their clients."

The waiter brought our entrées. Grilled salmon with an orange glaze and side of asparagus and wild rice for me, vegetarian lasagna for Isabel. Mine was delicious. We both ate for a few minutes without speaking.

"I understand Kurt's views – experiences – caused stress in his marriage," I said. "And with Tobias."

"To say the least. His ex-wife divorced him. And Tobias refused to consider that his father was telling him the truth."

"So you did know why they divorced. You avoided the question before."

Isabel shifted her martini glass so it sat in front of the center of her plate, directly between us. "I wasn't about to talk about Kurt's experiences. That was confidential. But Tobias told you, so now I can talk about it."

"And Kurt pushed Tobias to believe that he, too, had been abducted, and so had his mother, and Tobias and Kurt were hybrids?"

"It was a lot for Tobias to take in. It might have been better if Kurt let that go."

"Do you think Tobias has been abducted?"

Her frown deepened the lines in her forehead. "He's never talked to me about it, so I can't evaluate him."

"What do you personally think about this hybrid idea?"

"There's no proof of different physiology or altered genes in people who say they're hybrids. I'd expect to see that. Also, what I know about biology tells me it's unlikely aliens and humans could reproduce with one another. So I don't think there are hybrids in the way some of my clients do. I can see a more figurative sort of reproduction. A mental and spiritual joining to form a new being."

"Did Kurt agree about that?" I said.

"He thought our human range of testing wasn't sophisticated enough to spot the alien biology. We agreed to disagree."

"Any other running arguments?"

She lay her fork on her plate, tines down. "I didn't say we argued. We disagreed."

Isabel would make a good expert witness. She didn't let me reframe what she said.

"I heard you and Kurt disagreed about something else. Something he needed to decide. You told him to listen to you and to weigh the pluses and minuses, but he claimed he already had."

I was taking a chance she'd connect this information to Art. But it sounded to me like a long-running fight, so odds were more than one person heard it.

"I don't know who told you that." She pushed her plate to one side, a thin slice of lasagna left along with a few peas. "The only thing I can think of is we did talk on and off about Kurt selling his home and moving closer to Hyde Park, closer to me. I didn't think he'd like the commute to work."

I made a mental note to ask everyone I had already talked to, including Maria, whether Kurt ever mentioned this idea.

"I wasn't looking for that much togetherness. I liked focusing on my work during the week, then spending the weekends with him. I think he liked it too."

"Then why did he want to sell and move closer?"

"I think he was simply feeling the need for a change. He'd run his firm for decades, he'd lived in his home for decades, been with me for decades."

"Was he thinking of retiring?"

"He joked about it. But I couldn't imagine him not working."

Her comments weren't too far off from Art Feffor's guess that they argued about retirement. But Isabel made it sound like a calm disagreement, not a heated dispute. Though, as I knew from experience, when someone dies most people want to remember only good things.

I asked more about Kurt's desire for change, and Isabel claimed Kurt hadn't been unhappy about anything. Also that there was nothing else they argued about.

We agreed to split a slice of key lime pie with coconut gelato for dessert. The gelato was a bit grainy, but I liked the tangy pie.

"Do you think there's any way Kurt's alien experiences relate to his murder?" I said.

She smiled, looking for a moment more like my teenage

niece than a middle-aged psychologist. "Are you asking if I think aliens from another planet did it?"

I ate another bit of pie, unsure what to make of her shift into playfulness. And wondering why she considered that a joke if she really believed aliens visited Kurt and her clients.

"I'm asking for your gut feeling," I said. "Or your professional opinion. Anything about Kurt's alien experiences that could have caused his death."

Isabel pressed her lips together for a moment. "The only thing I can think of is if someone in the support group thought Kurt might expose their secrets. But I can't imagine him ever doing that. He understood the importance of keeping confidences."

Isabel told me the same things about the support group that I already knew from Art. Like Tobias, she had told the police about the group, but she also asked them to voluntarily contact the police. She claimed most of them had. And that none had been in Chicago the weekend of Kurt's death.

"You said you and Kurt didn't argue. But someone heard you arguing at the party the night before his death."

"Really?" She opened her eyes wider as if in surprise, then glanced away. "Oh, that was nothing. He'd expected me to stay the weekend. But at the last minute I got an invite to fill in for a colleague at the symposium."

"Someone in Kurt's office also overheard Kurt saying your hypnotherapy started everything. What was that about?"

The waiter picked up our dessert plate and left a leather folder with the bill. Isabel opened the folder and took out her credit card. "Split?"

"If you want to. But I'm happy to pay," I said.

"No, no. I don't feel I've been much help to you." She closed the folder and handed it to me.

"The phone conversation?" I said.

"I don't remember it. But it sounds like it related to Kurt's therapy so I couldn't share it with you anyway."

"Had you done hypnotherapy with Kurt recently?"

"I can't tell you that."

I glanced at the bill, which totaled less than I expected, reflecting the lower costs for rent and insurance in Hyde Park versus in downtown Chicago or Printers Row, where I live.

The server returned and ran our credit cards. She left separate receipts for us to sign.

"One of the people I talked to thought Kurt might have been considering breaking up with you," I said.

Isabel's pen froze mid-signature and she looked up. "What? Who would say that?"

"I can't share that." Two could play the confidentiality game. "But did he ever say he wanted to stop seeing you?"

"No. Never."

"Did you ever feel he might be losing interest?"

Isabel tucked her credit card receipt into her purse, took out a lipstick, and used the back of the spoon as a mirror as she applied it. "What's the longest romantic relationship you've had?"

"Three years." I didn't add that it had started when I was sixteen, which likely made it different from adult relationships.

"When you see someone for ten or twenty years, it's different. There are times when you feel the closest you've ever felt to that person, times when you wonder if the things that annoy you about each other have hit the point where it makes no sense to continue, and times when you drift along not happy or unhappy, just there. But you hang in because of the wonderful times. Because there's so much that works."

"That doesn't answer my question."

"Were there times I felt Kurt lost interest? No. But I'm sure sometimes he felt less interested than others. As did I."

"Any times recently either of you felt that way?"

"No."

"When was the last time you felt he might be less interested?"

"I was talking figuratively. Generally." She took her suit jacket off the back of her chair and slid one arm into it and then the other. "It's an ebb and flow."

"Sometime in the last year?"

She stood and started putting on her long wool coat. "No."

"Did he ever tell you he started seeing someone else?"

Isabel paused with one arm halfway into its sleeve. "Was he?"

"I've gotten a few hints of that."

She yanked the coat the rest of the way on. "I don't know if you're saying that to bait me or you really heard something. Either way, it's not true."

"You ever ask him about that?"

"I didn't ask because I didn't need to ask."

The restaurant had mostly emptied out. I waited with her for her Uber so she wouldn't be out there alone in the dark. Though our conversation was stilted, probably as a result of my last questions, Isabel asked the Uber driver to idle the car until I got into the Volvo and pulled away.

On the drive home, my head started pounding, an after effect of a long day and intense focus on every word Isabel said. At a stoplight I swallowed two Advil dry – a skill I'd learned during three-hour law school classes. The pounding dropped to throbbing by the time I drove into the garage. It took four tries to maneuver the car into my narrow spot, which is bordered by a wall and a concrete pillar.

Inside, I paced my condo, dictating notes into my iPhone and exchanging texts with Maria. She said Kurt never mentioned retiring or moving to Hyde Park. Tobias said the same when I texted him. But both told me Kurt might not confide his plans in them.

The pulsing in my head had eased by the time I stopped pacing and set down the phone. Movement sometimes helped. I took out my dinner receipt to scan for my expense app. Doing so reminded me of meeting Calista, and made me realize what nagged at me had nothing to do with our conversation. All the same, I'd just hit on a possible motive for Kurt's murder.

16

───────

I was in my office by seven the next morning sipping Earl Grey tea, ready to scroll through hundreds of pages of PDF files from the food cases when Rachel, my former therapist, returned my call.

My hand hovered over the receiver. I'd come in early to get this project done, not talk on the phone. But my schedule had no gaps later in the day, so better to talk now than play phone tag. I answered.

"Quille, so wonderful to hear from you. Sorry it took so long to get back to you. I was out of town for a few days."

I smiled and let my back rest against the back of my chair. Her voice, an alto with warm notes, sounded the same as I remembered. As quickly as I could, I explained about investigating crimes, sometimes as part of a legal case and sometimes not, and about what I'd learned so far about repressed memories. It still took nearly ten minutes. I kept an eye on the clock so I didn't take up too much of Rachel's time. Also, I had a nine a.m. conference call and still hoped to go through the PDFs.

"Your research is thorough, which doesn't surprise me,"

Rachel said. "I doubt it's worth your client's time to pay me for background when you've done so much already."

"Oh."

"Unless you need an expert, in which case I can refer you to someone. Repressed memories aren't my area of expertise."

I closed out an email from the Cook County court at the bottom of my screen. "Have you done any work in the area?"

"No. But I've worked with people suffering from PTSD, which makes me a bit skeptical. PTSD sufferers, and most people, are more apt to remember trauma, not block it out. To oversimplify, people with PTSD focus too much on what happened to them. It takes them over. The challenge is to help them stop reexperiencing their trauma. It makes it hard for me – this is my personal view here, not a professional opinion – to understand people who say they forgot a traumatic experience like being abducted by aliens, only to have it surface decades later."

"You think therapists are planting suggestions under hypnosis?"

"I'm just not qualified to say."

"All right. Well, thank you."

"You sound disappointed," Rachel said. "Anything else I can help you with? What else is happening in your life?"

"I, uh, I talked to my dad recently. About investigating the original Q.C.'s death. And, see, I still say 'original,' like you got me to do. Not the 'real Q.C.'"

"I'm glad that stuck with you. An investigation like that, a cold case I guess the term is, that's a big undertaking. And a lot of time you'll be spending, if you do it, on events that happened before you were born. Before you were conceived."

"Are you saying I shouldn't do it?"

"I haven't talked with you in fifteen years, Quille. Even if I were inclined to give former clients advice, I wouldn't with so little to go on. Why don't you tell me why you're doing it?"

"My mother brought it up. She was mad at me. Said I investigated these crimes for other people but never looked into Q.C.'s murder."

"So you're doing it to please her?"

"No. She changed her mind the next day when we talked more about it." I stood and paced in the three feet between my desk and my office mate's. "But the idea kept coming back to me. I think I might feel happier. Freer. If I could resolve the Q.C. crime or at least feel satisfied I did the best I could. Followed every lead, and there was no more to do."

"Every lead. That's a tall order. Tell me what you want to feel free of."

"The feeling that my entire family is about Q.C. No, that's not quite it. Gram's not only about Q.C. Dad's not. Maybe no one is only about her. But their lives are all defined as before Q.C. and after, and I'm the only one who doesn't have a Before."

"Can you get a Before by looking into the crime? You can't change what happened."

"But I can understand what happened."

"Understand what happened? Or understand your family? Who they were before the crime and after it."

I sank into my chair again. "Yes. That. Who they were. Because they were different. I never knew those people. Only what was left after."

"I'd like to talk with you more about all of this, Quille. I suspect it's the main reason you called me. Any interest? I can fit you in early next week."

My eyes flicked toward my computer's calendar icon. I didn't need to open it to know how crowded my schedule looked. Or to know that if it really mattered, I could make the time. During my third year of college when I was taking five classes and working twenty hours a week I'd seen Rachel at 7 a.m. Saturday mornings.

"That's not something I want to do right now."

"I'm always here if you think about it and change your mind."

"Thank you. Really."

"Any time. Good luck with your case."

After we hung up I stared at my screen. And finally clicked back over to the PDFs from the food cases.

———

NEARLY HALF THE cases included petitions that listed each firm's costs, like photocopying, meals out, or airplane tickets, so E. Drake Draper and King and Stillwell could get repaid for them as part of a settlement. On my first review I'd ignored them because E. Drake didn't challenge those in his lawsuit against King and Stillwell.

When I describe expenses I'm charging a client, I'm specific. My note for the previous night's meal read: *Dinner meeting with I. Verde, PhD re: her relationship with and psychological treatment of K. King.*

The petitions included similar notes. It took nearly an hour but I isolated airplane, hotel, and meal expenses with the client who complained about no one telling her Kurt died. She'd told me on the phone she met Kurt only a couple times and Bryan once. Yet the petitions for her cases included dozens of Bryan's bills for coffee, dinner, or drink meetings to discuss her depositions, class certification issues, and possible trial testimony.

While she might be mistaken about the exact number of meetings, I doubted she'd confuse one or two with twenty-five. And if she had met Bryan dozens of times for meals, wine, or coffee, I felt sure she'd remember who he was.

Because of my accounting background and how I was raised, I'm careful to separate and personally pay any expense that doesn't directly relate to the case. But I knew plenty of attorneys who ordered an extra glass of wine (or two or three) or stopped for an extra meal because the client was paying. To me, that was wrong. But not in the same class as claiming someone joined you for dinner who didn't.

The total for the extra food and drink added up to over two thousand dollars. In class actions, judges need to approve any expenses attorneys who settle a case want reimbursed. So if those bills were fake, along with cheating class members out of money, Bryan had lied to the court. He also put Kurt, who signed the petitions, at risk. When an attorney signs a document in court, they're swearing it's true. Falsely doing so could get Kurt and Bryan suspended from practicing law or disbarred.

I could see a pretty serious argument coming out of that.

But I doubted Bryan risked his law license for two thousand dollars. Which meant these expenses were legitimate, or there was a lot more stealing going on and I just hadn't found it yet.

17

I SPENT the second half of the afternoon remote accessing King and Stillwell's system and looking at its books and finances. At twenty to six, I called Tobias.

"I need to leave the office soon for an appointment," I said. No need to say it was for dinner with Gram and Ty. "But remember how you asked me to look at the books along with everything else? I'm running into some stumbling blocks."

I clicked on a menu item I hadn't tried before. But it brought me back to King and Stillwell's QuickBooks home page. I used that same bookkeeping program for my firm's accounting, but this was an older version. One that didn't seem to link to their online accounts or their other programs.

"What kind of stumbling blocks?" Tobias said.

"I see bookkeeping entries but can't find what they're based on for the last few years. There are no time sheets, invoices from court reporters, bank statements. Is there another part of the system where those are saved? Maybe with a unique password?"

I tracked my own timekeeping through an app on my phone that synced with my laptop. Then I added expenses and created month-end bills. I didn't expect King and Stillwell to use exactly the same system since they didn't bill by the hour or send monthly invoices. They got paid only when their cases settled or they won a trial. But they still needed to show the court why they ought to get fees, which meant they needed to prove what they'd done and spent on their cases. They also needed documents if they got audited. Which meant there must be something, I just couldn't see where to find it.

"My guess?" Tobias said. "There's another place, but it's not on the network. It's in my dad's office. Or in storage."

"I'm talking about for the last six or seven years, not decades ago."

"So am I. My dad wasn't exactly on the cutting edge of technology."

"That's – really?" I didn't even have a file cabinet in my office. Everything was saved electronically. A few boxes in a shared suite storage space stored those rare documents that still needed to be on paper. "But Maria gave me PDFs for the food cases. I'm assuming there must be other electronic records, too."

"I'm pretty sure that's the exception. Because of the fee lawsuit."

Each page of each PDF was numbered sequentially with the initials DRA, three or four zeros, and a page number. It's a process known as Bates stamping or labeling, once done with a hand stamp, so parties to a lawsuit can refer to the same pages when they use documents as evidence. When I reviewed the PDFs I saw the numbers and knew they'd been produced as part of the lawsuit. But it never occurred to me that King and Stillwell only used electronic storage for lawsuits and not their own records.

"Bryan didn't push to update the practices?" I said.

"He might have wanted to. I'm guessing Dad resisted."

I powered down my laptop. "So where's the storage space?"

"You'd have to ask Maria. You think something bad is going on?"

I stood and fished my CTA pass out of my shoulder bag. "The expenses on these food cases that may not add up. Which means Bryan and your dad might've had the wrong figures in their pleadings to the court."

"You're saying someone embezzled?" Tobias's voice, already more of a tenor than a baritone, jumped a register.

"I'm not saying that." I propped the phone receiver between my ear and shoulder and slid my coat on my other arm. "That's why I want to see the receipts. It could be I'm way off base. Or there were simple errors. Let's say Bryan hands Maria a list of expenses –"

"Why do you think Maria's involved?"

"I don't. There's nothing right now to be involved in. I'm giving you an example." I switched ears and maneuvered my arm into the other sleeve. "My point is that it's likely all three of them took part in putting together the petitions. There could be an error any step of the way."

"Okay. Okay, that makes sense. Because my dad would never try to cheat his clients. Or his firm."

I shut my office door and turned the key. There was a break in a couple years ago, so now I lock it, though the suite also gets locked at night.

"I'm also looking at whether it could relate to the murder." I paused near the reception desk, which was deserted. "If Bryan was cheating and your dad caught him, they might have argued."

"And it led to murder?"

"It could happen."

I thought about Beckwell's donut example.

"Maria can take you to the storage space. Help you find what you need. Just – do me a favor and tell her it's routine. Or related to work on the fee lawsuit. She's dealing with enough right now. Doesn't need to worry that she made some sort of mistake that might cause trouble."

"Okay."

I preferred to keep my suspicions to myself anyway unless or until I had something concrete. The last thing I needed was for anyone to get rid of evidence. But I wondered if Tobias's reaction meant the idea that his dad might have done something wrong appalled him or if he felt he needed to protect Maria. Or both.

———

GRAM SET aside Front Bar's small bites menu. "Oh, honey, what good can come of all that?"

We sat with Ty at a tall table in the front window. Gram had been downtown for the afternoon to join a friend's pottery making class at an arts center in Lincoln Park. Front Bar was a perfect place to meet and talk with her. Because it's adjacent to Steppenwolf Theatre, it attracts a crowd that skews older and therefore quieter than almost anywhere in that neighborhood. Also, once the play starts, the place tends to empty out.

"You don't think it's a good idea?" I said.

I had expected my mother, not Gram, to question my investigating Q.C.'s death.

"Spending your time on a crime that happened over thirty years ago instead of on your life now? It's not healthy."

"Did you just talk to my therapist?" I said.

"You're not going back to her, are you?" Gram said.

Therapy was one of the rare choices I made that Gram didn't exactly support. She saw it as wasting time musing about life rather than making changes to improve it. I tried to tell her it wasn't either-or, but the best she'd say was that if it helped me, I should go ahead but she didn't understand it.

Ty suggested we order, and we chose a few appetizers to share. He went to the bar to order.

When he returned, he said, "Don't you think it might help your family to know who did this to Q.C., Mrs. Davis?"

"Well, yes, of course." Gram squeezed my arm. "But the police and FBI couldn't solve the crime, and they had all the evidence and witnesses whose memories were fresh. I'm sure at least half the people at the party have moved away by now. Or died."

"But the police focused on Mom and Dad for so long," I said. "They might have missed things."

"Oh, I'm not saying they did a good job. They didn't. I blame their bungling as much as your sister's death for your parents never being the same again, and especially for your mother's mental state. But with all the time that's passed what are the odds you'll learn anything new?"

I drank some of my wine. Ty and I had ordered a bottle since we were taking the L home. It was a deep red Pinot Noir with a flavor that hinted of ripe cherries and cedar. "Is that the only reason you don't want me to do it? Because I know it's a long shot. I'm not expecting miracles."

"No, it's not just that. Looking into it, talking about it, none of it will be good for anyone. You said your mother's been doing better lately. Why drag her down that road?"

"I'm pretty sure she still thinks about it every day." I folded my arms across my stomach. My phone dinged, but I ignored it.

"Isn't there a chance it would ease her mind to know someone looked at this again whether or not there are answers?" Ty said.

"Maybe for some people. With Quille's mother, I doubt it." Gram looked at me. "Does your dad think this is a good idea?"

"He said Mom wants me to do it."

"Of course she does. Well, if your mother wants you to, I

guess that settles it." Gram tossed her napkin on the table. "Excuse me."

She stalked across the restaurant to the hallway with a glowing Restroom sign over it.

"Should we tell her that's the communal Unisex one?" Ty said.

"She's been here before," I said.

A server set down a plate of mushroom caps stuffed with blue cheese and spinach. Ty and I each ate one.

"I thought she was mad at me, but now I think it's about my mother," I said.

"I've never seen your Gram mad. Did she ever yell at you when you were a kid?"

"Oh, yeah. When she thought I was slacking on homework. And the first time I got paid directly from a theater and I spent all the money at once on a new TV."

"Such a wild girl you were," Ty said.

I laughed. "I was eighteen. I'd been watching a fourteen-inch black and white my aunt gave me for my room. Gram didn't mind my spending. She was just upset I spent the entire check rather than putting at least ten percent in the bank."

The server brought out a small cutting board with home-made ultra-thin potato chips on it. I checked my phone. Art Feffor had texted that Lauren and Joe could attend the next support group meeting. I thanked him.

Gram returned with her lipstick refreshed and her mauve and silver scarf straightened. "Sorry, honey. I'm not upset with you. And it's your choice to do this or not."

"But what did you mean of course my mother would want me to do this?"

She took a handful of chips. "I try not to criticize your mother to you. But this is – digging into everything, I'm concerned – oh, I'm just going to say it." She ate a few of the potato chips before going on. "You're an adult, you know what your mother is like. She frets and wallows in her feelings and makes sure everyone's life revolves around her. I sympathize, of course I do. And I tell myself she does her best. But so many times over the years I've just gotten so frustrated with her."

Three chimes sounded, and a woman dressed in black called out that the house was open. Shuffling sounds came from nearby tables as diners pushed aside wine glasses and grabbed their coats and bags.

"Losing a child must be terrible," Ty said.

"Yes. But you know who else lost a child? Quille's father. Who is my son. But did he get to grieve? No." Gram smoothed her napkin. "Because he had to take care of Brenda. Quille's mother. All the time. Still has to."

"Maybe that's how he coped," Ty said. "His way of grieving."

Gram brushed a few stray white hairs away from her eyes. "You may be right. Maybe that's what saved him from spending his life deeply depressed. But it feels like Brenda's pain drowned us all out. I lost a granddaughter. Quille's sister Kendra lost her little sister. And she and Quille both basically lost their parents."

"But you took care of us," I said.

"I did my best, honey, but I had to work, too, and so did your dad." Gram turned to Ty. "Quille and Kendra did more to care for their mother than the other way around. I've tried not to blame her for that." She shook her head and focused on me again. "But I moved hell and high water to get you all to come live in that apartment across the hall so you'd have some sort of structure. And I swear sometimes I wanted to grab your mother and shake her. It was as if she forgot she had two other children and a husband."

"Quille's other grandparents couldn't help?" Ty said. The distance in my family often puzzled him.

"Could've. Didn't. They moved east a month or two after

Q.C.'s body was found. And the grandmother died a year later. Stroke."

"And my mother lost touch with her father," I said. "She'd never tell me why."

Gram sighed. "If you're determined to investigate, someone will have to tell you. Like the police, he thought your dad did it. Your mother never forgave her father for that. It's the one time she showed some backbone."

"But I thought when Q.C. was found with that other poor little girl it ruled out both my parents," I said.

"It did. But your grandfather wasn't one to say he was sorry, and your mother refused to be the one to reach out. To tell the truth, I think he just couldn't forgive your father for not being at the party when it happened. But look at all the people who were there, and no one saw anything."

"Were you there?" Ty said.

"No. My husband – Quille's grandfather – had his first heart attack the day before. Needed open heart surgery. For almost a year after I lay awake imagining the party, imagining we were both there and saw something wrong and stopped it all. Or I imagined that our being there somehow shifted the entire day just enough that the killer changed plans. Didn't take little Q.C." She shuddered. "But that's like wishing he'd move on to some other child, isn't it? And yet I couldn't stop thinking it."

"You're sure it was a he?" I said.

"No. But it feels more likely." She gulped some water, then put her hand on my arm. "Can we talk about this another time? I wasn't expecting this when you said you wanted to meet me."

"Of course. This weekend maybe?"

"How about next? I've got a file of documents I'll show you."

She offered us a ride home. It wouldn't take her far out of her way. But she looked so tired I didn't want to add to her driving time. I said no. As we walked her to her car, I needed to slow my normal pace so as not to get ahead of her. I'd never done that before. And when she opened her car door she gripped the driver's seat with one hand, the other on the window, and eased herself in.

It was as if simply talking about my sister's death had aged her ten or twenty years.

18

TOBIAS SAID you asked about firm storage. It's in the building's sub-basement. Can take you down tomorrow with an hour's notice to make sure Bryan doesn't need anything.

The email came in at eight in the morning. I wished Tobias hadn't contacted Maria first. I'd wanted to see how she reacted when I asked. But at least the storage space was on site not in some warehouse hours away.

Today E. Drake Draper and I had a court status call in the fee lawsuit. You never see court status calls in movies or television shows. For a good reason. Not much happens at them. All the attorneys wait for the clerk to call out their case names. Then they stand in front of the bench and tell the judge what they've done – and a lot of the time what they've not done – and how much more time they need for the next steps in the lawsuit.

At least this one gave me a natural way to talk with E. Drake again. Except that he didn't stroll through the courtroom's double doors until the instant the clerk announced our case.

E. Drake strode straight to the judge's bench. Without giving me a second to speak, he told the judge he filed a motion the evening before seeking a ruling on his petition for his share of attorney's fees. The judge had stayed the petition – meaning it was more or less on hold – for over a year as the two sides traded information and tried to settle.

"We've tried and we've failed, Your Honor," E. Drake said. "The case was filed two years ago. We know the facts. The only question is how much we're owed, which is for you to decide. I see no reason to delay the hearing."

"Your Honor, if I may," I said.

The judge, who looked at bit like E. Drake, nodded at me.

"I'm Quille Davis and I represent King and Stillwell. First, I never saw this motion counsel is talking about. Second, as he knows, and as you'll see in the file, Mr. King, the named partner, passed away recently. Very recently. He represented the firm. I've only just entered the case. It will take me some time to get up to speed and respond to the motion. I don't know what timeframe Mr. Draper is talking about–"

"Two weeks for her response, Judge," E. Drake said. "And my apologies if Ms. Davis didn't get notice. Sometimes the system's slow. But we had the status set already, and it can't be a surprise that we want to move things along."

"The matter has been pending for quite some time, Ms. Davis," the judge said. "I'm afraid I don't see any benefit to dragging it out longer. Fourteen days should be ample time. I'm sure Mr. King or his partner had a response in the works that you can put the finishing touches on."

I gripped my legal pad. Never had a judge refused to give me time to learn the case. To do it when the previous attorney, who was also the client, died, floored me.

"But there is a benefit to allowing a little more time, Your Honor. I'm not personally involved the way Mr. King was. Once I'm up to speed, I'm sure counsel and I will have better luck negotiating with one another."

"With all due respect to Ms. Davis," E. Drake said, a sure

sign that his next words would in so many words say I was full of it, "however reasonable she is or how good at negotiating, and I'm sure she is, Mr. King was never the roadblock to settlement. His partner Mr. Stillwell stood in the way. Mr. Stillwell is still alive. And still in the way."

"I'd like a chance, Your Honor. First, I've no idea if what counsel says about who was a roadblock is correct. And if his view is based on settlement talks those are confidential and shouldn't be raised in court. Either way, though, Mr. King's death isn't something my client did purposely. In the interests of fairness and justice, as a new lawyer stepping in, I ought to have the chance to get to know the case."

The judge's eyebrows rose. "Far be it from me to stand in the way of justice and fairness, Ms. Davis. All the same, Mr. Draper is right. This petition has been pending too long, and the law that applies is clear. Fourteen days to respond. Mr. Draper, since you seem to be in a rush, seven days for a reply?"

In the petition, Draper set out why he should get the fees he wanted. The response was my chance to tell the judge our side. In a reply, Draper could answer anything I wrote that was new to him. Once the judge read everything, he'd bring us back to court and listen to us argue, then decide.

But Draper surprised me again. "No need for a Reply, Judge. My points are what they are."

The judge took off his reading glasses and looked Draper in the face. "You're certain? All right, up to you. Hearing one week following Ms. Davis' response."

E. Drake held the door for me as we left the courtroom. Out in the hallway, I said, "Some warning would have been nice."

He shrugged. "Better all around if this is resolved. That money in escrow does none of us any good."

The fees sat in an account neither side could access.

"That's not the point," I said. "I'm new to the case. Common courtesy suggests giving me a heads up, especially when you ask for something that ridiculous."

"This judge hates cases sitting on his docket. No matter what you said or what you knew ahead of time, it wouldn't have mattered. But you handled yourself well."

"I'm not looking for validation. Just civility."

"Heh." That annoying half-chuckle again. "The facts are what they are. It's why I don't need a reply."

"Or you really, really need that money."

"Who doesn't? See you at the hearing. Unless Bryan decides he wants to make a counter-offer first."

E. Drake disappeared into another courtroom, and I headed for the elevator alone.

———

DUST FLEW, making us both cough, as Maria and I pushed a cardboard box off a stack and onto the carpeted floor.

She fished a tissue from her purse, handed it to me, then took another for herself and blew her nose. "As you can see, no one's been down here for a long time."

I glanced around the narrow storage room. A single rectangular window ran alongside the door leading into the dimly-lit hallway. Black metal file cabinets lined the walls. Rows of cardboard boxes stacked six deep filled the center of the room, creating a U-shaped aisle between them and the file cabinets.

"Don't know why not," I said. "So cozy."

Maria laughed, then coughed again.

It was nearly six p.m. Friday evening. We'd been buried in the storage room for over half an hour sorting through papers and setting aside documents. Though I tried not to be obvious, I was most interested in comparing expenses in cases Kurt handled alone to cases Bryan handled alone, as well as to ones where the two worked together. That ought to tell me if Bryan, Kurt, or both, padded expenses. I also wanted to see tax files, but we hadn't gotten to those yet.

The sub-basement's heat had shut down at five-thirty. But today was warm again for early November. Over fifty-five the entire day. The storage area still held plenty of heat. Too much, in fact, with no air circulating. I wiped sweat from my face. My blazer lay over one of the file cabinets. Dust coated my arms.

"One more." Maria yanked a batch of about a hundred pages fastened with a silver clip at the top. When it came out the rest of the file thumped onto the carpet. The cloud of dust made my eyes water.

"Thanks. They ever vacuum in here?" I swiped at my eyes with the back of my hand, then flipped through to a fat section of the packet. I peered at the signature on an oddly-shaped receipt.

"They probably charge extra for vacuuming," Maria said. "Something particular you're looking for?"

"Just getting a better sense of fees and costs sought over the years. Who prepares the petitions for the court?"

I wanted to trust Maria. Way back when we were in the play together, she'd always asked how I was doing backstage and made sure I had a ride home. And she'd been with King and Stillwell a long time.

But the Chicago Daily Law Bulletin reported a story when I first became a lawyer about an office manager who filled out all the expense reports at a small firm. The attorneys needed to sign them, but not everyone read what they signed. She stole seventy thousand dollars over twelve years by putting in for reimbursements no one looked closely at.

"I pull out a previous one and fill in as much as I can," Maria said. "Then Bryan or Kurt change it to fit the case. Now it would be just Bryan."

"Do you copy the receipts to attach?"

She nodded. "They each had their own firm credit cards to pay expenses, then the firm reimbursed them. Bryan entered his own into QuickBooks, but I entered Kurt's. When it was time to do a petition, I created a report. And pulled the paper receipts. But now more and more are electronic."

"What if there's no receipt? Or if someone paid cash?"

"Kurt especially isn't – wasn't – great about that. He'd dig around his suit jacket pockets and glove compartment and see what he could find. Half the time I'm sure he never got reimbursed at all, and we never charged the file, because he forgot things."

"And if he couldn't find a receipt but knew he paid for something?"

"He did the final –"

The lights snapped off, not just in our room but in the corridor, plunging us into darkness.

19

———

"Damn," Maria said. "Have we been down here that long?"

The combination of soft surfaces, like carpet and cardboard, and the metal file cabinets that reflected sound made it seem like her voice came from more than one part of the room.

"That long?" I said. "Oh. The timer."

Like Kurt's bookkeeping, the sub-basement lighting system was old school. When we entered, Maria had flipped a dial that began ticking and turning as soon as she released it. People rarely came down to the storage area. It was there to ensure no one walked out and left the lights on all night or, in our case, all weekend.

"I thought I set it for a full hour," she said.

My phone's screen cast a bluish glow, highlighting the shadows in her face. "It's only ten after six."

She sighed. "I'll go reset it."

"I'm coming with. I'm sure you spun it all the way around. Isn't that an hour?"

"Should be. Old technology."

That made no sense, though. It was one thing to set a timer on my phone and scroll to forty-five minutes rather than an hour forty-five. Or have the voice assistant not hear me correctly. But the dial timer here was mechanical. If it spun all the way and started ticking, which it had, I didn't see how it suddenly sped to the end.

"Shouldn't we lock it?" I asked as the door to the storage room swung shut.

Maria fumbled in her shoulder bag. "Damn key. Ugh. Must've fallen all the way to the bottom."

I started to shine my flashlight into her bag, but she said, "Let's just go. The dark is creeping me out, and nothing in there's valuable. You took your wallet, right?"

"Yes." If living in Chicago teaches you anything it's never leave a purse or wallet unattended. My wallet sat inside my shoulder bag, which I'd grabbed the moment the lights went out. "But we ought to lock it."

Maria, though, had already gone around the corner. The storage room could only be locked with a key, a precaution against anyone being locked inside by mistake. I hurried after her, training my phone's flashlight on the scratched white tile floor. It looked so old I guessed it still contained asbestos. Our footsteps echoed in the corridors. Around us, the building creaked.

We turned a corner and a musty smell rolled over us.

"Ugh," Maria said. "Flood plain."

"What?"

"A section flooded way, way back. Never quite cleaned up right."

"I didn't smell that before," I said.

"You're right. Someone must've – that's weird." She shone her phone's light down a side corridor. "That door's never open."

A footstep sounded behind us. I spun and aimed my flash-light at a silhouetted figure that darted toward us.

The figure charged, arms in the air. I sidestepped. My

assailant brought something down on my shoulder. Pain seared from it along my arm, and my phone flew from my hand. Bluish light bounced off the walls as I dropped to the floor. My right knee hit the tile floor and pain shot through it. I yelped and rolled toward the wall. I ended on my back, knees to my chest, uninjured arm wrapped around them.

Maria lay on the floor next to me, panting and howling. Her phone had hit the floor, too, and blinked out.

20

———

The attacker's footsteps pounded away from us.

"Maria?"

She made a strangled sound. I rolled onto my side. She lay curled in a ball, her back to me.

I scrabbled to a sitting position, my shoulder and knee still throbbing. I touched her arm. It felt warm. At least she wasn't in shock. "How badly are you hurt?"

"Not...bad. Where...he go?"

Her breathing stopped for a second, then she drew in a deep, shuddering breath.

"I'm not sure." I strained my ears but didn't hear any footsteps over her breathing.

Maria struggled to sit.

"Rest," I said.

"No...just winded." She sat, looking like a ghost with her pale skin, and put one hand to her nose, which was bleeding.

I placed my phone so it shone on the opposite wall and provided a circle of light around us without shining in our eyes. "You're okay?"

She nodded. "He hit my stomach with...whatever it was. A

board? I doubled over. Then fell face down. Didn't do my nose any favors."

"Did you get a look at him?" I said.

"No. Was it a him?" Maria said.

I thought about it. "Maybe not. Taller than me, though. Broad shoulders. Lots of power in that swing." I rubbed my injured shoulder.

Anchoring myself with my good hand against the wall, I stood and took a careful step. Despite knee pain, I could walk.

Maria got to her feet, too, and retrieved her phone, which lay a few feet away. "Screen's cracked, but it's working. Sort of."

We both tried to make calls, but the second level underground didn't lend itself to good reception. Or any reception.

"I lost my sense of direction. How far are we from the timer?" I said.

"Should be around the next corner. I hope."

I didn't love wandering the sub-basement, but standing still wasn't a better option. My flashlight beam shining, we linked arms and moved slowly forward, ears straining.

Maria was right about the timer being around the corner. I flipped it all the way. All the corridors lit.

Maria looked at the double doors that led to the elevators and stairwell. "Should we go back for the records?"

"I'm thinking No. Not alone."

I ACHED EVERYWHERE, but my injuries were limited to bad bruises. Maria's nose was swollen and a black eye was forming. The paramedics whisked her away to the hospital to rule out a concussion.

The police officers who came to the scene found no one in the sub-basement. But the stack of files Maria and I set aside had disappeared. Tobias contacted the building management but didn't have much hope of obtaining helpful video. They told him the security cameras showed two entrances to the building from outside and the dock door but that was it.

Tobias's shoulders slumped. I sat across from him at the conference table, ice packs on my shoulder and knee. He had found them in the office kitchen freezer where Bryan kept them for his runner's aches and pains.

"I never should have asked you to look into this. And now Maria – if she's got a concussion or worse, I'll never forgive myself."

"She told the paramedic no dizziness, no vision problems, no loss of consciousness. They're being extra careful. I bet she'll be out in a couple hours with no issues."

I didn't want to tell him how much experience I had with injuries. I doubted it would make him feel any better.

"Well, we're not risking anyone else getting hurt. This is it. The end. No more investigation."

21

———

"THAT'S something I like to hear." The voice came from behind me.

"Ty?" I twisted in my seat. Darts of pain shot down my arm from my shoulder.

He stood in the conference room doorway. "Glad to see you intact. Didn't hear me come in?"

"I must be slipping," I said. I had called him right after the police, both because we had plans later and because he'd want to know I'd been hurt.

Tobias leapt to his feet. "The front door's not locked?"

It was barely after six-thirty, a time when most lawyers I knew were still working. But my office suite locks its doors at six. If someone arrives after that our very sophisticated system requires that they bang on the door hard until someone squirreled away in an office hears them.

I was a little surprised Bryan, the only person in the office when Maria and I headed downstairs, didn't lock the door when he left.

Tobias left to lock the outer door. Ty rolled a chair near my injured side and took over holding the ice pack on my shoulder.

I wrapped my right hand around the chilled fingers on my left to warm them.

"Any chance you'll consider stopping the investigation?" Ty said. "It's not personal. Not like the others were, where friends needed your help. Or where it was Marco."

Marco was my former boyfriend, the one whose death I'd looked into.

I shook my head. "I'll stop only if I have to. It's the first time someone hired me to do this thing that I love doing. If Tobias'll agree, I want to keep going."

Ty flipped the ice pack. The side that had been open to the air felt much icier and more soothing. I shut my eyes and felt both my shoulders drop.

"Love it?" Ty said. "I knew you liked it, but... you want to change careers?"

"Not change. Keep doing it. As a side job. That doesn't always pay."

"And that can get you killed," he said.

"I'm not convinced the murder investigation led to the attack."

Tobias came back and plopped into the chair at the head of the table. I told him what I'd just told Ty. He ran his fingers over the drooping edges of his mustache. "Why else would anyone attack you and Maria?"

I drew my chair into the table. Ty let the ice pack drop and wheeled his chair next to mine.

"I'm not sure hurting us was the goal," I said. "It might've been to draw us out of the storage room and be sure we stayed out for a while."

Tobias spun his wedding ring around on his finger. "So whoever it was could steal the files?"

"Or figure out what I was looking into. Which could be about the expenses I'm questioning. Not the murder."

"Then it can't be my dad who submitted fake costs," Tobias said. "He obviously didn't attack you."

"But you could've," I said. I doubted he had but was curious to see his reaction. Also, stranger things had happened to me.

Tobias's head reared back. "You're accusing me? I could go down in the storage room any time."

"I'm not accusing you. Just keeping an open mind. You knew Maria and I would be down there. You knew roughly what I was looking for, but not what files or types of documents I needed to see. This way you could find out and hide any evidence that your dad did something wrong."

"But he didn't do anything wrong."

"Wouldn't you have recognized Tobias?" Ty said.

"It happened fast," I said. "The attacker ran straight at me. And he wore a hoodie and something over the lower half of the face."

"I don't even have a key to the sub-basement," Tobias said. "You need one to get into the storage area, then another for the room itself."

"I only have your word for it that you don't have keys," I said.

"What about Bryan?" Tobias's cheeks reddened. This wasn't the best way to convince him to let me keep investigating. "You told the police he was the last one to leave the office tonight."

"He was. But he gave us the keys. He'd been down there last, and Maria told me there's only one set for the office."

"He could've made copies," Tobias said. "And it makes more sense he'd submit fake expenses to the firm than that my dad did. Dad owned eighty percent of the shares. He'd be stealing mostly from himself."

"There might be a tax benefit," I said. "Say he gets reimbursed $10,000 in expenses a year. That's $10,000 the firm's not paying taxes on because it's not showing as profit. Your dad has an eighty percent share, so he saves whatever the income tax would be on $8,000."

"Seems like a lot of risk for not much reward," Tobias said.

Ty asked if anything else pointed to Bryan.

"A lot of extra meals with a client."

"So he does more wining and dining than work?" Ty said.

I shook my head. "It's not that. The client claims she only met Bryan once."

Tobias, calmer now, scratched his head. "Wouldn't the client notice fake expenses?"

"Yours probably would. Mine definitely would. Their computer programs flag anything on my bill that doesn't match their records. But class action plaintiffs don't get bills, and they don't pay costs themselves. King and Stillwell petitions the court to get reimbursed out of the money awarded to the whole class. But the client did meet with Kurt a number of times. Maybe she mixed up him and Bryan."

"I doubt it," Tobias said. "Dad was over thirty years older."

"These cases have gone on for years and years, so the client's memory might not be great," I said. "Who else could get into the sub-basement?"

"Probably a lot of people," Ty said. "All the building tenants must have keys. Former tenants might have kept theirs, too."

My phone vibrated with a text from Lauren. She confirmed she and Joe were both free to go to the next alien experiencer support meeting. I texted back a thumbs up. If Tobias stuck to his view that I needed to stop investigating I'd explain to her later why they didn't need to attend. After I did everything I could to change his mind.

"Former?" Tobias said.

"No matter how hard management companies work at getting passes and keys back when tenants leave," Ty said, "they never get all of them."

"So we've narrowed it down to everyone everywhere," I said.

Ty spread his hands wide. "Just trying to help."

I rubbed my forehead. "If the motive was to see what I was

doing, it needed to be someone who knew Maria and I were heading down to the storage room tonight. Which brings us back to Tobias and Bryan. But Bryan – he's a bit full of himself, but he is smart. He'd have to know he'd be the obvious suspect."

"Anyone here for meetings today?" Ty said.

"Not when I was here. But there could have been earlier when Maria was on the phone with Tobias or with me. Also, Bryan uses speakerphone a lot, and sound travels up from Maria's workspace. Long shot, but if he had someone on speaker and his door was open, that person could have overheard."

"He definitely does that," Tobias said. "Couldn't hear myself think when I worked in my dad's office for a day."

"If he wants to clear himself, maybe he'll tell us who he talked to today," I said. "Or he'll tell the police. I'm sure they'll question him."

Tobias stood. "I'll ask Maria. I'm going to the hospital to check on her."

I stood, too, though I needed to press my hand against the table for a boost because my knee still throbbed. "Before you go. I know your first reaction was no more investigation. But finding the person who killed your dad is the best way to protect everyone."

"I wish I felt sure about that." Tobias smoothed his hair. "I need to think about it. For now, it's on hold."

22

———

"ON HOLD? SERIOUSLY?" Lauren sliced her blueberry scone in two. It was late Sunday morning, and she was meeting a client to show her South Loop condos in half an hour. "But Joe and I are going to that meeting tomorrow night."

In two days, the temperature had dropped twenty degrees, and a fire burned in the fireplace inside Café des Livres. My friend Carole and her husband, both from France, own the place. Ever since I helped her when a friend was missing, she has the staff comp all my meals. Lauren's too. We both risked our lives during the investigation.

"I know." I sipped my *chocolat chaud*, a favorite of mine on the menu. It's very rich but not sweet because Carole uses gourmet 85% dark chocolate and steamed whole milk.

"Tell me you're not asking me to skip it," Lauren said. "I could've done a showing. Right here in our neighborhood. Two of them actually."

"You didn't need to do that," I said. "Reschedule showings."

"Of course I did. I'm not missing a chance to be abducted by aliens. And to make Joe play along."

I laughed. It was fun hearing about, and seeing, Lauren

tease Joe. He and I met when he was eighteen, which seemed very grown up to me, and I was a kid. He looked out for me in the Chicago theatre scene. All the older actors did, really, but Joe especially. He was very serious about it, and I rarely saw his lighter side even now.

"You're sure you feel safe going to the meeting?" I said. "Knowing someone attacked Maria and me?"

"But that wasn't about aliens."

She had a point. I twisted strands of hair around my fingers. "Still, Tobias hasn't given me the go ahead yet. Although...."

"You've got a way around that. You do, don't you? Have a way around that? Because the next meeting's over two weeks away. Who knows what could happen by then?"

"I'll try again to persuade Tobias. But until I do, I'll focus all my work on the fee lawsuit. Which I have now told you I'll be doing. Now if you're so curious and so excited about the meeting that even knowing I'm no longer investigating the murder you still want to go, I can't stop you."

Lauren finished the last of her scone. "All those rationalizations work perfectly well for me. But should I tell Joe that Tobias called it off? I might not have mentioned that to him when I told him about the attack on you. Which I actually might have said was more like a theft rather than attack."

"What you tell him is up to you. It's your relationship."

"It's your investigation."

"Not investigating anymore, remember? Just lawyering."

She huffed, making her blond bangs bounce. "I reserve the right to blame you if he gets mad."

I lifted my mug to her in a mock toast. "You're awesome, you know that?"

"Oh, totally. You're welcome."

———

"I'VE GOT INFORMATION FOR YOU," Detective Sergeant Beckwell said when I answered my phone.

"Really?" I squeezed Ty's arm and left him in the Icon movie theater's concession line. We had tickets to see the latest DC superhero movie. Not my favorite franchise, but Ty enjoyed it.

"First, you know I can't officially share confidential files and so on," Beckwell said.

"Full disclaimer noted." I stationed myself at the windows overlooking Roosevelt Collection. It's a U-shaped luxury apartment complex with retail on the ground floor and landscaped sitting areas and a park in the center. Workers were busy stringing white winter lights through the trees at the center. It made the gray November afternoon feel cheerful. "I'll find another way to learn whatever you're about to tell me. But I'll find it quicker knowing what to look for."

"I'm less concerned with saving you time than saving you getting attacked again, which I heard just happened."

"How did you hear?"

Ty joined me, and I inhaled the scent of freshly buttered popcorn.

"Let's say your name is known around here. And I might keep an ear out. One of the people you're investigating has a criminal past. Pled down to a misdemeanor, but the original charge was a felony."

"I ran everyone through a database." I subscribed to several for my mix of litigation and investigative work. No one at King and Stillwell showed convictions for any crime, and neither had Isabel, anyone at E. Drake Draper's firm, or Tobias or his mother.

"It was expunged. So you wouldn't see it, and it can't be used in court. But it came up in the national crime database. And it's not who you might think."

"How could you know who I think?"

"You know the statistics as well as I do. I'm guessing you've focused on men."

"No, but I agree," I said. "Statistically they're a lot more likely to shoot someone to death."

"This could be unrelated, but you might want to look at women. Specifically, the office manager."

"What were the charges?"

"Embezzlement."

23

———

"You knew this and didn't tell me?" I stared at Tobias across the square table at South Branch, a restaurant along the Chicago River two blocks from his office. It was quarter to six Monday night and already dark out.

Tobias's glass of wine sat untouched. "It was expunged."

"But still happened."

"That's why she's so grateful to my father. It took years to get it off her record and no one else was hiring her. And she needed full-time work for the health insurance."

"I specifically asked if anyone had been arrested, served time, or been convicted. You said No."

In addition to my own research, I'd asked Tobias that. But one of many challenges of both practicing law and murder investigations is that clients hold back information. Sometimes it's because I don't ask the right questions in the right way, but I've learned to be careful how I word things. Other times, like now, they decide it's not important.

Tobias stared at his own reflection in the window. "Obviously she didn't kill my father, so what does it matter?"

"One, her former employer brought criminal charges

against her. That's not an everyday thing. Two, I told you I saw discrepancies in the books, and she was charged with embezzlement. And, three and most important, there's no obviously. If anything was obvious the police would have whoever killed your father in custody already."

He looked at me. "Ask her about it. Once she explains, you'll see she's not a criminal."

"The State of Illinois begs to differ." I sipped my whiskey sour and rolled my aching shoulder, trying to loosen it. The injury and a long day with lunch at my desk had prompted me to break my no-alcohol-in-a-client-meeting rule. "It's not that police and prosecutors never make mistakes. I know they do, and I wouldn't have leapt to conclusions about Maria. But I can't do my job if you don't tell me the facts."

"I asked you to stop doing it anyway."

"My contact on the department called me, I didn't call him. And you still want me to handle the fee case and check out the firm's finances. You didn't think someone charged with embezzlement working at the firm might be relevant?"

Across the river, a train pulled into the underground part of Union Station, its warning bells clanging loud enough to be heard through the windows and over the hum of conversation around us.

"Maria didn't embezzle." Tobias's hands, resting on the table, closed into fists. "It's – she'll tell you about it."

"She told me she fills out a lot of petitions and the expense reports. There's a chance she's the one submitting false expenses."

"But she didn't attack herself. Someone else was in the sub-basement. Someone else stole the files."

The firm's receptionist had given me a list of all the calls and meetings the day Maria and I visited the sub-basement. Bryan had a video conference call with E. Drake Draper and three other attorneys. But Bryan took the call in the conference room with the door shut. The receptionist told me he couldn't hear any of it. He also was sure no one on the other end heard anything going on at the firm.

If he was right, we were still left with only Bryan, Maria, and Tobias who knew she and I would be down in the storage area. The receptionist had known as well, but said he didn't tell anyone, and he'd met friends for drinks after leaving the firm at five that night.

"Maria could be working with someone else," I said. I'd been thinking about that all afternoon. "Staged an attack to scare me off."

"That's pretty far-fetched."

A text came in from Lauren.

Almost there. No second thoughts?

I set the phone down next to my glass. Maybe I could change Tobias's mind before I answered, making it okay all around that Joe and Lauren were attending the support group meeting tonight.

"But possible," I said. "I'll talk to Maria again, hear what else she has to say. And I hope you'll do one thing for me. Restart the investigation."

"The thought of you and Maria being attacked–"

"If the murder's related to the finances or the fee lawsuit, stopping the criminal investigation could put me in more danger."

He frowned. "You believe that? Or you just don't want to let it go?"

I stirred my drink. "It is hard for me not to finish what I start. But I believe the possible embezzlement and the murder are related. It's a lot of coincidence otherwise. Two crimes, one firm."

"Coincidences happen."

"Yes. And you knew from the beginning there was risk in investigating."

"But now it seems real. And I feel responsible."

"You're not. Whoever attacked is. And don't you want your dad's killer found?"

"You can't guarantee that'll happen."

I opened the folder with the bill and took out my black business Visa card. "But there's a better chance than if we do nothing."

"I'll think about it." Tobias reached across the table and slid the bill folder toward himself. "Let me get this. I insist. I'm driving you crazy, at least I can buy drinks."

I probably shouldn't have, but outside, as I waited for an Uber, I texted Lauren.

Go for it.

———

THE MORNING after the support group I asked Joe and Lauren to meet at Lou Mitchell's for a late breakfast at 10:30 a.m. That's when the diner is least likely to be crowded. Founded in 1923, it's jammed for pre-work breakfasts and during the lunch hour each day. People line up out the door on weekends, as it also draws tourists. Lauren was walking over from a meeting at the Willis Tower, and we ran into each other at the intersection of Wacker and Adams.

"Oh my God, seriously," she said as soon as I was close enough to hear. "How do none of those people at least see the flaws in each other's stories?"

"It is a support group." I took off my knit hat. Despite the chilly day the sun felt too hot on my hair. "Traditionally not about picking apart what other members say."

"Oh, fine, if you want to be logical." We hurried across. "But, speaking of logic, there is none there. Zero. Though the people were all pretty nice. And one of them is thinking of selling a rental condo he owns in West Town and might want to list with me."

"Really? What about the whole anonymity thing?"

"Yeah, that's the 'might' part," Lauren said. "Only know his first name so far. But I gave him my card."

Joe was waiting just outside the entrance. Inside it smelled of powdered sugar and frying bacon. The greeter gave Lauren and me boxes of Milk Duds. The diner is on the edge of the neighborhood known as Greektown, and the practice comes from the Greek tradition of giving sweet treats to welcome women and children guests to a home. Some days it's house made donut holes, which I like better, instead of Milk Duds.

We slid into a booth toward the back and opened our laminated menus. I sat next to a pile of our coats, gloves, hats, and shoulder bags, with Lauren and Joe across from me.

"What did you think of the meeting?" I asked Joe after we ordered.

"The members surprised me." Joe poured cream into his coffee and stirred. "In a way I didn't expect."

"That's absolutely what a surprise is," Lauren said.

He smiled. "Right, yeah. But I expected to find their stories surprising. Not the people themselves."

"How so?" I said.

"They seem so normal," Lauren said. "People you'd see at Whole Foods. Or seriously any grocery store. Trader Joe's. Jewel."

"You didn't think alien experiencers would eat?" Joe said.

She lightly jabbed his side with her elbow. "You're the one who said they're surprising."

"I meant I expected half of them to be talking about crystals or Tarot Cards or New Age energy," Joe said. "And the other half to be uneducated. Maybe people who didn't get far in life and deal with it by making up fantasies about aliens."

"But did you think they *were* making things up?" I said.

Lauren and Joe exchanged glances, and Lauren shook her head. "Mostly no because they believe what they're saying. Though these two guys think aliens harvested their sperm when they were teenagers. No details, but, honestly, there's some serious guilt issues over their moms catching them alone in their bedrooms if you see what I'm saying."

Not far off from Art Feffor's comments. "Was Art there?" I said.

"He introduced us to everyone," Joe said. "Gave the cover story we agreed on. That Lauren went to therapy for anxiety, started remembering being abducted from her parents' house as a kid."

"I did an awesome job by the way," Lauren said. "Almost convinced myself I'm traumatized."

"You didn't overdo it, did you?" I said. "I don't want Isabel Verde to guess my friends snuck into the group."

"Lauren reined it in," Joe said. "Dr. Verde wasn't there, but almost everyone talked about her."

"Especially this woman, Jill." Lauren drank some of her cappuccino and wiped a trace of foam away from her lips. "She's in her forties, veterinary assistant."

"So of course Lauren told her she hates dogs," Joe said.

Lauren waved her hand, almost knocking over Joe's water glass. "Well, I do. And I figured it was authentic. So it didn't seem like I was pretending to get along superwell with every-one. Anyway, Jill said the Grays – that's what they call the aliens – stuck needles in her right side and then her left side starting when she was, like, twenty-five, but she didn't know why. Until in therapy with Isabel Verde it came to her telepathically. The aliens were taking her ova to create alien-human babies."

"Everyone believes in hybrids?" I said.

"Not everyone," Joe said. "They all agree it's possible. Alan, the guy Lauren mentioned–"

"He's some sort of vice president at one of those discount

shoe chains. Thick head of dark hair," Lauren said. "Think George Stephanopoulos when he was younger and supercute."

Joe's eyebrows rose. "You think George Stephanopoulos is cute?"

"Not now. Well, sort of still now. But definitely when I see those YouTube clips from twenty years ago."

"Can we stay on track?" I said as the waiter set down our plates. Lauren and I had gotten short stacks of pancakes, mine chocolate chip, and Joe had a sunny side up egg with crispy bacon.

"It's so coincidental, don't you think, that these Grays have big eyes and squat bodies and look like they came right out of Close Encounters or ET?" Lauren said.

"Maybe it means the filmmakers did their research," Joe said. "See? I could've played the believer, not the skeptic."

"The meeting?" I said.

"Okay, let me tell it," Lauren said. "We met in a semi-private room in an Italian restaurant. Sparkly lights all over. Besides Alan and Jill, I talked with this woman, Freya, a graphic designer, and a guy who claimed to work in advertising, Jameel. No last names other than Art's, but everyone was pretty open about their jobs. Makes me think they're not as worried about staying totally anonymous as Dr. Verde told you they were."

"Anyone talk about Kurt?" I said.

"They did to me," Joe said. "We told everyone we met Art through Tobias, who I knew from our years on the board together. I made it sound like Tobias filled us in on Kurt's hybrid beliefs and that he sympathized with my trouble believing Lauren. Then a group member told me that when Tobias was a teenager, he told Kurt to stop visiting him or coming to any of his school events. Up to and including Tobias's college graduation. And his wedding. They only started spending time together again when Tobias and his wife had kids."

"I knew their relationship was strained," I said. "But that seems extreme."

"Tobias never let Kurt be alone with the kids. He was afraid Kurt might start telling them about aliens and hybrids," Joe said.

"Did he?" I said.

Joe shrugged. "Not that anyone mentioned."

"We heard about Isabel, too," Lauren said. "Joe absolutely made a great skeptic. He said he thought my therapist influenced me too much by having me watch a documentary about alien experiences, then hypnotizing me. It got the rest talking about hypnosis to reassure him."

Joe cut his bacon strips into smaller pieces. "That guy Alan, the one Lauren's smitten with, said Isabel helped him deal with his memories through hypnosis. Also said Isabel helped Kurt do the same."

Lauren swiped a piece of bacon from Joe's plate. "Though everyone absolutely talked about Isabel and Kurt as a couple, not like she was his therapist."

"So she hypnotized him as a favor?" I said.

"Sort of. The way you might give me some legal advice and not charge me I guess," Lauren said.

I ate more of the chocolate chip pancakes as I thought about what they'd said. "Alan talked about dealing with memories, not recovering them?"

"His story is seriously sad," Lauren said. "I had to step outside for some air so I wouldn't cry in front of him."

"I didn't hear this," Joe said. "What happened to him?"

"Well, obviously I think nothing other than what he imagined. But he says the aliens take blood samples from him, not the other thing, and it started when he was in grade school. Each time as soon as they brought him on the ship, he ran and hid in these storage bins. Or under lab tables. But the Grays always found him."

"It sounds scary," I said. "But why did it make you cry?"

"Getting there." Lauren's cappuccino cup was empty. She reached across Joe's plate for his coffee mug and took a gulp. "When he recovered those memories through hypnosis, he felt petrified. But then he switched to Isabel Verde. She guided him to re-experience his memories from an adult perspective. And it hit him he never needed to be afraid."

"Because?" Joe said.

"Because the aliens were really playing hide and seek with him. Something he never got to do as a kid. His big brother had leukemia, and his parents never had time to play with Alan. And they didn't let his friends come over for fear of disturbing his brother. That's when the aliens started visiting Alan. And now he's seriously grateful they came to him when he needed friends."

"Did this seem more dramatic told by a guy who looked like George Stephanopoulos?" Joe said.

She frowned at him. "You don't think that's sad? This poor guy had such a lonely childhood that he needs to believe these beings from another planet crossed galaxies just to play with him."

I wondered if the story affected Lauren so much because she was an only child. Maybe she identified with Alan.

"Self-delusion is sad," Joe said.

I pushed aside my plate. "It sounds like Isabel helped him reframe his memories so he felt better about them. Maybe she did that for Kurt, but it affected him in some way she didn't expect. Or like."

Lauren finished the last of Joe's coffee. "Makes sense. No one said anything about that, though."

The waiter brought the check. I glanced over it and took out my firm Visa. "Anything else interesting?"

"Joe talked to Art Feffor about his investments."

"He's in your range?" I said. Joe worked with people who had over $5 million in assets.

"Apparently," Joe said. "And he got this far without an adviser. My good luck."

"You two are quite the power couple." I handed Lauren her purse across the table and slid out of the booth. "Networking at the alien support group."

"It's a good group for that," Lauren said. "Makes me wish we could keep going."

At Lou Mitchell's you pay as you leave. On the way to the lunch counter register, Lauren said, "Oh, I almost forgot the most seriously important thing. Jill mentioned a writer who's not an experiencer, so he wasn't there. But he's taking oral histories from them so they can publish a book together. She had Art text me his info because my story would fit so well. Told you I did an awesome job."

As I buttoned my coat, Lauren texted me the writer's information. I stored it in my phone for now. Before I got to him, I had a meeting with Maria to ask about her embezzlement charges.

24

———

"I WAS AN IDIOT." Maria sat across from me in the firm's conference room. "But I didn't embezzle. Someone I worked with did. Someone who I also happened to be dating."

"Did you help him? Or her?"

"Him. I didn't help him take money. But he came to me saying he made a terrible mistake, and I tried to help him cover it up."

I grimaced. "Bad idea."

"Oh, yeah. I was very young. And very gullible."

Maria told me she worked as a teller at a bank for five years while acting in plays at night. She started dating an audience member she met at an after-show meet and greet. When he was laid off from his job as a waiter she recommended him to her boss. Two months later he came to her in a panic.

"Said he lost a packet of ten-dollar bills. A hundred of them."

"How do you lose a thousand dollars?"

"The way we did things at the time, it could have happened. We counted out at the end of our shifts, filled out a sheet balancing it all, and took this heavy zipper bag with the cash

167

and checks to the safe. It was down this long hall past the break room."

"You all had the combination to the safe? Or keys?"

"No, no. You fit the bags through this slot. It was just wide enough. No way you could get anything out of the safe through it. I was the last teller open that night. My boyfriend finished earlier and said he stumbled in the hall. He hadn't closed the bag. Everything flew all over. He scrambled around, looking for all the change rolls. Thought he got everything. But he was kind of shaken, so once he zipped it all up again he stopped to have a cigarette in the break room. To calm down."

"I would've taken it straight to the slot. To be sure it was done."

"Me, too. But, well, he was my boyfriend. I didn't question him. One cigarette led to two and then three. And in the meantime, the janitorial staff was cleaning the lobby and halls. Larry said he took the bag to the slot and that's the first time he thought to recount, be sure he found everything. That's when he saw a packet of tens was missing."

"And you still thought he was telling the truth?"

"Honestly? Infatuated as I was, I knew he wasn't the brightest guy I ever met. Or I thought I knew that. I figured it really didn't cross his mind to recount until that moment. Looking back, though, he was bright. Very bright. He hid it well and that's how he got away with things. After I helped him search all over for almost an hour he mentioned the cleaning people. Said one of them might have taken it. Or accidentally swept it into the trash."

"Doesn't seem all that likely. The trash part."

"No. But I could imagine someone seeing cash while cleaning and taking it. Or, honestly, I wanted to believe that more than I wanted to believe my boyfriend was playing me."

The landline on the credenza buzzed. Maria answered,

talked for a few minutes about a court filing due date, and returned to the conference table.

"So you helped him cover it up?" I said.

"First I tried to convince him to call the supervisor. But he was so new he was sure he'd be fired. Probably he would have been. He begged me to help him rejigger his daily entries so he'd balance. Promised he'd borrow a thousand dollars from his dad the next day to pay it back. Then we could reverse the transactions."

"You could do that?"

"Could. Did. It wasn't like now. Customers didn't have online access to their accounts. As long as it was all a wash before the next time the customers came in and their passbooks were updated, no one caught on."

"That really worked?"

"Not in the long run, obviously. But this one woman who made a deposit that day had a high balance. The records showed she only came in every few months. We took a thousand out of her account. My boyfriend borrowed six hundred from his dad and four hundred from me – I know, I know – deposited it in another account the next day that was usually dormant, then transferred it to the high balance woman's account. All before the end of the month. Neither of them ever noticed."

"How did you get caught?"

"We wouldn't have, except he kept doing it. Which I didn't know. Not borrowing and repaying from his own money. Finding accounts with the right patterns of deposits and withdrawals to shift funds around. He withdrew from one, repaid from another, which he then repaid from a third, and so on. Always balancing out the withdrawals just in time. He stole nearly twenty thousand dollars by the time he got caught."

"And they traced it back to you because you loaned him that money?"

"No, that was in cash. They traced it back to me because he used my teller login. I didn't give it to him. He must have watched over my shoulder. Lucky for me, I'd been there five years and my supervisor knew me well. She vouched for me with the prosecutors and the bank. Told them she believed I didn't know about the thefts."

"Seems like there were some serious flaws in the bank's procedures."

"Oh my yes. Lots of tightening up after that."

"Was there a trial?"

The receptionist popped his head in. "Back from lunch."

I hadn't heard him come in, just as I hadn't heard Ty the other night. Supporting the idea that it was unlikely anyone on Bryan's conference call overheard Maria and me talking the day of the break in.

"I plea bargained. I had a public defender who told me I wouldn't go to prison and the probation wouldn't be that big a deal, which was true. But he didn't tell me how hard it would be to get a job with misdemeanor theft on my record. Not to mention no reference from the bank."

"But you got it expunged."

"Ten years later. I waited a lot of tables before that. Long hours, no health insurance. And this was before you could buy it on your own if you had any problems, and I have asthma. Then I met Kurt at a Goodman Theatre event for the board members. He's the one who told me I could get it expunged. And suggested he'd consider hiring me down the road if I earned a paralegal certificate."

"You talked about all of it to him that night?"

"It was a rough week. The restaurant I worked for went out of business. Since he's a lawyer I thought maybe he'd have some advice for me, and he did. And he referred me to a friend who did the expungement cheap."

"Sounds like he was a kind person," I said, though that

didn't quite fit with how he treated Tobias. Kurt might have believed, though, that he was doing what was best for his son.

Maria looked down at the table. "He was. Not one of those attorneys who pretends to be for the little guy to make a lot of money. Kurt wanted to make the world better for people."

She seemed sincere, but she was an actress.

"Did you ever date him?" I said.

Her eyes widened. "Kurt? No. He's been with Isabel forever."

"If he wasn't with Isabel would you have been interested?"

"He was an attractive man once you got to know him. But not my type."

That wasn't exactly an answer. I filed that away to think about later.

25

———————

Bryan frowned. "I'm sorry someone attacked you and Maria. But I already talked to the police. I don't know why you're questioning me too."

After talking with Maria, I worked in Kurt's office until Bryan returned from lunch. Now he sat in the one visitor chair I'd cleared of Kurt's files.

"When someone assaults me, I ask questions," I said. "Of everyone."

"Well, the someone wasn't me."

"But you're the one who didn't lock the front door when you left."

He leaned forward, elbows on the chair arms. No trace of a smirk for a change. "Sorry about that. I wasn't thinking. We lock the doors at six. I left well before that, about five minutes after you went downstairs."

"You didn't think about how you were leaving the suite empty?"

"It was stupid, but I didn't. I guess I thought you two would grab a few files and come right back upstairs."

"Which way did you leave?"

"Through the building next door. But if you're looking for proof, they don't have cameras on the exit I used. Found that out the one time I parked my car out there and someone banged into it and drove off. No cameras. Now if I drive in, I suck it up and pay the garage rates."

"And you drove in that day?" The garage was beneath the building next door and, if nothing else, must keep records of parking passes or license plate numbers.

He shook his head. "Walked. I was heading out for drinks and wanted to take an Uber home."

How convenient that Byran left using an exit he knew lacked video surveillance. On the other hand, I cut through buildings all the time. In downtown Chicago, they connect in ways you'd never notice from outside.

A series of underground passageways known as the Pedway links key buildings like the Thompson Center, City Hall, and the Daley Center. Some side-by-side structures feature adjoining floors. Others, like the building where King and Stillwell's firm was located and its next-door neighbor, have narrow alleys between them and matching side revolving doors. People can walk from one to the other in a few strides. It's a great way to limit outdoor time if it's pouring rain, freezing cold, or snowing.

"Who do you think might have attacked us?" I said.

"E. Drake Draper."

Rumbling came from outside the window, probably a large truck bouncing over a scored patch of asphalt where the city was working on the street.

"Why him?"

"He was here late Thursday to talk with me about a new case. And he snoops. One time I caught him leaning over the front desk when our receptionist stepped away. If Maria left her calendar open and it showed visiting the storage space with you and when, he saw it."

"But you didn't see him looking at her calendar?"

"No, but it's not like I walked him out."

"What's the motive?"

"You said he asked for a crazy short date on your response. He could've wanted to slow you down more. Make it harder for you."

"I've run into lawyers who are rude to everyone to make cases more frustrating. But assault?"

"You don't know class action plaintiff attorneys. We fight more with each other than with the other side."

"So these fee disputes like the one I'm handling for you happen all the time?"

He waved his hand. "We don't sue each other all the time. But there are always issues over how to split fees, who runs the case. This old guy, Fred Varnes–"

"I met him."

"Well, he brought in a client literally eight years ago on one of our cases. Never did another thing. But now it's settled and he wants twenty percent of the fees. Claims Kurt promised him twenty percent back in the day, conveniently not in writing. But if he did, that's when Kurt thought the case would wrap up in a year. It took eight."

My shoulder still ached from the attack. I moved my elbow off the desk and let my arm drop to my side. "Will he get his twenty percent?"

"Not if I have anything to say about it. Our last hearing like that Fred made such a scene the judge held him in contempt and had to call the bailiff to take him away in handcuffs. This is a different judge, though."

"Any chance Fred wanted Kurt out of the way?"

"Kurt would've given him a lot closer to the twenty percent, so I doubt it."

If that was true, it was another reason Bryan might want Kurt gone, though.

———

ON MY WAY OUT, I asked Maria if her calendar showed us visiting the storage room. She said it did, but she always locked her computer before leaving her desk. She also said she never noticed E. Drake snooping and didn't have any reason to think he'd attack us.

"What's your view of Fred Varnes?" I said.

"Laziest attorney I ever met."

"Any chance he'd attack us to get into the storage room?"

She laughed. "I don't see him expending that much effort. Fred complains if he has to click a mouse to open an attachment to an email. Says it's too much extra work and I should paste in the information instead."

Yet a judge had ordered him to be taken away in handcuffs.

———

DESPITE ALL THE other work I needed to do I dropped in at Fred Varnes's office on my way back to mine. Like me, he shared space in a larger suite. His office was down at the end of a long row of offices on one side and file cabinets on the other. His desk was made of pressboard and listed to the right, making me think he assembled it himself.

He stood when I appeared in the doorway. "So you're Quille Davis. Lot prettier than Bryan. He should have you negotiate our fees. I'd give you a deal."

I wasn't sure how to answer the harassing comment that he probably saw as a compliment. But I had already achieved one thing. Fred Varnes was about three inches shorter than me and forty pounds heavier. Definitely not the assailant.

"I'm hoping to get your take on something."

He gestured toward the rickety-looking chair in front of the desk. "Sit. I got fifteen minutes or so."

I told him about the attack and asked for his views on whether E. Drake Draper, Bryan, or anyone else on the cases they shared might have done it and why.

"Huh." He rubbed his chin, which was covered with two-day gray stubble. "Don't see anyone doing a terrible thing like that to two girls. And for some paper? Not like you've got bars of gold down there, is it?"

I agreed that King and Stillwell did not. "But let's say there was something valuable. Any of the attorneys you think might physically attack other people to get it?"

"Had some big fights myself in the day. But these guys – they're soft. Stillwell gets his nails buffed. Can't see a guy like that attacking anyone. Changing world I tell you and not for the better."

"And E. Drake?"

"Well, he's a horse of a different color as they used to say. But he's a bit of a dandy, too. Monogrammed cuff links, thousand-dollar suits, that kind of thing."

"So you think men who dress well and take care of their appearances wouldn't fight physically?"

He drummed his fingers on his desk, making it shudder. "Doesn't seem likely, does it? And I can't see E. Drake Draper wasting his time with fighting when he makes so much in the courtroom. Next week he's getting three million for a case he spent half a year on. Think of that."

Fred had nothing to add about any of the other attorneys on the team.

"Stop by any time," he said as I rose to leave. "We need more pretty girls around here. Though, you know, one of those power dresses the ladies on TV like these days, that'd show your figure more than a pants suit. Might help your chances in court."

I'd been about to thank him for his time. I switched to a simple good-bye in case I needed to get any information from him later and left.

Back in my own office I typed out notes about the meeting. Then I wrote a motion in the chocolate chip brownie case, which ought to be over but wasn't. I took a break to get a ham and brie croissant downstairs and bring it back to my desk. As I ate, I reviewed a transcript of a client testifying in a deposition about his brother literally locking him out the factory they inherited from their father. I highlighted typos, including a missing Not at a key spot. That surprised me. I use the same court reporter whenever I can because she rarely makes mistakes.

I sent the changes to the client, then entered all my time into my timekeeping app. Then I shut everything down and headed out to meet Ty. We were meeting for a quick dinner and to play ping pong at SPIN Chicago, a club in the River North neighborhood. On my way down in the elevator I texted Art Feffor to ask if he knew the writer Lauren mentioned. I preferred to tell the writer that Art referred me rather than using Lauren's name. I didn't want anyone in the support group to link her to me.

Art answered right away and agreed to my plan. I felt tempted to return to my office and try to squeeze in a quick call. But I'd barely seen Ty for anything fun lately. It was time for a night off. I'd contact the author in the morning.

26

———

I RARELY ANSWER calls from numbers I don't know, but the next morning the writer did.

"Xavier Dopson."

"Hello, Mr. Dopson. My name is Quille Davis. Art Feffor gave me your information."

"Did he? So either you need a book ghostwritten, you want to tell me an alien abduction experience, or you have a very bad toothache and Art thought my brilliant wit might distract you from the pain."

I smiled. "None of the above. Though I am interested in alien experiences. I'm an attorney, and I've been looking into the death of Kurt King. His son asked me to."

The last two sentences were literally true. But they were misleading unless I made it clear Tobias also asked me to stop investigating. I spun my chair sideways, away from the diplomas hanging on my wall.

"For some kind of lawsuit?"

"Oh, no, no. I'm trying to help solve the murder."

"Hmm. Tobias doesn't trust the authorities to do it, huh? Sounds like he might be a little like his old man after all."

"You know Tobias?"

"No. Feels like I do, though. Heard an earful about him. But as I always say, one side of the story is one side, and the truth isn't flat. It has multiple dimensions."

"Based on my legal experience and the murders I've looked at, I agree."

"And you're trying to put together the dimensions and figure out who killed Kurt."

"Yes. Can you help?"

"I'm willing to. Less sure I'm able."

"I'm hoping while writing this book on alien experiences you picked up some things that could help me understand Kurt and the people around him. At least those he knew from the group."

"It's possible. Can't share anything told me in confidence, though."

I'd never met so many people dedicated to keeping secrets.

"You're planning on publishing, aren't you? How confidential can anything be?"

"Not everything's going into a book. And a lot of people will be under pseudonyms, not their real names."

"Including Kurt?"

"Not sure if can tell you one way or the other."

The suite door banged open. I peered out my office door to be sure the receptionist was there. She was.

"You can't tell me if he planned to use a pseudonym?" I said.

I didn't see how it could be confidential whether Kurt wanted to use his own name or not when I already knew who he was.

"You took me by surprise. I'm not trying to stonewall you. Just need to think a bit before we talk."

"I understand. With a murder investigation, though, sooner is always better."

He chuckled. "I'll think fast. Sorry. Just hit me none of this is funny. We can talk later this week."

"I'm happy to buy you dinner if you've got time."

I find it easier to get a read on people when I meet them in person, but my eyes flicked toward my purse. In the past three weeks I'd charged court reporter fees for deposition transcripts, routine maintenance by my new IT person, a large photo-copying bill, and breakfast with Joe and Lauren. My credit card payment wasn't due for another twenty days, which meant this week's charges would be on the bill, too. I hoped Xavier didn't have expensive taste.

"No need, no need. I might want to pick your brain, too. Sounds like you have an interesting professional life. But if you want to meet in person, you'll need to come my way. I'm on a tight deadline. Usually take a half-hour break around two each afternoon, though."

He told me he ghostwrote memoirs and autobiographies, mostly for sports figures, in addition to books where he took down and edited people's true stories.

Unfortunately for me, he worked at a coworking loft in Rogers Park, a residential Chicago neighborhood on the border of Evanston, the northern suburb that's home to Northwestern University. That meant at least a forty-five minute drive or L ride each way, wiping out an entire afternoon of work.

I arranged to meet him the next day anyway, despite that I'd need to reschedule a conference call.

"It's a plan," Xavier said. "This'll be a much more fun break than my usual spin the K-cup tower and try whatever flavor it lands on."

I had only twelve minutes until my next call, but I felt I needed both to warn him and come clean about Tobias.

"Sounds like you have an exciting work life," I said. "There's something you should know. Or two things. First, someone attacked me and the office manager at Kurt's firm."

"Maria? Is she alright?"

"I — yes, she's fine. You know her?"

"Met her once. When I ran into her and Kurt at a restaurant. They seemed pretty close."

I set down my pen, unsure what to do with that information. It was a small fact that might support Fred Varnes's speculation about Kurt and Maria, which on its own struck me as Fred being gross. Better to ask Xavier about it in person, though. It was now only ten minutes until my call.

"The other thing is that Tobias was very upset when that happened," I said. "He asked me to stop investigating the murder. But I think he's wavering, or I hope he is, and in the meantime I don't want to lose the thread."

"Wavering. So he hasn't said to go ahead yet?"

"No. But I'm still following leads wherever they cross over with the other work I'm doing for Kurt's firm."

"I sympathize. Curiosity has killed many cats for me. But then I am more of a dog person. And I want to see whoever did this caught. But I don't feel right meeting with you unless Tobias is on the same page."

I frowned at my framed law license, wishing for a moment I were someone who could ignore it and feel fine lying. "But you'll talk to me if he is?"

"That I will."

"I'll get him on board then."

In the six minutes left before my conference call I stared out the window at Dearborn Street below, trying to think of how to convince Tobias.

27

———

GRAM TOLD me you're investigating Q.C. Need to talk. Zoom tonight at 7.

The message from my sister Kendra came in while I was on the phone with my officemate, Danielle, about cases she'd handled where partners embezzled from their own firms. Danielle, a criminal defense attorney, was on trial all week in Lake County, but she'd called me during a break. As we talked, I made a list of what else to look for in the King and Stillwell expenses. Starting with whether the vendors who provided services were real companies.

When I saw Kendra's text, I asked Danielle a few more questions, thanked her, and hung up. I'd planned to spend this evening having dinner with Lauren. She and I had spent less one-on-one time since she started dating Joe, and I missed that. But when I texted Kendra to see if she could talk another night, she claimed she couldn't.

I gritted my teeth and agreed, not wanting to wait who knows how long to hear what she had to say.

Kendra and I are eight years apart. We never shared clothes or talked late into the night or went out for cocktails together once we grew up. But she did teach me how to tie my shoes and draw stick figures and straighten my hair. And walked me to the local drugstore to buy popsicles every Friday night in spring and summer until the store went out of business.

As adults, we mainly see each other on holidays. My niece and nephew, her two children, visit me more than she does. They love taking the Amtrak train to the Chicago area to visit Gram and me. And they always spend New Year's Eve with me.

Kendra and I used to talk on the phone more, but a year ago she asked me to check out her husband's activities. She didn't love what I learned. She apologized later for how badly she reacted. But my best guess was she wasn't saying she needed to talk now because she wanted to encourage my investigation.

I forced my mind away from my family and signed remotely into the King and Stillwell system. Danielle's comments gave me ideas about where else documents might be stored. None panned out, but eventually I found a trove of supporting tax documents in a mislabeled folder.

"Jackpot," I said to the screen. Probably wishful thinking, but I felt entitled to it.

When I left my office half an hour later I had at least the semblance of a plan for talking to Tobias. I texted him.

Can we meet tomorrow? More red flags in firm's books. Want to talk about a forensic audit.

———

LAUREN CAME over to my place anyway, and together we cooked butternut squash ravioli and asparagus. After we ate and loaded the dishwasher, she made us whiskey sours just how I liked them. Fresh squeezed lemon, simple syrup, Templeton Rye, and egg white, heavier on the sugar and lemon than the rye.

"You deserve something for dealing with your family."

Lauren dropped onto my couch, turned on my television, and popped on her noise cancelling headphones. "I'm expecting a full report after."

"You got it," I said, but she didn't hear me.

I climbed the ladder to the sleeping loft above my bedroom area and set up my iPad on the student-sized desk in the corner. My friends from theatre and I created the space right before Marco died. It was meant for when his son came to stay with us.

Kendra answered from her half-finished basement rec room. The recessed lights shining down made the silver strands in her blond hair stand out. For the first time they looked more like gray and less like highlights. Her peaches and cream skin, which I always envied, had reddened around the sides of her nose.

I shifted the iPad so my face didn't fill up quite so much of the screen. "You wanted to talk about Q.C.?"

"Yes," she said. "It's about time someone took another look."

"Really?" I let my hands fall still on the desk.

"I told Mom years ago they ought to hire a private investigator."

"I never knew that."

"Why would you? You were in high school. It came up when Mom said they were moving back to Edwardsville and leaving you with Gram. And I told her you just don't do that. You don't take off and leave your fifteen-year-old."

"I was sixteen by moving day."

"Sure, that makes all the difference."

"It wasn't so bad," I said. "At least I didn't need to be in the room when Mom called Aunt Cathy to talk about the fabulous Q.C."

I had been called Q.C. at the time too, but no one ever wondered which of us my mother meant.

"She was fabulous," Kendra said. "You didn't know her."

I took a long swallow of the whiskey sour. "Having trouble keeping up here. You're criticizing our mother? Or supporting her?"

"Neither. Look, I'm sorry. What I was saying to Mom is if you love your living teenage daughter you don't move 270 miles away to be near your dead daughter's grave."

"You thought she didn't love me?"

To be fair to Kendra, I thought that a lot, though by the end of therapy I'd come to believe, in my head at least, that my mother did love me. But she feared feeling it deeply or expressing it because she couldn't handle more loss in her life.

"Sure, she did," Kendra said. "She loves me, too. But not like before. You know, she used to play Crazy Eights with us when we were home sick. And make milkshakes and popcorn for dinner once a month on a Saturday night."

Kendra had told me all of that the night before her wedding when she drank too much wine. But she might not remember. "Sounds nice," I said.

"And she listened to me," Kendra said.

"What do you mean? She did what you told you her to do?"

"No, she listened. When she got home from teaching, she came into my room and asked me how my day was. And she listened to me tell her about it."

That I had never heard. It was harder to imagine than my mother making milkshakes.

"Like you used to do with me," I said.

"You remember that?"

"But you stopped." My shoulder felt stiff, worsened by a long day of computer work and tense phone conversations. I switched to the futon, lying on my back with the iPad propped on my chest.

"Well, you were still making things out of paste and construction paper when I started high school. Obviously, I became far too cool to hang out with my little sister."

"Obviously."

"And you started going to that theatre group, and I started hanging around with boys who weren't good for me."

"Gram always worried about that."

"She never worried about the right guys, though. I could've told her which ones were really trouble."

I wondered if Kendra considered her husband to be one of those. Best not to ask.

"So you told Mom she should hire a private investigator?"

Kendra tucked her hair behind her ear. "Oh, right. Basically, I said if she and Dad were still that focused on Q.C. maybe it was because they had no answers and it was time to hire someone."

"And?"

"Mom yelled at me for being disrespectful to Q.C. How was that disrespectful? But she burst into tears. Dad took the phone and said moving wasn't about Q.C. It was about Mom missing her home and Aunt Cathy. And that they moved to LaGrange to give you and me a stable home with Gram. But now I was gone and you were almost grown up and moving back could help mom's mental state."

"So you still think it could help Mom if I can do it? Find out what happened to Q.C.?"

"I think it's worth trying. That's why I wanted to talk to you. See if I can help. Though I was only seven. So there's that."

"But you were there that day."

"Yeah." Kendra looked away from the camera. "I don't remember anything, though."

28

I SAT UP, back against the futon's armrest, iPad perched on my knees. "Nothing?"

"The car ride there. Q.C. and I rode in back. She was so excited she kept kicking the front seat. Dad was in the passenger seat in front of her, kept turning around to tell her to stop."

"Wait, our mother was driving?"

During bad times my mother could barely stand riding in a car. Or leaving the house. I'd never known her to drive.

"She used to like driving."

Kendra also remembered running to the video arcade game section of the pizza parlor.

"And that's it. I don't remember the guests arriving or what Q.C. did. Nothing. Until the background music shut off suddenly and Mom screamed Q.C.'s name. She must've been looking for her for a while before that," Kendra said. "It was so quiet after she screamed. Like a physical weight pressing in on me from all sides. Because nobody answered."

"Is your memory – is there a blank for the time of the party?

Or more like things blur together and just those moments stand out?"

"Neither really. I just – it's just that's what I remember."

Her next memory was all the adults pulling the kids out of the ball cage and away from the machines, herding them into one corner away from the front and back doors. Aunt Cathy kept an eye on them while the other adults searched everywhere.

"Did anyone look outside?" I said.

"They must have. But I don't know for sure. Then there were sirens. All these sirens. So loud I held my ears."

"When did Dad come back?"

She shook her head. "No idea. But I remember him and Mom sitting at a table with this old policeman. Who knows if he was old, really. Thirty probably looked old to me."

"Did you think he looked old compared to Mom and Dad?"

Kendra's eyes turned upward. "Yeah. Because I didn't think of them as old. So he must've been, what, at least thirty-five or so."

"And he wore a uniform?" If so, that made him a police officer rather than a detective. At least that's what it would mean now in Chicago.

"I think so. I remember the badges on his shoulder."

"What next?"

"Grandma and Grandpa MacLean took me to their house."

"Not home?"

"No. I guess Mom and Dad thought it was better for me to be out of the way. They told me Q.C. got lost and the police were helping Mom and Dad find her."

Kendra didn't remember anything else about that day or most of the days that followed. She stayed at our grandparents' house.

"The next day I asked Grandma MacLean to take me to the library. I found this book about Edwardsville and tore out the map. I kept it so I never got lost. Plus I thought if I found Q.C. we could use it to get back home. I got caught, though. Grandma paid for the book and never told Mom and Dad."

"Why would they say she was lost?"

"It sounded less scary than kidnapped? But when Gram visited she took me outside and sat with me at the picnic table and told me a bad person came and took her. So I should always stay by adults. And if I was ever alone and a stranger tried to talk to me, I should run away."

"But the police didn't think it was a stranger."

"I didn't know that."

Kendra's cell phone rang. She muted the Zoom for a few minutes and disappeared off screen.

When she returned, she said, "For years I dreamed Q.C. and I were playing together at a playground, except it was inside the pizza parlor. And I convinced her to play tag, and I was It, and I never found her."

"Do you think you played tag that day?"

"It's a dream, Quille."

"Memories might surface in dreams." I wondered if there was any chance hypnosis could recover Kendra's memories.

"What? Parlor tricks? I don't think so," she said when I suggested it.

"It wouldn't hurt to try."

"How do you know? You're not an expert. And I don't need to have those dreams again. You don't know what it was like. Waking up in a panic, then relaxing when I realized it was a dream, then remembering Q.C. was really gone."

"But if it could help find the truth?"

She frowned. "I don't think it can. Look, I've got to go." She reached for her mouse.

"Wait, wait. Can you send me a list? Who you remember being at the party and anyone else you remember seeing or talking to that day?"

"I'll try."

———

TOBIAS WAS WORKING a half day the next day. His only free moments were during his walk to the Ogilvie Transportation Center to catch the train home. I met him outside the Civic Opera House again.

"The amount the firm spent on case-related costs jumped five years ago. By a lot more than inflation did," I said. "Lots more dinners, more travel, more photocopying. That last is strange because everyone was shifting to e-discovery. Way less paper traded back and forth. There could be an explanation, but it needs to be looked at."

We crossed the bridge over the Chicago River on Madison Street. It shook slightly as cars, taxis, and trucks sped past us.

"Can't you do it?" Tobias said.

"You'd be paying me to do something a forensic accountant can do better and faster. I can refer you to someone."

We entered the sprawling Ogilvie Transportation Center through a revolving door. The wide corridor inside smelled of dark roast coffee. "There's someone we use at work, but sure, send me some info."

Tobias veered toward the Starbucks pick up line.

I lowered my voice. "I told you before that financial fraud could be the motive for your father's murder. It looks like there's enough at stake for that to be true. Which means by digging into it I'm poking the bear whether I focus on the murder or not."

"If that's true, all the more reason to step away."

"But you need answers or you could face some serious IRS issues down the line. And it's more likely the person who killed your dad will remain out there. Free to harm other people."

He swallowed hard. "The police might catch whoever it is."

"And if they don't?"

A barista called his name. He grabbed his coffee and started up the ramp toward the first-floor retail area. I hurried alongside him.

"It's – I don't know. I just know I don't want you or anyone else in the line of fire," Tobias said.

"Look, this is something I understand. From experience. You might think you can live with not knowing who killed your father. But it eats at you. Not just not knowing who did it, but why they did it. You can't put it to rest, and it won't only affect you. It'll affect everyone who knew and loved your dad. And who knows and loves you."

He stopped in front of a toy store. A castle made of red, white, and blue plastic bricks filled the window. Two commuters swerved around us, one of them cursing.

"You're talking about your sister."

"Yes. I can't prove my parents and everyone else would have better lives if the murderer had been caught. But I feel it. I know it."

"I'm sorry your family went through that. But it might be influencing you to push ahead here when it's better not to."

"Could be," I said. "And I did go ahead with the murder investigation and learned something important. Your dad talked to a writer, one who writes memoirs and biographies, about his alien experiences and his beliefs about being a hybrid. And about you. The writer's planning to publish a book."

Tobias shifted from one foot to the other. "It'll include Dad's name?"

"The writer won't tell me more unless I have your okay to go forward."

"But you already talked with him."

"Briefly. By phone. I have an in-person meeting at two today, but I'll cancel if you tell me to. I have to warn you, though, as long as I'm handling the fee case and helping with the finance issues, I can't promise I won't be learning about the murder, too. Because I don't see how they can be separated, at least not for me. And probably not for you. It's why you hired me."

"I can't look for a new lawyer now, I don't have time." As if his words reminded him he needed to catch a train, he glanced at the escalators that led up to the Metra station, then at his phone.

"I'm not saying I'll withdraw from the other work. But I know myself. If I come across anything at all that might relate to the murder, I'll be right back at your door pushing you to let me follow it up."

He looked at the escalators again, then back at me. He sighed. "You're right. I asked you in the first place because of the murder. Just please be careful."

I promised him I would. He took off for the escalators. I texted Xavier to confirm. My phone dinged as I headed back to Starbucks to pick up a sandwich for lunch.

Looking forward to it. 4 blocks from the Howard Red Line stop. Lots to tell you.

29

———

Tobias may have agreed on my visiting Xavier. But the weather
didn't, and neither did my iPhone.

A minute after I exited the Howard L station in Rogers Park,
thunder cracked. Two seconds later, rain drove down so hard it
splattered up off the sidewalk. My thighs and calves got
drenched despite my full-sized umbrella from the Art Institute
– with, ironically, a print of Gustave Caillebotte's painting *Paris,
A Rainy Day* on it. I gripped the umbrella with one hand, struggling as the wind threatened to wrench it away, and held my
iPhone in the other so I could follow its directions.

I walked on the north side of the street, following the
numbers to what ought to be the right address. But fewer and
fewer buildings lined the street with each block. Siri insisted I
keep heading east. When I peered ahead and saw that would
land me in Lake Michigan, I stopped.

With no desire to become wetter than I already was, I back-
tracked to the L station. Chicago is laid out on a grid. Most
blocks cover one hundred in street address numbers. So if
you're at 200 South Michigan Avenue and you walk four blocks

193

south, you'll be at 600 South Michigan. Once you understand it and know where the zero is on the grid (the intersection of State and Madison Streets downtown), it's easy to find your way around so long as you know what direction you're heading. And if you falter on that, you can look for the Willis Tower, which stands on the west edge of downtown, or ask someone where the lake is. It's always east.

Based on the grid, Siri had sent me the correct way – east toward the lake. I was definitely on the right street, so I headed west instead, wrong as it seemed. After a block, the street numbers jumped abruptly to 100 West Howard, though on the Chicago grid that address made no sense. Four more blocks brought me to the coworking space on the third floor of 500 West Howard. Which is when it hit me that, whether my iPhone's maps knew it or not, this side of Howard must be in Evanston, not Chicago. Evanston, unlike the near west suburbs I was more familiar with, must have its own numbering system.

Inside the lobby I took a plastic umbrella bag from a dispenser that sat beneath a wall directory. The coworker space was on the fifth floor. My jeans and wool coat were still soaked. My boots were water resistant, so inside them my feet were only damp.

Shivering, I dripped my way to the elevator. It opened onto a wide-open space with exposed beams across the ceiling and hardwood floors. A few people sat typing away at laptops at long tables. A row of offices lined the far wall.

"Xavier?" I said into the void.

At the far end of one of the tables sat a plump man with a pasty complexion that contrasted his dark long-sleeved T-shirt. He stood and headed toward me. "Quille? I reserved an office for us." He looked me over. "But unfortunately, no towels. I can offer hot drinks. You can mix flavors."

He led me to a kitchen bar with a Keurig coffeemaker and a

separate machine with multiple buttons and flavor packets. When it comes to office kitchens non-coffee drinkers like me rarely get choices beyond one or two types of black tea, generic herbal, and Swiss Miss chocolate powder packets hardened with age.

Xavier pointed. "One packet here, one here, hit this button. I'll see if I can find any towels."

I opted for hot chocolate with vanilla crème syrup and stood under a heat vent as the machine whirred and clicked. Xavier rummaged through the cabinets and found a roll of paper towels. I used some to dry the front of my leather Frye shoulder bag until my drink was ready.

It didn't taste as good as my friend Carole's *chocolat chaud*, but nothing did. And for the equivalent of vending machine hot chocolate it was pleasantly rich and creamy.

Xavier took me to an office with four boxy arm chairs arranged around a round coffee table. He perched opposite me, looking as if he might spill forward out of the chair at any moment. Rain pelted the windows behind him and obscured the view of a similar building across an alley.

"This book of alien experiences you're writing," I said. "It included Kurt's?"

"A short version of them. Because there's also this." Xavier clicked keys on his Surface tablet, then flipped it to show me the words Attorney Abducted in large scrolling letters across the screen. Kurt's full name was listed below the title. "Kurt hired me to ghostwrite his memoir. That's not the cover. Just what I use for myself."

I stopped smoothing the pages of my damp legal pad and peered at the screen. "He was putting his real name on it?"

"That was the plan."

"When did he hire you?"

Xavier spun the tablet to face himself again. "About three

months before he died. Did three interviews with him so far. Well, three interviews. I looked over my notes from our conversations, thought about what I can tell you. What might be important."

"It'd be more helpful if you tell me everything. Then I can figure out what might relate to the murder."

What I really wanted was to see his notes, but he wasn't likely to hand them over to someone he met five minutes ago. Or possibly ever since they were his creative work.

"But there's a lot," he said. "Tons of information that might not ever go into the book. I don't know where to start."

"From the title, I take it you're focusing, or Kurt was, on his alien abduction experiences. But I had the impression he kept that part of his life quiet."

"He did. This was going to be the first time he went public. If it came out after the experiencer book he was going to have me use a pseudonym in that one so his book would get more attention."

I could think of a lot of people who wouldn't be happy about that.

"Did he tell anyone he was planning to do this?"

"If he did, he didn't tell me. I kept pushing him to tell Tobias, and Kurt kept putting it off. Said his experiences embarrassed Tobias and he needed to find the right way to tell him."

Tobias struck me as wounded, angry, and abandoned more than embarrassed. But as Xavier said, the truth wasn't flat.

"But Kurt meant to tell him sometime before the book came out?"

I wondered if Kurt told Tobias the night of his fortieth birthday party. It didn't seem like much of a present if he had and might have made Tobias angry. While Tobias had a stronger alibi than Isabel, Maria, Bryan, or E. Drake, it wasn't one that completely ruled him out.

"I told Kurt he needed to. And soon. Some people like surprises. But not if the surprise is a book that includes your name and makes your dad look crazy in the eyes of your coworkers and most of the rest of the world."

"But you weren't aiming to write a book that made Kurt sound crazy."

"No, but that's how a lot of people feel about alien abductions. It's how Tobias felt. Regardless of the proof."

A spiky-haired guy in a suit opened the door. "Is this 5A?"

"B," Xavier said.

"Sorry." He walked off without shutting the door. I closed it and returned to my seat.

Xavier frowned. "These kids. Sign a mile wide on the door, but they can't read anything that's not on a smartphone screen."

"What proof?" I said. "Of alien experiences?"

"Eyewitness accounts."

"So Kurt didn't have, I don't know, an implant that was removed from his body or photos of aliens, or reports from neighbors who saw a spaceship over his home?"

"Not that he told me." Xavier clutched his tablet to his chest and thrust his head forward. "Have you uncovered something?

"No. I'm just covering the bases." I flipped a page on my legal pad. "Was there a reason Kurt decided to do this now?"

"He felt he'd made enough of a name for himself that it wouldn't have a huge impact on his law firm. And he thought the story of a prominent attorney's experiences could help people believe aliens visit the planet and want to help us."

I thought back to the argument Art Feffor claimed he overheard between Kurt and Isabel. It could easily have been about Kurt's plan to write the memoir.

"What happens with the memoir now?"

"I'd like your opinion on that. I don't have enough for a full book, but if I could get just two or three other experiencers like him – Art Feffor might do it – to share more of their stories under their real names the publisher might be interested. But everything's on hold now."

"And you need Tobias's consent, as the heir."

"Not legally. Kurt signed an agreement giving me the right to publish what I had if anything happened to him."

30

My hand stilled in the middle of writing a note. "Kurt thought something might happen to him?"

Xavier frowned. "Not the way you mean. Not murder. He thought the aliens might take him home, as he called it, any time. Or I should say hoped. Kurt never felt quite right in this world. So he wanted his story out there if he was taken that one last time."

"No humans he was worried about? No one in the support group, maybe someone unhappy he might expose who they are?"

"No humans. Sorry. That would have been helpful, wouldn't it?"

"Did Kurt tell the group about the memoir?"

Xavier scratched his head. "They're all pretty close. Wouldn't surprise me if he did."

I flipped to the page of topics I'd written out during the L ride. "You said on the phone that you ran into Kurt out with Maria. When was that?"

"A week before he died? Maybe a little longer."

"Did you talk about the memoir in front of her?"

"We didn't really talk about anything. Kurt introduced us. My wife and I headed for our table."

"Did Kurt tell Maria you were a writer or how he knew you?"

"Oh, yeah, he did. He said I was a writer he knew from his support group."

"Did he say what type of support group?"

Maria had given no hint that she knew about Kurt's abduction experiences. My memory for what people say is near perfect, and when we met she told me she didn't know what Kurt's "unusual beliefs" were.

Xavier's forehead creased. "Don't think so."

"What did Kurt say about Maria? How did he introduce her?"

"Hmm." He rocked a bit in the chair, pushing his toes against the carpeted floor. "That she was from his law firm. Something gave me the impression she wasn't a lawyer, so maybe he said paralegal. Or assistant. Something like that."

Xavier's memory for exact words obviously wasn't near perfect. But, being a writer, maybe his observational skills were better.

"Did it seem like they were on a date?" I said. "Before he said anything."

"I thought so at first, and I was surprised because I thought he was seeing Isabel Verde."

"What made you think it was a date?"

"Just that it was at Geja's. You know, the fondue place with all the candlelight and secluded booths? We were there for our anniversary. It's a romantic place."

It was, but I went there more often with friends than with Ty, who wasn't a fan of eating that much cheese or of leaving smelling like the hot cooking oil set out for patrons to cook the main course items.

"What was their body language?"

He shut his eyes. "Could go either way. They were definitely focused on each other, good eye contact, didn't notice us pausing at the table until I said something."

"Did you hear what they were talking about?"

"Some book on the New York Times best seller list. They both thought it was bad. Always like to hear what people think about books."

I shifted in the chair and crossed my legs. My jeans still felt damp and clammy against my skin. "You said at first you thought it was a date. Something changed your mind?"

"When he said they worked together. Also, it was a weeknight, Monday or Tuesday."

Geja's was miles from King and Stillwell's office, though, so Kurt and Maria didn't just pop over after work for dinner.

"Did you ask Kurt later if he was seeing Maria?"

"No reason I would."

"Isn't that important to a memoir?"

"A memoir's not a biography. It's not a history of a person. We mainly talked about his alien experiences from childhood to now, not his relationships."

"You knew he was seeing Isabel, though."

"Because he was dreading telling her. She thought if anyone knew about his experiences it would damage his reputation as a lawyer. And maybe hers as a therapist and professor."

"He used the word dread?" Dread sounded a lot more serious than, say, concern.

"Huh. Not sure the exact word."

"Could you write the book without mentioning Isabel's name?"

"We talked about that. But it'd be hard. They were involved for twenty years. Even if we used a pseudonym for her, Kurt worried people could figure it out."

"You couldn't leave her out entirely?"

"No. Kurt learned a lot about abduction experiences from

her, found the group through her. She did hypnotic regressions with him. Leave her out and there are a lot of gaps."

"When did she do the regressions?"

He tilted his head, eyed the ceiling. "Two, three years ago? A psychiatrist hypnotized him decades before that. That's when he realized he was being abducted. But he wanted to see if working with Isabel, someone he felt so safe with, might reveal more."

"And did it?"

Xavier tapped his fingers on his knee. "He said it brought him more peace. And it's when he realized the aliens eventually were going to take him home."

That might fit Kurt saying to Isabel that her hypnosis started it all. Maybe it started his view that the aliens planned to take him, which made him feel freer to start talking, and writing, about his experiences.

"Did you ever meet Isabel?"

"A few times at MUFON conventions. I speak at some because of my books recording abduction experiences."

"Did you feel Kurt's worries about people figuring out who she was were valid? That is, they could figure it out, but why would anyone bother?"

His eyes lit up. "That's what I said. My books are for people already interested in aliens and UFOs. Maybe they've experienced something similar. Sure, I get a few emails or online messages where people say I'm perpetrating a fraud, blah, blah. But mostly people who don't believe aliens exist, or don't think they visit our planet, don't read my books. And those who do, if they did want to figure out Isabel's identity, it would be to become her clients."

"Did he say anything else about Isabel?"

"Nothing specific."

I sipped my vanilla crème chocolate. It had gone cold and tasted too sweet. "But?"

"I got a sense of trouble in paradise. Like they were going to put up a parking lot."

"Sorry?"

"The song? Paved paradise...never mind. I sensed all was not well, at least from his perspective. Now that I think of it, that might be why the idea of a date popped into my head when I saw him with Maria."

"You're saying Kurt and Isabel were fighting a lot?"

"It felt more like...inertia. A body at rest stays at rest. You're with someone for decades, you're not quite happy, there are things you can't resolve. But it's easier to stay in than make a change."

"Sure," I said, though, as Isabel had pointed out, I didn't have personal experience with that. It might apply to my parents, though. "What things couldn't they resolve?"

"No idea. It's just a feeling I got, and I had a note to explore it, see if it related to the alien experiences." He grimaced. "And now the thought of a body at rest seems disturbing with Kurt dead."

"Did anything prompt your gut feeling?"

Xavier ran his index finger along the edge of his tablet's screen. "Kurt told me his only regret if the aliens took him soon would be if the firm fell apart and Maria lost her job. He worried she'd have trouble finding another. Said she practically ran the place and it'd be a shame if she were caught in the lurch."

"Nothing about Isabel? Or Tobias?"

"Nope."

I felt for Tobias. The two had been estranged for so much of their lives that I would have thought it would be Kurt's biggest regret. And while I knew why Kurt worried Maria might have trouble finding another job, there had to be a greater reason than that for him to talk about her and not Isabel.

Which added another thing he and Isabel might have

fought about the night of Tobias's party or when Art overheard them from his swimming pool. I tried to imagine Isabel bringing a gun to the coach house. Rage taking over her face, prompting her to reach into her coat pocket for a small handgun. Maybe one she carried for protection. Or brought to Kurt's home with a purpose.

It was possible. Danielle always told me you don't know what anyone holding a gun will do in the grip of strong emotion. On the other hand, men are far more likely to shoot someone to death than women.

"Did Kurt ever talk about his law partner, Bryan Stillwell?"

"We hadn't gotten to talking about his work yet, other than Isabel's view that this memoir would damage his reputation."

"Did Kurt seem concerned about that?"

"No. Hold on." He clicked keys again. "Nope. No concern. Here's his exact words: 'I made all the money I need. I want to keep helping people, but if I can't do it through the courts anymore because of this, I can't. Telling the world what's happened to me, what it means, why the aliens come here, will do more good than a billion lawsuits.'"

"Any reason you wrote that down word-for-word?"

"I thought it might be a good quote at the beginning of the book."

Xavier told me Kurt hadn't talked much about his clients or the lawyers opposite him in cases. The name E. Drake Draper didn't ring a bell.

I asked Xavier about other memoirs he ghostwrote. He gave me one title, that of a former Chicago Bear, where his name was on the book. Otherwise, he told me he did true ghostwriting, with confidentiality agreements that kept his role secret.

I drained the last of my too sweet and no longer hot chocolate. "Any chance you'd let me see your notes for the memoir?"

"I figured you'd ask. And I thought about it a lot last night. Kurt authorized me to publish, so he didn't see a need for confidentiality. You seem like you really care about finding the truth. If you're willing to sign something saying you'll never use the material or publish anything based on it, I'll put together my handwritten notes to send you."

I felt safe promising not to write about alien abduction experiences. And hoped I'd be able to read his handwriting.

"Is there anything I haven't asked you that you think I should know?" I said.

It was a question I'd learned from Danielle. She often asked it at the end of interviews with her own clients. I was surprised how often, though, witnesses for the other side in a case volunteered something useful when I asked it.

"You didn't ask whether I think Kurt was abducted."

"Do you?" I wasn't sure that would help in a murder investigation, but he clearly wanted to talk about it.

"His experiences are consistent with what others report."

"Not really an answer."

"But it is. When I ghostwrite for someone, whatever the topic, I'm in it with them. I become them. It's not my job to sort out what's true or not. It's to tell their stories."

"How about before you started writing these books. Did you believe in alien abductions?"

"It's a vast universe, most of which we know nothing about. It could include aliens who travel here to study humans. Who am I to say it never happened?"

"Do you think Kurt's abduction experiences relate to his murder?"

He rested one hand on his rounded belly. "In my gut? Yeah, I do. Can't say exactly why, though."

At the exit, he shook my hand and thanked me for working to find Kurt's killer. "Any of this help?"

"Everything helps," I said. "I'll have a better idea how when I read your notes."

31

———

THE RESTAURANT and bar The Train Car stood four blocks from King and Stillwell. The owners had gutted a literal old train car from an Amtrak train. Inside, a polished wood bar stretched almost the entire length of the car with leather bar stools in front of it. About three feet separated the backs of the stools from the opposite side of the car, making it a real claustrophobia trigger, especially when filled to capacity. After seven on weeknights, though, the crowds thinned out. Here and there two or three seats in a row were empty, making it easier to move around without bumping other diners.

Six months ago, I might have felt safe talking with Maria at the firm alone at night. But the way my last investigation ended had made me more cautious despite training twice a week with my ex-police academy instructor. Also, my injured shoulder, though mostly healed, still ached from time to time, reminding me of the basement attack.

I arrived early to stake out a spot far from the restrooms so fewer people would be squeezing past and overhear us. The bartender, a young guy with three piercings in his right eyebrow, asked what I wanted.

"Could I get a whiskey sour, very light on the whiskey?"

"So fresh squeezed lemonade with egg white, splash of whiskey?"

I smiled, happily surprised he knew how to make one the right way. Usually only the older bartenders did. "Yes. Barely a splash. Do the same if I order another."

I ordered the cocktail because I guessed Maria would talk more freely if she saw this as a night out for drinks together rather than me interviewing her, but I wanted to stay as sober as possible. I was ready with a story for the bartender about why I needed to drink less. Most bar patrons don't ask for light pours, they complain about them. But he said fine and returned a few minutes later with my drink. It's one of the things I love about living in a big city. Strangers don't want to know your business.

Maria arrived and set a dripping umbrella on the bar. "You started without me."

"Long day," I said. "How was yours?"

"Ugh." She waved to the bartender and asked for a glass of Zinfandel. "Bryan's scrambling with last-minute filings for a key final approval hearing."

"Big deal?"

She slid onto the bar stool next to me. "Finishes the whole case. And it's when we get paid. Usually that doesn't happen until about four weeks after the hearing. But this corporation wants it on the books this month for some reason. So the second it's approved, the fees get wired out."

"And the money's in the firm's account?"

"Yep. And no fights over who gets paid what. This one's clearly covered by our agreement with E. Drake. We've got another like that coming in a month."

The bartender brought Maria's wine in a wide glass. I said I needed a few more minutes to decide on food, not wanting the evening to pass too fast. Maria and I were meeting so I could ask a few more questions about the fee lawsuit. At least that's what I'd told her. I hoped to get her talking about the way expenses were handled. And about Kurt.

"What do you think of E. Drake Draper personally?" I looked at the menu without really seeing it. I'd planned out my food choices online this afternoon so I wouldn't be distracted. "Everyone at the firm seems to know him pretty well."

"Well, he's around our office a lot. He and Kurt liked to talk through things in person. Kind of old school. Which Bryan always thought was a waste of time – unless he was doing the talking."

"Does Bryan like E. Drake?"

"He says he doesn't." She glanced up from the menu. "Potato skins? Not healthy but they're sooo good."

"Nothing's healthy here." The Train Car offered a wide selection of bar food, most of it fried. "I'll split them with you. So you think Bryan is an E. Drake fan?"

"I think he's jealous of him. Bryan's always strutting and puffing out his chest, but E. Drake has that thing where he walks into a courtroom and looks like he owns it."

"You've seen him in court?"

"Couple times. At class certification hearings where I helped run tech. Bryan's probably better at the legal arguments, but E. Drake is a man who can tell a story."

We gave the bartender our order, adding fried mushrooms. Might as well double down on the bar food.

"Did E. Drake ever question any of King and Stillwell's expenses on the food cases? Or did Fred Varnes?"

Maria's elbow bumped her umbrella and she slid it off the bar and onto the empty seat next to her. "Not that I heard. Why?"

Neither had mentioned expenses, but it saved me from admitting I was the source of the questions, which might make her defensive.

"You said before you pulled paper receipts and matched them with the amounts. Is that all the time?"

"I used to do that. But now I just fill in the amounts and Bryan attaches PDFs from his hard drive."

I sipped my whiskey sour. It tasted a lot like fresh squeezed lemonade. "His hard drive? Not a networked drive?"

No wonder I couldn't find all the documents.

"No, his. Because he's the one who pays everything."

"You never pay the bills?"

"I don't. Kurt doesn't." She blinked and looked down for a second. "Didn't. Only Bryan. Oh, and Bryan said it's all more secure on his hard drive rather than the network. Because some of the vendors put their Tax I.D. numbers on their invoices."

"Really?" Tax I.D. numbers are like Social Security Numbers. I couldn't imagine a company putting one on an invoice. "You've seen that?"

"I – you know, I'm not sure. Maybe Bryan just told me that."

"How long ago did the procedure change?"

She tapped one finger on the bar. "It was a while after most vendors started emailing their invoices. Bryan started saving them on his computer once he paid them. That was maybe, hmm. Four years ago? Five years?"

Right around when the firm's expenses skyrocketed.

"You're sure it was Bryan, not Kurt, who suggested it?" I said.

"I'm sure. Kurt didn't pay attention to that kind of thing."

"At all?"

"Oh, he looked over petitions and at quarterly income statements." Maria waved her right hand, which held her wine glass. Some wine sloshed over the rim. "But if Bryan wanted to use a different software or change a procedure, as long as it didn't cost a fortune or make Kurt's job harder he left it to Bryan."

"I saw Kurt signed all the petitions. Does that mean he was the main attorney on them?"

"No. Kurt signed everything because he thought it carried

more weight. Bryan thought that was stupid. Do judges care who signs?"

"Not that I've noticed." After a couple more swallows of my drink, I scrolled to copies of invoices from two years ago on my phone. "Does the court reporter service Scribe and Scrib ring a bell?"

"Oh, sure. That's Maggie Vella's firm. She's our favorite court reporter."

"Her firm is Scrib and Scribe."

"That's what you said."

"It's not. See?"

I showed Maria a PDF of one invoice with the name Scribe and Scrib and the other with Scrib and Scribe. "These are from two different fee petitions."

She peered at the headers on the invoices. "That one – that's weird. Typo?"

"On the court reporter's invoice?"

"Well, I create our letterhead on our computer. If they do that there could've been a mistake in their program that they fixed."

"Except I checked. The two names are used interchangeably throughout the last five years. It's not like there was a mistake and then it was corrected."

"But who – what would that accomplish? We use online banking, so the bank would still transfer the funds from us to the court reporter's account – oh." She blinked rapidly. "No. No, that – huh."

"What?"

Maria set her wine on the bar. "Payment might not go from the firm to the court reporter. If the attorney puts something on their Visa card, the payment goes to the attorney as reimbursement but it's coded with the court reporter's name."

"So if Bryan created these invoices he could pay himself for non-existent Visa charges and it would be coded as a court reporter payment?"

"Right. And if Kurt ever looked at the file, or I did, we'd see a court reporter bill and not think anything was wrong. Or if there was an audit of some type."

"No one checks the attorneys' credit card statements?"

"No. I mean, Kurt and Bryan are both partners. Who would check that? And why? As long as there's a receipt for the expense." She glanced again at the invoice on my phone. "Except now it looks like a fake receipt."

"The firm's accountant doesn't go over payments?"

"No. We just send him our QuickBooks file every year and he does the taxes."

Some accountants do an in depth review of a client's books each year, but only if the client wants that. And is willing to pay for it. The process Maria described was less expensive and more common for small firms, including mine.

Part of me was shocked, though, that King and Stillwell had no checks on what the partners did. But I handle everything myself. No one verifies my expenses unless the IRS decides to track me down. Kurt had started as a solo attorney. And, like a lot of attorneys, his undergrad major was political science, not business.

"Did Kurt ever suspect Bryan was doing anything wrong with expenses? Or finances generally?"

"No, never." Maria took another swallow of wine.

"And he would have told you if he did?"

"Yes. I'm sure of it."

"Because you're the office manager. And he'd want you to know so you could keep an eye out," I said.

"Right. Exactly."

"Because he trusted you."

"Yes. He did." Another drink of wine. "He really did."

"And, knowing your history, he wouldn't want you to get in trouble or for Bryan to pin anything on you."

"You're right," Maria said. "He'd be especially careful of that."

"Especially since you were seeing each other."

"Right. He –" She broke off and stared at me. "How did you know?"

32

IT WAS an old trial lawyer strategy. Get the witness saying yes, yes, yes to questions that didn't set them on high alert. Then ask the one that mattered. A little extra wine to lower inhibitions didn't hurt.

"A couple people mentioned things, and I put it together," I said. "But why did you deny it when I asked you before?"

She looked at her hands, which were folded in her lap. "I felt bad. He hadn't told Isabel – Dr. Verde – yet."

"How long were you seeing each other?"

"Only a few weeks. But we were friends for so long, and there was always a little bit of a spark there. But he was with Isabel, and I was living with someone. Until we split up last Christmas."

"And when did things start to change with Kurt?"

She had said three weeks, but she might be underestimating to make it sound less troubling. Or have miscalculated.

"Not for a long time. The firm closes from Christmas to New Year's. When we were back, Kurt asked if something was wrong. I was too quiet, I guess. I told him about my break up, and he took me out for a drink." She gestured to the bar. "Right here, actually. But it was just two friends. Then I was in rehearsals most of the time, or performances, in winter and spring. But I hit a lull, and we started both hanging out late at work and talking more. It'd get late. He'd give me a ride home. Then in late August we decided to see a movie. And we picked up a pizza after and took it to my place. Drank some wine. And he stayed the night."

"What did he say about Dr. Verde?"

"He said things were a little rocky. That they disagreed on some professional things and it was seeping into their personal relationship."

"Professional things? Like what?"

"He didn't say, except that it shouldn't be my problem. That I didn't need to be his therapist. Which I appreciated. My ex, over the years I did start to feel like his therapist. And his cheer-leader and his coach. And he wasn't much for reciprocating. It was like he didn't think I ever needed a listening ear. Kurt knew that, and he didn't want to fall into that same pattern." Maria closed her eyes for a moment. "He really was pretty wonderful."

"Do you think he ever told Isabel about you?"

She shook her head, setting her long hair swinging. "I know he didn't. He was going to the afternoon of Tobias's birthday party. Isabel was supposed to get there early, and Kurt said he'd talk to her then. Their schedules just hadn't matched before that, and he wanted to tell her in person. But I got to the party and there she was, cutting the cake with him, wishing him another wonderful year. With her."

"That couldn't have been fun."

Maria puffed out her cheeks. "It wasn't. And do you know I'm the only one she never offered a piece of that cake to?"

"Did you talk to Kurt about it?"

Now that she was sharing, Maria didn't hesitate. She must have been longing to tell someone, and it didn't occur to her that she was painting a picture that could lead to jealousy, rage, and murder.

"It was an hour before I got a minute alone with him, if you can believe it," she said. "He told me Isabel ran into bad traffic and only got there as the first guests were arriving so he didn't have a chance to talk with her."

"He didn't text you to let you know she ran late? So that at least you wouldn't be surprised when you walked in?"

She tightened her grip on her wine glass. "That's the point I made. He claimed he kept thinking she'd be there any minute and they'd talk. And then it got too late and Tobias and his wife arrived."

"You didn't text him sometime before you got to the party to ask how the conversation went?"

"I didn't want to be that person," she said. "I told Kurt early on I wasn't going to keep seeing him if he didn't end things with Isabel. It was up to him to do it."

Kurt might not have wanted to break up with Isabel. Or he had trouble with conflict and kept putting it off. Which, oddly, is something I find not that unusual with lawyers. While some become attorneys because they like fighting with people, a lot of others thrive on conflict in the courtroom but hate it in their personal lives.

Whatever Kurt's motives, the whole scenario was a recipe for getting both Isabel and Maria angry at him.

"When you found out he didn't talk to Isabel, did you break up with him?"

"No. But I told him before we took the next step he needed to do this."

"Next step? Sex?"

I'd assumed that spending the night together meant sex, but it might not have.

She waved her hand. "No, no. That happened. And was

great, by the way. But Kurt wanted to meet my family. And tell Tobias about us."

"He wanted to meet your family and tell Tobias but not break up with Isabel? How was that going to work?"

"You see what I'm saying."

That definitely suggested he was serious about Maria. If she was telling the truth.

"So what happened?"

"He said he'd tell her that night after everyone left. But he called me later to say they argued about something else during the party and she left before he could."

Our food had arrived. I ate a fried mushroom and burned my tongue.

"Any idea if that's true?" I said.

Maria slid a potato skin onto her plate and added a spoonful of sour cream. "I didn't see them argue. But I was so frustrated with him I left early. Around nine. He called me at eleven. Said he'd call Isabel the next day and break up over the phone."

"Did you believe him?"

"Weirdly, yes. He didn't want to tell her over the phone before, but he sounded like he'd had it. And maybe she had, too, and ending it was just a formality."

"Did you make plans to see him later in the weekend?"

She nodded, cleared her throat, and glanced around the bar before going on. "We were supposed to have brunch. On Sunday. But, obviously, that never happened. I told him we could talk then. And to – to leave me alone in the meantime."

"And did he?"

"No. But my sister was visiting and I just didn't want any more drama with him. So that's – that was the last time I talked to him. He called a couple times Friday. But I didn't answer. And he didn't leave a voicemail. So that was it."

Maria drank the last swallow of her wine and waved at the bartender.

"I'm sorry," I said. "This has to be really hard."

She pressed her lips together and nodded. The bartender brought us two more drinks.

"So you're back to investigating Kurt's murder?" Maria said.

I sipped my barely spiked lemonade. "I didn't exactly stop. But yes. Tobias gave me the okay."

"Well, make sure you find out who did it. Whoever it is deserves to pay."

———

IN THE MORNING, Tobias and I spoke together to a detective from the Violent Crimes Unit, though not the same one who interviewed him about Kurt's death the first time. We met in the conference room in my office suite. While the fake invoices and the other bookkeeping questions didn't prove anything about Kurt's death, they raised a motive for Bryan. Also, Isabel now had two possible motives, the memoir and Maria. And Maria's relationship with Kurt was new information.

The detective from Violent Crimes didn't seem impressed, but maybe he was good at keeping his expression neutral. He did say he'd look into all of it. And he brought with him a second detective from the Property Crimes division. She asked more questions about the potential embezzlement charges. We spent over an hour explaining why I was involved, what I'd learned so far, and what additional research the forensic accountant was doing.

I sat alone in my office afterward staring at my task list for ten minutes, feeling like I ought to be able to put all of this together. And worrying that I shouldn't have shared the information because it made it less likely I'd be able to take Isabel by surprise when I asked her about Maria. I tried calling her but got her voicemail. I asked her to call me, adding that if possible I'd like to meet with her again soon.

For the rest of the day, I worked on the response in the fee lawsuit and caught up on other cases. I also went over my notes on my interviews with my dad and Kendra. Tomorrow was Saturday, and I was visiting Gram. She'd promised to show me her file of documents about Q.C.

33

Unlike L trains, Metra trains run on the railroad line and have two levels. I like to ride on the upper deck. It's all single seats, so I never end up sharing and I can always look out the window. This morning I had my choice. Not too many people take the train from the city to the western suburbs on Saturdays at 8:30 a.m.

Once the train rumbled out from underneath Union Station, reception returned to my phone. I checked email and saw that Xavier had sent his memoir notes. Before I could open them, though, my phone rang. It was Bryan Stillwell. Normally I don't talk on the train but since no one sat near me I didn't see any harm in answering.

"Embezzlement? Seriously?" he said.

I braced a hand against the wall as the train jolted over a rough spot on the tracks. "What's this about?"

"As if you don't know. Two detectives. Questioning me."

Two. That could mean the Property Crimes detective and the detective from Violent Crimes. But if they questioned Bryan about murder, I felt sure he would have led with that.

"What did you tell them?" I said.

"Nothing. I told them I wanted an attorney before I answered anything. So you accomplished nothing by pointing a finger at me."

While it didn't prove anything in a legal sense and couldn't be used against him in court, Bryan asking for a lawyer immediately added to my sense that he had faked expenses. Given my parents' experiences, I'd ask for a lawyer early if a detective hinted I was a suspect. But none of the background information I'd found about Bryan suggested any past with law enforcement.

"Were both detectives from the Property Crimes division?"

"Where else would they be from?" Bryan said.

It hadn't occurred to him that he might be on the hook for murder, then.

My phone buzzed with a text from Isabel Verde.

Downtown this afternoon. Can meet you at 1:30.

Mentally I reviewed my schedule, which included singing tonight with Danielle and Joe, our first job in a long time. I missed whatever Bryan said next.

"Sorry, what?" I said to Bryan.

"What did you tell the police about me?"

"I'm guessing that's not something they'd want me to answer."

"Tobias is going to hear about this."

The line went dead. I texted Tobias to suggest he share nothing if Bryan called him. Tobias texted back an OK sign.

I messaged Isabel and arranged our meeting. I wondered if the detectives, or at least one of them, had come to see her, too.

The train pulled out of the Riverside station. Despite the overcast sky, the trees and grassy areas leading down to the Des Plaines River still looked beautiful. Usually from there until LaGrange, where Gram lives, I stare out the window, enjoying the changing landscape as the towns roll past. I find it relaxing. But the thought of seeing Gram's Q.C. crime file intruded.

I took out Xavier's notes. With three stops left, I might as well get a little more done.

Kurt's typical abduction experience now. Not taken from bedroom (as when he was a kid), taken from coach house.

Many weekday nights drifts to sleep at his desk. Leather chair's comfortable, likes reading there with a glass of wine. Dozes, then wakes and goes to bed. Once a month, sometimes twice, aliens come to him. (But sometimes four or five months pass with no sign of them.)

He feels warmth on his face. Opens eyes. Bright light streams down through skylight. Kurt is floated upward. Shuts his eyes. Opens again and he's in large space full of plants. Vibrant flowers with finger-like petals. Among the plants are infants. As if the plants are holding them, but some float in the air. No walls he can see but knows he's on a spaceship.

These look like human babies but they're not. Kurt's not sure how he knows that. He more feels it than knows. He sings to the infants. Songs he sang to Tobias when he was newborn. Also talks to them about human life so they'll be prepared when they're put on earth. They can't smile, but Kurt feels they're smiling inside.

This care, this singing and talking. No one did that for him because he was one of the earliest hybrids. The system wasn't good yet. Now the hybrids are prepared. Tobias fell in between. Some things were better for him, but not as good as now. Kurt wants these early days to be good for all the new hybrids.

I ask why these babies are on ship if they're hybrids. Wouldn't they be embyros in their mother's uterus?

Develop like human children? Kurt's not sure. Thinks maybe they appear as babies to him because that's more familiar to his brain but they are really at a much earlier phase. Probably two-celled zygotes invisible to the naked eye. A day or two after conception at most. Kept here for a few days, then transplanted to–

"LaGrange."

The conductor's voice interrupted my reading. I jumped to my feet, grabbed my wool coat and shoulder bag, and stumbled down the metal steps, phone in my hand. On the main level, I pushed open the double doors to the vestibule as the train squealed to a halt. My boots clanged on the metal steps down to the platform outside. My coat hung open.

The weather forecast had promised no precipitation, but a light, icy rain drizzled down. I stood on the side opposite the train station, but there was a brick shelter with a few benches. Inside it, I stowed my phone and buttoned my coat. I thought about fishing out the bright pink Totes umbrella that's always in my shoulder bag for emergencies but decided it wasn't worth it.

That turned out to be a good choice because as I crossed the tracks the clouds shifted and bright, warm sunlight beat down on me. Just past the bank, I turned the corner and headed for the row of three vintage apartment buildings in the heart of the downtown business district. All the while thinking about this man I'd never met who believed he was an alien-human hybrid. His parents abandoned him to a sister who abused him and locked him in closets. But the aliens, according to him, put him in a space without walls and allowed him to care for babies in a way no one had ever cared for him.

34

———

I KNOCKED A SECOND TIME. While I have keys to Gram's apartment, I always knock as a courtesy unless she tells me ahead of time to just walk in.

Another few seconds passed. I unlocked the door and pushed it open. "Gram?"

Gram prefers I take off my shoes, but I hurried through the empty living room to the kitchen, the soles of my boots slapping the floor. The kitchen smelled of hazelnut coffee but was deserted. The counters were clear, but that didn't mean much. Gram always cleaned up before she left home. I put my hand on the dishwasher, an ultra quiet Bosch I'd bought her last year for Christmas. It felt cool and still. Scraped dishes and a week's worth of coffee mugs filled three-quarters of the inside.

Both bedrooms stood empty. Gram's was in perfect order. A floral comforter lay over mauve sheets and pillows on the polished wood sleigh bed. Color coordinated, but without shams or other frills that take extra time to put together in the morning. As a child, I'd curled in that bed while Gram read me bedtime stories, often falling asleep next to her rather than in my own room in my parents' apartment across the hall.

I returned to the kitchen. A whiteboard hangs over the microwave there. Gram writes reminders on it in red marker. Underneath one about her bridge group she'd written "Quille Saturday 9:07-9:10." So like Gram to estimate my arrival time based on the train schedule plus how fast I was likely to walk the five blocks.

Yet she wasn't here.

I dialed her cell phone and got voicemail. After leaving a quick message, I texted, then crossed to the back door. An outdoor wooden staircase zigzagged between wide landings on each floor. The parking area behind the building had four spaces. Three vehicles sat there, but not Gram's Honda Accord.

Knowing she drove somewhere made me feel a little better. At least paramedics hadn't carted her away. But I'd never known Gram to miss an appointment for any reason other than a true emergency.

After checking my phone and texting again I crossed the hall. The neighbor, a woman about twenty years younger than Gram, answered right away. I asked if she had seen Gram today.

"Oh, Quille, hello. Your Gram headed out around nine. Since you're here, could you help me turn a planter? My rubber tree plant's been reaching for the windows for far too long but it's too heavy for me. Was just about to try anyway, though."

"Sure." I followed her inside. "Was Gram in a rush? Or worried about anything?"

Her apartment was the one I had grown up in and was a mirror of Gram's. On another day I might have felt nostalgic, but too much else filled my mind.

"No, dear, not at all. Stopped to ask if I wanted her to pick up anything from Target."

We crouched and turned the heavy ceramic pot that held the rubber plant. "She went shopping?"

If Gram was in a store, I didn't see why she hadn't answered my text asking where she was.

The neighbor straightened up, one hand on her back. "I think just stopping at Target on her way back from some sort of meeting."

She offered me coffee or tea, but I thanked her and went back across the hall. If Gram was at a meeting, she'd have her phone off. But she wouldn't have asked me to come over. Standing in the middle of the living room, I texted my mom and dad in case there had been a family issue. But they knew nothing. My mom helpfully pointed out that Gram was in her late seventies and might be becoming forgetful.

She's never been before, I texted back.

Happens to everyone eventually.

I frowned. My mother could make light of it all she wanted, but this wasn't like Gram.

My dad called. "You were meeting with her about her Q.C. file, weren't you?" he said. "She mentioned it earlier this week."

I sank onto the couch. "Yes. She said she'd go over it with me."

"Maybe it was too much for her. I doubt she's looked at it in, well, probably in three decades."

"But she'd say so. Not let me come to an empty apartment. And she didn't forget. She's got a note on the board."

"I'm not saying purposely. A slip. A Freudian slip. I'm sure she's fine, honey. But I'll keep trying to reach her, too."

"Okay."

I didn't know what else to do. I couldn't very well call the police because Gram didn't answer my texts, and nothing in the apartment gave me any sense of where she might be. I just hoped she'd get in touch soon.

The next train to the city wasn't until 11:06. Metra trains don't run often on weekends. I took out my iPad to start research for a new case about the sale of a pool hall that fell through. But after a few minutes I walked into the kitchen and stared at the whiteboard again. I'm not prone to anxiety, but I couldn't set aside the idea that if one of my investigations over the last two years, or this one about Kurt, angered someone, they might take it out on people I cared about. Or that whoever killed Q.C. somehow learned Gram was about to share her file of documents with me.

But that was ridiculous. I walked to the back porch again and looked at the empty parking spot. Gram took her own car. She talked to the neighbor. Everything suggested she'd simply forgotten.

After texting Gram again, I set a timer to go off in thirty minutes. If I didn't hear from her by then I'd call a few of her friends. Then I returned to the dining table and forced myself to research partial offers.

When my phone rang I grabbed it right away. But it wasn't Gram. It was Detective Sergeant Beckwell.

"Thought you might want to know. Bryan Stillwell's been arrested."

"For embezzlement?" That seemed fast. I hadn't expected the Chicago police to take my word for it about the iffy expenses.

"No. For the murder of Kurt King."

35

———

The police had searched Bryan's office looking for evidence to support an embezzlement charge. They seized his laptop. And found a gun. The type that, based on the bullet, was used to kill Kurt King.

"He kept it in his own file cabinet?" I stared out at Gram's empty parking spot, but I saw the wooden file cabinet with gold locks behind Bryan's desk.

"In the back of the bottom drawer, hidden in an accordion folder."

"If he used that gun to kill Kurt, why keep it? And especially why keep it there?"

"You'd be surprised, Quille," Beckwell said. "We catch a lot of wanted men because they were driving around with a tail light out."

Danielle often told me the same thing about her clients.

"I didn't know you could get a search warrant so fast," I said.

"We can. Didn't have to, though. Tobias King gave permission."

"Tobias? Can he do that?"

"Owns the firm, so yes."

"But he doesn't. He inherited his father's share, but that was eighty percent. The other twenty –"

"Oh sh—don't tell me."

"Bryan Stillwell. King and Stillwell? No one thought of that?"

A heavy sigh. "Not my case so no idea what anyone was thinking. Or more like not thinking. Always a joy to speak with you. Now I've got to point this out when in no way should I have been talking to you. And by the way, I never talked to you."

"Got it. Just point out the whole concept of the named partner in a law firm. That's what it means. You're named in the firm name. You're a partner."

"What about these hundred-year-old law firms with long strings of names? Those guys can't all be alive."

"They can die and the name stays. But once there was a living partner for each name."

Another sigh. "Fantastic. Might as well tell me the rest of your thoughts. You believe this guy stole from the firm, but he wouldn't murder Kurt King to cover it up?"

"He might," I said. "I just doubt he'd keep the murder weapon. Feels more like someone planted it there."

"And he didn't notice?"

"Bryan was doing his best to move all the records to digital. Probably never went into that filing cabinet."

"Making it a good hiding place."

"Maybe." I returned to Gram's kitchen, inhaling the comforting coffee smell. I didn't like the taste, but the scent reminded me of her. I wanted to ask Beckwell more questions but Gram called at last. I ended with Beckwell and clicked over.

"Quille? Honey, I'm so sorry."

I pressed my free hand to my chest. "You're all right? Everything's fine?"

"Yes, yes. The final planning meeting for the November benefit was today. I had the phone on silent."

"But –"

"It was in my head that I was meeting you tomorrow. I am so sorry."

"It's right on your board. For today."

"I know. It's in my phone app, too. Just wrong in my head. I'll be home in twenty minutes."

A glance at the microwave's clock sent a jolt of adrenalin through me. "Can't. Gotta catch a train." I grabbed my coat and pulled it over one shoulder. "Did you leave the file for me?"

"No, no, I'm sorry. It's in my safety deposit box at the bank."

I stowed my iPad and double locked Gram's door on my way out. "Then how were you going to show it to me?"

"I thought we'd walk to the bank together."

I started down the stairs. "On Sunday?"

"No, no, you're right. Makes no sense if I'd thought for a minute. I'll come downtown this week. Bring it to you."

Outside the icy drizzle had returned. I reached for my umbrella, but I'd left it on the side table just inside Gram's door. If I went back, I'd miss the train. I hurried down the block.

"Why keep it in a safety deposit box?" I said.

"I put it there a few months after you all moved here. I didn't want you or your sister to run across it by accident."

Before I hung up, Gram apologized again for the mix up.

My dad had been right. Freudian slip.

———

THE TRAIN GOING into the city was crowded, but I found a lone seat on an upper deck. I brushed off my coat and spread it out to dry on the wide metal shelf where commuters store briefcases and bags. During the ride I texted with Maria. Happily, she answered all my questions without asking why I wanted to know.

I emerged from Union Station thirty minutes later into a

day that felt completely different from the one I'd left in LaGrange. Lake Michigan's temperature changes more slowly than does the air, so the lingering warmth from the summer keeps downtown much warmer through fall and early winter than it is in the suburbs. Usually by at least ten degrees.

Plus there were no clouds here. Sunlight sparkled across the Chicago River, making it look greener and less murky than when I'd crossed it that morning. I found a quiet spot on the plaza along the river, stripped off my gloves, unbuttoned the top buttons of my coat, and took out my phone and dialed.

Tobias answered right away. "Thank God it's done," he said.

"Bryan may not be the one who killed your father."

"What? How else did the gun get there?"

A seagull waddled over to me and cocked its head. I shook mine. I had no food. The bird seemed to understand and hopped away.

"The individual offices at your firm aren't kept locked. Attorneys in the plaintiff's group were at the firm for a meeting yesterday, including E. Drake Draper and Fred Varnes. Also, Isabel is in town. Your dad might have given her a firm key somewhere along the line. She could've planted the gun. And obviously Maria has access any time."

"But none of them knew that I'd authorize a search today."

"The gun might've been there for a while. Also, the more I think about it, the less Bryan's embezzlement – if he did it – feels like a motive for murder."

"Of course it is. Dad found out, Bryan got angry, they fought."

"Maria thinks your dad would've told her if he suspected Bryan of cheating him. And with his dislike for business and numbers, it seems like he would've asked for her help sorting it out."

I didn't want to reveal Maria's relationship with Kurt unless or until I needed to. It was up to her to tell Tobias. Or not.

"But you just included Maria as a suspect. Why trust anything she says?"

"I don't. But if she were lying, I imagine she'd lie to help make Bryan look bad. Say that your dad did tell her he suspected Bryan."

"Maybe," Tobias said. "I don't see Dad combing through the books on his own. And the firm's accountant said Dad never asked him about it."

"Also, if your dad didn't know, killing him was a sure way for the truth to come out. Someone would look over the books to value the firm if nothing else. While your dad, if he lived, might never have caught on."

"So you want to keep looking into this?" Tobias said.

"Yes."

As I spoke, though, I felt doubt. I'd never before charged anyone for investigating. It felt odd to ask Tobias to keep paying me after an arrest. But he agreed.

Next, I left a voicemail for Bryan. His phone was likely in police custody for the moment. But he'd get the message eventually.

"Bryan, it's Quille Davis. I heard about your arrest. I don't know if the police are right or wrong about you, so I'm still looking into Kurt King's murder. If you know anything that might help, call me when you can."

Guilty or not, I hoped he'd be desperate enough to talk to me.

Three blocks north, I clambered down a long flight of outdoor stairs and boarded a bright yellow boat. Chicago's water taxi was the quickest way to get to the restaurant, and I enjoyed a ride on the river even in cold weather. It pulled away, made a U-turn in the water, and headed north and then east. The boat swayed beneath me as I stood on the bow with a handful of other passengers, my hands resting on a metal railing. I inhaled the mixed scents of fishy river water and chocolate from the Blommer Chocolate plant. It's in the Fulton River District neighborhood, and when the wind is right makes downtown smell of rich, dark chocolate.

I watched the waves and made a mental list of what else I needed to know from Isabel Verde.

36

———

RPM Seafood overlooks the Chicago River. When the weather's warm, you need to reserve a month in advance to get a table outside or in. The walls fronting the river on both floors fold open, making the bar and entire restaurant indoor-outdoor in good weather. It's pricy enough that I only go there for special occasions. But I agreed when Isabel suggested it. I wanted her to relax and talk, and she'd be more likely to do that if she chose the place.

To my surprise, she sat at an outdoor table on the upper level. Two tall heat lamps warmed the area enough that I unbuttoned my coat. Isabel waved to a bottle of Syrah from Santa Barbara. "Hope you like red. Half-price during lunch, and if I'm going to tell you everything, I need alcohol."

"I do."

I sat, grateful that she'd also gotten glasses of water. As with Maria, I wanted to keep my wits about me. Alternating with water meant drinking less wine. So would food. I scanned the menu QR code with my phone and looked over the appetizers.

Isabel flicked away a single white hair from the shoulder of her black blazer. "Cats. Who knew they shed so much?"

I glanced up from my phone. "You just got one?"

"My sister's. About a month ago. Turns out her youngest is allergic. She begged me to take it so the kids can at least visit."

We agreed on the cheese-baked focaccia bread with olives and the citrus-cured salmon.

"So what do you want to tell me about?" I asked after the waiter disappeared inside.

"A few months before his death, Kurt told me he wanted to write a book about his abduction experiences. Under his real name. That's what we were arguing about at his party."

I put my phone in my shoulder bag and set the bag at my feet. "Why didn't you tell me this before?"

"I assumed Kurt didn't tell anybody but me about the book. So how could it relate to his death? But I've been thinking a lot since you and I met for dinner, and now I'm pretty sure he must have."

"And something I said changed your mind?"

"In a roundabout way. Do you know the biggest difference between introverts and extroverts?"

"Extroverts like interacting more with people."

"Not necessarily. But the ways they interact or the reasons they do differ. For instance, faced with a question or problem to solve, introverts think things through on their own. Then they tell other people. Maybe. But usually by that time they're sure of their plans, which sometimes surprises friends and family. Extroverts, though, think by talking. They bounce ideas off other people. And Kurt was the consummate extrovert. Which means he likely talked to quite a few people to try to decide what to do."

"Still, wouldn't you be the first one he'd bounce something off of?"

"That's where you come in. Two years ago, maybe a year ago, I would have been that first person. But you asked about distance between us recently."

"Which you denied."

"Which I denied. Because I was in denial. Ironic for a therapist. But there's plenty of physician heal thyself in our profession, too." She rubbed her thumb along the stem of her wine glass. "Kurt's death is hard enough without admitting to myself I was already losing him. He wanted to live what he called a more honest life. Be open about his alien experiences. I felt it would come back to bite him. But also me." She sighed. "More so me. So now I think maybe I was the last person he told, not the first. Because he knew I'd try to discourage him."

A strong scent of bread, cheese, and rosemary filled the air as the waiter returned with our appetizers. Isabel ate an olive. I bit into the warm, cheesy focaccia. And finished a whole section of it before talking again.

"This doesn't answer why you're telling me now. Did the police interview you again?"

"No. Art Feffor called. He had an attack of conscience about introducing your friends to the support group."

Nice of him to fill me in.

Isabel stabbed a thin slice of salmon and slid it onto her plate. "Which doesn't make me happy. That group's supposed to be a safe place. But if Kurt talked to anyone about writing a book, he talked to the group."

"And no one told you?" I said.

"I don't attend. But your friends did, and I figured you'd find it suspicious I never mentioned the book to you. So I'm here to explain it."

"Then explain. You told me about Kurt's abduction experiences. Why hide that he wanted to write a book?"

Coming forward with it now reminded me of the way attorneys front evidence that looks bad for their clients at trial. You tell the jury about troubling facts in your opening statement so you can frame them in the best light. Also, the jury doesn't think you're hiding anything and is less likely to see the bad facts as a smoking gun.

Isabel looked out over the river. Despite the chilly day, joggers, dogs, and dog walkers filled the riverwalk on the other side.

"I wasn't hiding it. I just didn't feel the need to tell you everything. Tobias trusts you, but I don't know Tobias very well. I don't know you. And it's a painful topic for me. Once upon a time Kurt valued my opinion." She bit her lip. "And cared whether something might hurt me. Admitting that he didn't anymore was hard. Is hard."

I wasn't sure if I bought Isabel's attempt at vulnerability. She seemed sincere, but just as she didn't know me, I didn't know her. And I'd been fooled before. People lie to protect themselves, and a murderer has a lot to protect.

"Seems to me he could care about your opinion," I said, "and not want to hurt you, and desperately need to tell his story. At sixty-five, he might have felt afraid if he didn't do it soon he'd miss his chance."

Her lips curved into a half-smile. "Sixty-five isn't exactly death's door."

"I don't think it is." If I did, I'd really need to worry about Gram. "But it's a time a lot of people retire. Or shift to a new phase of life."

She brushed her white hair away from her face. "He kept telling me I ought to shift gears. That I didn't need to work so hard anymore so what did it matter if I got fewer clients or tussled with the University over the alien issue."

"But I take it you didn't feel that way? I don't think I would."

I'd been working since I was ten. I couldn't imagine not wanting some type of career, whether it was law or investigating crimes or something I'd yet to think about.

"No, I didn't. I love my work. I love my clients. I love teaching. No interest in retirement."

"Kurt didn't love his work?"

"It was wearing thin. All the in-fighting especially."

I ate another section of focaccia. "So for the third time – why tell me now?"

Isabel drained her glass. "Because I need something from you."

"What?" I said.

"Information. About Maria."

37

———————

WHEN I STARTED LOOKING into Kurt's death, no one appeared to have a motive. Now it seemed everyone did. Bryan didn't want Kurt to find out about the embezzlement. Isabel was jealous of Maria, and she didn't want Kurt to tell his story. Any number of other people, including Bryan, Tobias, and any of Kurt's co-counsel, might feel the same way. Maria was angry at Kurt for not ending things with Isabel. And Tobias had been angry at Kurt forever.

Isabel refilled her glass and returned the wine bottle to the edge of the table. "Were Maria and Kurt seeing each other?"

"What makes you think they might have been?"

"I talk and you don't?" she said.

"Tobias asked me to report only to him."

She pursed her lips. "Fine. The way she looked at me when she walked into his living room the night of the party. Like she was surprised I was there. Then she turned and walked right out of the room."

"How did Kurt react?"

"He didn't see it. He was talking to Tobias, and I was cutting his birthday cake. And you know she's the only one who never asked for a piece of it?"

Maria had mentioned the birthday cake, too, but she'd complained that Isabel didn't give her a piece.

"But Kurt never told you he was seeing her? Or anyone else?"

"No. But he did tell me he signed a contract with someone to write the book. We went off on that and I never came back to why Maria was upset. That's why I went to the conference. I was on the fence about it, but I was so angry I couldn't see spending the weekend with him. If I had –"

I touched her elbow. "There's no use thinking about that. Whoever killed him is responsible, not you."

Unless she had killed him.

Isabel nodded.

"Who else do you think Kurt might have talked to when deciding whether to write the book?" I said.

"His law partner. Bryan. Aside from me, that's who might be affected the most. Oh, except for Tobias and his family. But I have to think Tobias would be less open to the idea than I was, so I doubt Kurt talked to him about it. He probably would have told him a week before it was published."

"What about the other lawyers Kurt worked with? The ones he shared cases with. You think he'd talk to them?"

"If he decided for sure to do it. He'd want to give them a heads up if it might be raised in court. You know better than I if that would be an issue." She swirled her wine in her glass. "It feels pretty bad to think he might have told them and not me."

"But he did tell you. You said it was an on-going argument. Then the night of the party he told you he went forward anyway."

And if he'd told Isabel about his book contract, he might have told other people as well. One of whom could have returned Friday night to kill him.

———

DANIELLE, Joe, and I had a singing job that night at a café on the North Side of Chicago. One great thing about a cappella singing is you don't need to lug instruments. And this place had its own sound system, so we needed to bring nothing other than ourselves.

I stopped home to change clothes. Usually when I sang I just used scarves, bracelets, or other jewelry to dress up my office uniform of a tank top or long-sleeved T and jeans. But lately I'd been experimenting with dresses. I tried a bright green peasant dress with knee-high leather boots. In between reapplying my makeup and starting on my hair, I texted Fred Varnes. I asked how it would affect the plaintiff's attorneys as a group if a judge knocked Kurt's firm out of a case.

He responded as I styled the last section of my hair, turning tighter curls into loose waves.

No change for me. Unless it meant no recovery for the class. Might be good for E. Drake. He could become the only lead counsel.

Anyone else who might step into that role?

Not in cases I'm on.

I texted Maria to ask if there were other firms like E. Drake's that Kurt partnered with. Firms a judge might consider experienced enough to be lead counsel. She couldn't think of any.

Which meant E. Drake might have been thrilled if Kurt revealed his plan to write about alien abduction and being a hybrid, causing judges to see Kurt as too unstable to represent the class. As sole lead counsel, E. Drake might then get a greater share of the fees.

Ty's knock on my door put an end to the twists and turns my mind started taking. We headed over to the venue together.

———

I HAD a great time singing with my friends. After, we went out for drinks and then breakfast at one of Chicago's few late-night diners.

For most of Sunday and part of Monday I worked on my response to E. Drake's motion in the fee lawsuit. The next evening, I headed to King and Stillwell, taking Ty with me.

Bryan's office was in a shambles after the police search, but I was interested in Maria's area. Because she was an employee, not a partner, Tobias clearly had the legal right to see anything she kept at the office or on her firm laptop. I didn't feel great invading her privacy, but I needed to do it. Everyone else was gone for the day, so it was the perfect time.

Ty sat at the reception counter watching streaming videos on his tablet and keeping one eye on the door. Though it was locked, I didn't want to take a chance on anyone getting in and surprising me. It took me an hour to go through Maria's desk and file cabinets and find her password. It was taped inside a file cabinet drawer. While I had access to the firm's network drive with the remote login Tobias gave me, I wanted to see if Maria's hard drive or personal email included anything about Kurt or the expense fraud.

A personal desktop folder named Fun included a Microsoft Paints portrait of Bryan with a pitchfork and devil horns. Maria's calendar included her sister's visit, which Beckwell had told me the detectives on the case confirmed. The calendar also listed Kurt's party and the brunch Maria had planned with him for the following Sunday.

I clicked over to her drafts of fee petitions. As best I could tell, Maria had told the truth. She simply filled in the expenses based on receipts the attorneys emailed her or what she found in the files.

A recent settlement approval order looked like it matched the attorney fees Maria mentioned at the Train Car. The firms combined had gotten fourteen million dollars, most of that split between King and Stillwell and E. Drake Draper and Associates, with a million each going to three other plaintiffs' attorneys.

Shocked, I switched to the bookkeeping program. I didn't remember ever seeing over six million dollars at once coming in to King and Stillwell. And I was right. Plus, last year as a whole they'd earned less than half that. Which sounds like a lot until you subtract rent, salaries, malpractice insurance, employee benefits, and all the other expenses of running a law firm. The recent settlement, though, would pay a lot of bills. And bonuses.

A hearing in another case was scheduled in two weeks, this one for five million total. Three plaintiffs, Alan Schmeter, Freya Watson, and Jill Teegan, representing a class, had sued ABX Restaurant World. ABX was a conglomerate that owned several coffee chains.

Something about the petition to approve the settlement nagged at me. I printed the first page. Maybe seeing it later would jog something in my mind.

As the printer whirred, I heard a buzzer from downstairs. The front door camera linked to the firm's computer system. I clicked over. E. Drake Draper stood outside. He wore a dark blue cashmere coat and a gray wool scarf. No gloves or hat.

"See what E. Drake wants," I called down. "But make sure he knows there are two of us here."

Ty is great at getting people to talk. It's part of his business, and I was curious whether E. Drake might open up more with another man. Or at least with someone who wasn't investigating a murder or representing the opposing party in a lawsuit.

E. Drake claimed to have a meeting with Bryan at six-thirty. Ty told him Bryan wasn't here and commented on today's Bears game. The firm's networked calendar told me E. Drake did have a meeting with Bryan this evening. I supposed Bryan had better things to do in jail than text E. Drake.

As I scrolled through more documents on Maria's computer, I half listened to their conversation downstairs. They agreed on the new Bears quarterback – no better than the last. But contrary to Calista Zopp's comment that class action plaintiff's attorneys all own boats and planes, E. Drake told Ty he didn't own a boat.

I clicked to Maria's draft file in her personal email tab. She'd written an email to Kurt the Friday of his death.

Seeing you and Isabel together at the party really hurt my feelings. Not sure you get that though I said it and texted it. So I feel like I need to be more clear. I don't want to talk to you unless you broke up with Isabel. Text me a Yes and we'll move forward. If not, we're going to have a very different conversation. Soon.

Because this is just

According to the program, Maria last edited the draft at 3:11 p.m. Friday. I didn't find a finished version anywhere, including in the Sent or Trash folders. She might have called or texted instead. Or gone to Kurt's home to have that conversation.

I printed the draft email. Downstairs, Ty asked E. Drake if he liked his current office location. E. Drake said he did except that his landlord kept raising the rent. Ty asked how much longer he planned to practice.

"Another decade at least," E. Drake said as I came down the stairs.

I smiled at E. Drake. "Ty never stops working." That wasn't exactly true. As a commercial real estate broker, a lot of his work is socializing and he enjoys it. So he gets to relax and work at the same time.

"Heh. Neither do I." E. Drake glanced around the empty first floor. "Had a meeting with Bryan today but looks like he forgot."

"Since you're here, how about an extra week or two on my response to your motion?"

I was nearly done. But if he agreed I could fine tune my response without working twelve-hour days tomorrow and Wednesday. I worked more late nights and weekends now that I worked for myself than I had while working for a large firm. Something I ought to think about at some point.

He crossed his arms. "And put off next week's hearing? No chance."

"This case has gone on two years. You can't wait another week?"

"Why should I?" E. Drake rested one elbow on the counter. "I've heard the arguments for years. None of them holds water."

"You've heard Kurt's arguments. Not mine."

The more I learned about the lawsuit the more I concluded that Bryan was right. Kurt's heart hadn't been in it. The year before a mediator tried to help settle the case. Kurt wrote a statement filled with four-line sentences and meandering prose that badly needed editing. E. Drake laid out a clear, simple story. No surprise the mediator leaned toward E. Drake's side.

"Same facts," E. Drake said. "How different can they be?"

I smiled. "I heard you're a great trial lawyer, so there's no way you believe that."

He stood straight. "Who told you that?"

"Maria."

"Heh. Lovely gal. Well, I'll concede. Different storytellers, different stories." He squinted at me. "But you think you're a better storyteller than me?"

"We'll see," I said. "There's also the law."

E. Drake's writing showed him to be either uninformed

about the law or comfortable misrepresenting it. Much like Gram complained most people did with the Bible, E. Drake grabbed a line here and a helpful phrase there and ignored the rest.

E. Drake glanced at his phone. "Still nothing from Bryan. Must have better things to do. See you next week."

After the door clicked shut behind him, I turned to Ty. "Any sense from talking to him if he knew about Bryan's arrest?"

"No idea." Ty tapped his key fob on the counter. "But at the risk of being late for dinner, I've got an idea about the attack on you outside the storage room."

38

———

TY RAN a few searches on the receptionist's computer. "Here it is," he said.

"What?"

He spun the monitor around. "See that? E. Drake's office address for eight years ago."

I peered at it. "Near here, right?"

The 600 West part of the address told me E. Drake's old office had been about six full city blocks west of State Street. I was pretty sure that meant it was around where Ty and I sat now, though I didn't know offhand how far west Jefferson Street was.

"It is here," Ty said. "Almost. That's the building next door. It's got a Washington Street address because the main entrance faces Washington, while the main entrance here faces Jefferson. And...." He spun the monitor to face him and clicked a few more keys. "Yep. What I thought. The sub-basements connect."

"So if E. Drake kept his key, no problem getting in."

"Right. But why steal from the storage room?"

"Same reason Bryan might've. To see what I was doing. Or he suspected Bryan was inflating expenses and wanted proof."

I returned to Maria's area to put things back in place using pictures I took with my phone before I started. I did my best to line up her framed photos just so on the edge of the desk. One showed her holding a plump orange and white tabby cat in front of a Christmas tree. In another, she stood arm and arm with a slightly younger woman who looked a lot like her. Possibly the sister she spent the weekend with.

As I shut Maria's middle desk drawer, my phone rang. It was Bryan.

I sank onto Maria's chair. "When did you get out of jail?"

"This afternoon. After the bond hearing. I've been trying to reach Tobias and he won't pick up."

"Can't imagine why," I said.

"I didn't kill his father."

"You might have a hard time convincing him of that." Not to mention the embezzling, but I didn't want to raise that unless Bryan did.

"Did you mean what you said in your voicemail? You're not convinced I'm guilty?"

"I'm not. So if you're innocent and you know anything that might help me, now's the time."

"I'm telling you the truth. I didn't kill Kurt. But I know who did."

———

I THOUGHT Bryan might talk more if I met him alone, but Ty insisted on coming with despite that we planned to meet in public. He said he'd let me down before, and he wasn't about to again.

The three of us sat in a booth at the back of Miller's Pub, a dimly lit bar and grill on Wabash Avenue. It's been there forever and sports signed photos of celebrity guests like Marilyn Monroe and Frank Sinatra on its walls. It's usually crowded and noisy, but Monday nights after eight are pretty slow anywhere downtown. Half the booths around us sat empty.

"Your attorney okayed you meeting with us?" I said.

I hated to look a gift informant in the mouth. But I couldn't help but ask. No good criminal defense attorney should let the client talk alone to someone investigating the crime he was charged with.

"No. But I don't care. I didn't kill Kurt, I have a solid alibi, and no way am I going through all of this if there's a way to catch the killer."

"Solid alibi? You said you were home reading. You live twenty minutes from Kurt's home in bad traffic."

The waiter set our drinks on the table and took our food order. I got barbeque Canadian baby back ribs, a pub specialty. Ty chose a cheeseburger with tomato and bacon and Bryan ordered a plate of French fries to go with his beer.

"I wasn't at home," Bryan said after the waiter left. "But before I say more, one thing. No questions about expenses or this ridiculous embezzlement theory you and Tobias cooked up."

I nodded and sipped my Pepsi. "Fine. Embezzlement's off the table. Where were you?"

If he really had a good alibi, I couldn't see why he'd keep it from the police. If it checked out, he might have avoided his arrest. For murder at least.

Bryan shifted, sitting very tall, and his eyes darted around the room. Then he sighed and looked at me. "I'm seeing someone. We met when she was married, but she was already planning to leave her husband. Now she's in the middle of a messy divorce. She doesn't want anyone to know we're involved. She'd lose her mind if she knew I told anyone."

"I'm not a family law expert, but I'm pretty sure her seeing someone can't change her divorce settlement," I said.

"Right, Illinois is No Fault. But if her ex finds out he'll drag it out longer for spite. He's already made her life hell."

"But you told the police all this?" Ty said.

"No. I can't make things worse for her. It's only two months and it'll be final. Then she'll sign a statement that I was with her. And it's not like I'm sitting in jail."

"Why aren't you?" Ty said.

"I made bond."

I asked how much, and he told me a million cash. Not unsurprising for a murder. The cash part meant that rather than paying ten percent of the bond to the court, which is typical for less serious crimes, and being charged the full amount only if he disappeared, Bryan had to deposit the entire million dollars. He or his family had a lot of money easily available. Or a very large line of credit.

"But what if the prosecutor doesn't believe your friend? Or the jury doesn't?" I said.

"We flew to a bed and breakfast her sister and brother-in-law own in Maine the weekend of Kurt's death. Got there mid-afternoon Friday, came back Sunday morning. The sister and other guests saw us, and if it comes down to it I know they'll testify to that. But I can't ask now in case it gets back to the soon-to-be ex."

"You don't want to tell the police, but you weren't worried her husband would find out about you traveling together?" Ty said.

"I didn't say we're always smart. But he was on vacation for two weeks in Florida with their kids. I wanted to cheer her up, and he hates New England. Never goes there. No family there. We decided it was worth the risk."

If true, it let Bryan off the hook. But there was no way to check if he wouldn't turn over the information.

"For the sake of argument, say I believe you. Who do you think killed Kurt?"

"It's obvious. Maria."

39

"IT'S NOT OBVIOUS TO ME," I said as the waiter set our plates on the table. I ate a few of the French fries. They were hot and crispy.

Bryan slid the plate of fries toward himself. "Maria's got easy access to my office. She's always in early, could've planted the gun any time. Also, she and Kurt were close. I'm thinking seeing each other close."

"You never mentioned that before," I said.

"No one put a gun in my file cabinet before. I thought a lot harder about it since then, and Maria shot dagger eyes at Isabel all night at the party. What else would that be about? And no question Kurt would let Maria in if she came to his door at whatever time. Or, who knows? He trusted her with all the office keys. Maybe she had keys to his place, too."

I thought back to when Maria took me on the tour at Kurt's and I admired the crystal swan on her keychain. Kurt's house and coach house keys had been on that keyring. Not on a separate ring like the keys for the sub-basement and the storage room. And I'd seen two keys today in Maria's middle drawer. I opened my phone and flipped through the photos. There it was. Two keys on a University of Denver Law School keyring.

"But then who attacked her and Quille in the storage area?" Ty said. "You?"

His chin pulled in. "Funny. Sure, I came here to tell Quille I attacked her. No, that had to be E. Drake."

"What's his motive?" I said. "And how would he know Maria and I were down there?"

"I don't trust E. Drake, but I talk with him a lot. Keep your friends close and enemies closer. And that afternoon I told him you and Maria were going to dig through old files."

"Why tell him that?"

"Because he kept saying how he was going to win everything in the fee lawsuit. I told him you weren't going to roll over the way Kurt did. That you're thorough and smart and were spending that afternoon combing through all the old files."

"Never knew you thought so highly of me."

Bryan smirked. "Don't let it go to your head. I said it to tweak E. Drake."

"And yet you're here," I said. "But what about him as the murderer? Maybe he worried there was evidence against him in the storage room."

"Like what? A note from Kurt saying if he's found dead, E. Drake did it? No, he wanted to get a look at your strategy in the lawsuit. See what you were digging for."

"Or frame you," Ty said. "Get Quille thinking you attacked, looking more closely at you for the murder."

"But E. Drake's way worse off with Kurt gone," Bryan said. "You saw the file. Kurt did the least work possible on it. E. Drake would much rather have him running the case."

"What about Dr. Verde?" I said. "Isabel? You said she and Kurt fought that night. What if you're right? Kurt was seeing Maria and Isabel found out?"

"It wasn't that kind of fight." Bryan made a sideways cutting gesture with his right hand. "She was irritated and frustrated. Not jealous and angry."

Jealous and angry don't read the same for everyone. Isabel struck me as a controlled, measured person. She might very well sound calm when expressing anger. While Isabel on the surface had the least chance to plant the gun, anyone determined or angry enough to commit murder could find a way. Especially if she had a key to King and Stillwell.

"What we need is a way to force whoever did it to show their hand," I said.

I used "we" on purpose. If Bryan was the killer and believed I saw him as part of the team, he'd be more apt to slip and reveal something. And if he wasn't, he might have some good insights.

"I don't like the sound of that," Ty said, no doubt remembering how some of my investigations ended.

"No risk taking," I said. "At least, I'll minimize risks. But if I plant a seed that the police are closing in, the person might panic and run. Or try to hide evidence."

"But no one will worry once they hear I was arrested," Bryan said.

"Unless I suggest you were let go because evidence excluded you."

He gripped the side of the table. "You can't use my alibi."

"I'm thinking DNA."

"I thought it was too much of a mess to be helpful," Ty said.

"The police told Tobias that was likely. But they're still waiting for the test results. They could find something useful. And most people think everything's like CSI or those other murder shows with a fingerprint or some saliva on a wine glass solving the case."

Bryan frowned. "But it can't be the saliva on the wine glass or the killer already would have panicked."

"It can't be anything the killer realizes they left behind." I tapped my finger on the table. "But it needs to be something Maria, Isabel, and E. Drake have in common. So I tell a consistent story in case they talk to one another. I'll be back in a few minutes."

I left them in the booth and sat at the end of the bar near the entrance. It was deserted other than two guys in sport coats and jeans at the far end, but the smell of beer hung in the air. After getting a glass of ice water, I shut my eyes and recalled my meetings with Maria, E. Drake, and Isabel, concentrating on what I saw rather than what I heard. At first, nothing jumped out at me. My mind drifted to this afternoon at Maria's desk, then my conversation with Isabel at RPM.

I opened my eyes. "That's it."

The bartender glanced my way.

"Talking to myself," I said. "Looks like I'm an introvert."

He shrugged and emptied the last bowl of peanuts.

40

———

"Animal hair." I sat in my office, having gotten in early to make the last edits to my response in the fee lawsuit. Murder investigation or not I needed to keep up with all my cases.

"You're kidding," Maria said.

"I'm not. White animal hair. Bryan said the police found some in Kurt's coach house loft. He didn't have any pets, and they're sure it belonged to the killer based on where the hairs were."

From Maria's photo, I knew she had an orange and white tabby cat. The photo collage in E. Drake's office had included a black and white dog. And Isabel had brushed white cat hair off her shoulder when she sat down at RPM. Kurt didn't own a pet. Neither did Bryan or Tobias. So it made an ideal fake clue.

"So Bryan's off the suspect list because of pet hair? What if he was at a friend's house who had a white cat right before he went to Kurt's?"

Interesting that she assumed cat when I said animal.

"He's not off the hook yet. But there's a new technique where they might be able to get human DNA from the hair. The killer's DNA. Bryan's positive that will rule him out, and he claims he has other evidence that will, too, but his attorney won't let him tell me what."

I knew next to nothing about DNA techniques. But forensic science was always advancing, so I didn't think anyone would doubt me. Also, Beckwell had confirmed that, unlike on television, it often takes months for DNA to come back with the backlog Chicago has. Murder takes precedence, but there wouldn't be real DNA results that conflicted with my story any time soon.

"If it can pinpoint the killer, it's great news," Maria said. "How long will it take?"

My computer beeped with a calendar notification for later that day. I ignored it. "I'm checking with my contact in the department, but hoping by the end of the week. I thought you and Tobias should know because you know Bryan well. Don't tell anyone else, though. I want the real killer to think Bryan's still the main suspect."

I hoped to control who found out when. That way my friends and I could track the movements of each person who heard the false story.

"What about the embezzlement charges?" Maria said.

"Police are still looking at that."

Maria thanked me for telling her. I didn't hear anything but happiness in her voice. But from what I remembered and everything Joe told me, she was one of the best actors Chicago storefront theatre had to offer. That told me she could not only play a part but make it seem natural. In small theatres the audience sits a few feet from the actors, and sometimes right on stage. It requires a far more realistic and less dramatic style than playing to a large auditorium.

"Before we hang up – do you have your own keys to Kurt's home?" I said. "Since you were seeing each other?"

"We really weren't seeing each other that long."

"But you're an old friend," I said. "And you might have needed to get into his home office at some point."

"No," Maria said. "He never gave me keys."

Tobias had told me that he'd given Maria Kurt's house keys on a keyring from his law school, the University of Denver. Which must be the one I saw in Maria's desk drawer. It seemed unlikely she'd taken time to work the keys off that ring so she could add them to her swan keychain, give me a tour of Kurt's house, then return them to Tobias's keyring. Which meant she had used her own keys.

After hanging up with Maria, I texted Tobias. He was spending the day sorting out papers in Kurt's office. And keeping an eye on Maria. While I hadn't ruled him out completely as a suspect, if he was the murderer, I figured I could still trust him to report if Maria did anything suspicious. Also, I doubted he'd killed Kurt, then hired me to investigate the crime.

My next call was to my paralegal, who works remotely in another state. I asked her to see if E. Drake Draper had any court appearances tomorrow. That would help me figure out where he might be and when I could share my fake news about the animal hair in person.

Then I called Lauren. She was doing some digging on Bryan. We talked about her progress, and I filled her in on my conversation with Maria.

"If it's a woman scorned, though, I'm seriously betting on Isabel," Lauren said. "Maria was seeing him, what, a few weeks? And she knew he was involved with Isabel for twenty years. She couldn't have been that surprised he might take a while to end it."

Tomorrow I planned to place other dominoes, but for the rest of today I had other work. I opened my online case file for my chocolate chip brownie case. The plaintiff's lawyer had emailed rejecting our offer of five hundred dollars and asked for four thousand instead.

As I dialed my client's number a text came in from Tobias. *Maria looks upset and is heading out. Will follow.*

The client answered. She told me she'd rather pay me forever than give a four thousand dollar reward to the plaintiff for filing this ridiculous lawsuit. But finally she agreed to raise our offer to a thousand dollars when I pointed out that just finishing the briefing on the current motion would cost twice that.

I called the associate at the firm that represented the plaintiff. He'd be more pleasant to talk with than the partner.

"I don't see the client taking a thousand. Any chance of more?" he said.

"Getting that much was a tough sell," I said.

"The judge might deny your motion this time around."

"It's always possible," I said. "But I still only have a thousand dollars to offer."

My efforts to catch up on other work went well for most of the day. Around four-thirty they were thwarted, though, when my cell phone rang. It was Calista Zopp, the attorney from my old firm, answering a text I'd sent early that morning. I had a lot of questions for her.

———

"IF SOMETHING bad came out about one lawyer for the class does that help or hurt the others?" I said to Calista.

"Something about a lawyer? Or a named plaintiff?"

"I thought you said the plaintiffs didn't matter?"

"Sometimes they do. I defended one class action where the plaintiff died and her law firm never told the judge. Three years later we learned of it during our research and told the court."

"How could that happen?"

"The cases go on forever and the plaintiffs almost never come to court. The lawyers obviously weren't keeping in touch with her."

"So what happened?"

"That's the ironic thing. If they had told the judge, they would have gotten time to find a new plaintiff to represent the class. Instead, they were so afraid the judge would cut them out of the case that they settled before it could happen."

"And if a lawyer is cut out of the case?"

"The others take over. If they score a win or settle, attorneys who got shut out still get paid something. But it's a lot less."

"Besides a plaintiff dying, what might be a problem for a judge?"

"Well, the plaintiff and the lawyer are there to represent class members who never appear in court. If either has serious mental health issues and can't make good decisions, the judge wouldn't keep them in the case."

It seemed likely most judges would think a person who believed he was part human, part alien had a mental health issue. But I didn't think Kurt planned to tell the judge that.

"Also, the lawyer-client relationship can be too close," Calista said. "For example, you can't be the lawyer for a class where your mom or your boyfriend is the named plaintiff. The court worries you'll care more about them than the class members."

Her words made me think of the petition for the five-million-dollar settlement. I'd printed its first page while going through Maria's area. As I flipped through my file looking for it another text came in from Tobias.

Maria tossed keys in a garbage can on the street. Retrieved them with a napkin. Look like my dad's.

Thx. Keep following.

Calista was still talking. "But you can know the person

socially. One plaintiff was a golf buddy of the attorney. That was okay."

"Can you hold on a minute?"

I finally found the petition page. The plaintiffs were Jill Teegan, Freya Watson, and Alan Schmeter. I opened my notes about Lauren's and Joe's visit to the support group and scrolled to the member names. Joe and Lauren only knew the first names, but three of them matched the first names of the three plaintiffs in the case.

I tried to think how best to phrase the question.

"What if the attorney knew the plaintiffs from a church group? Or an AA meeting?"

"Just being in the same group might not matter."

"But it could?"

"Well, if the attorney's their pastor, that might be a problem. Or with AA, if the attorney is the plaintiff's sponsor. Especially if you can show there's some threat to a member's anonymity."

I thought of Art Feffor saying Kurt had been a sort of mentor to him.

"And why does that matter?"

"The attorney might have too much influence over the client. That client, the plaintiff, is supposed to represent the whole class. But if the client knows the attorney too well, the two of them might work together to get the best deal for themselves, and who cares about the class members."

That could apply to Kurt and his friends from the support group. Or other group members, the ones not in the case, could have been afraid the media might find out about them because of the lawsuit. Which meant a whole new batch of people who might be angry at Kurt. I dropped my head into my hands.

"Quille? Are you there?" Calista said.

I took a deep breath. One thing at a time.

"You said if a court found a relationship was too close, the attorney could look for new plaintiffs. How long would that take?" I said.

"I've seen it take anywhere from a month or two to a year."

That made me think of E. Drake. If he thought word of Kurt's book might get out and bring to light his connection to the named plaintiffs, he might have worried the whole settlement would be delayed. But I didn't know if Kurt told E. Drake about the book. Or about the clients belonging to the alien support group.

I asked Calista a few more questions, but needed to hang up when my phone rang again. It was Gram. She'd felt so bad about missing our visit Saturday that she'd brought a copy of her Q.C. file downtown. I was supposed to be meeting her in the South Concourse of Union Station right now to go over it.

"I'm so sorry," I said, clicking keys to lock my computer. "I lost track of time."

"Seems I'm not the only one who forgets things," she said. "And you thought it was my age."

"I'll be right there."

41

———————

GRAM PUSHED a thick file folder across the table. "Last time I read any of it was before I put it in the safety deposit box."

We sat in a bar and grill inside Union Station, as she planned to get the train straight back home when we finished. The mixed smells of diesel, roasted Starbucks coffee, and caramel corn wafted in.

The initial police report included the details I expected. The date and place of the kidnapping, my parents' information, and Q.C.'s age and description. It matched what my dad and Kendra had told me. But there was one part I hadn't heard.

———————

Witness Brenda Davis told this R.O. that her daughter was within her sight at all times except when said daughter left the ball cage to walk down the hall to the Girls' Restroom. Witness's eyes appeared bloodshot. She swayed when standing and her breath smelled of alcohol. She admitted to drinking at least two martinis at the bar, which is situated on the north end of the dining

area. Four video arcade games partially block the view of
the play area from the bar.

Witness admitted to taking a painkiller at around 11
a.m., an hour before the party started. She said she
strained her back while lifting a large box.

"Martinis and a pain pill," I said. "I thought she just had a
glass of wine."

More information that was wrong in my memory.

"She said the martinis helped the pain more than the pill."

"She must have felt so guilty."

"She did." Gram sighed. "And I made it worse. Blamed her
more than anyone else for not seeing what happened."

"She'd really hurt her back, though?"

"Your dad said yes. Claimed he insisted she take the pain
pill. It was left from when he'd broken his ankle the summer
before. She was in so much pain, and he didn't want her to miss
the party."

"What kind of pain pill?"

"It's in one of the other reports. I want to say Tylenol with
codeine. Not an opioid."

"Codeine is an opioid."

"Is it? Shows what I know. They used to prescribe it left and
right back then."

I sifted through black and white copies of old newspaper
clippings. A photo of Q.C. stared up at me, eyes wide, her blond
hair in pigtails. Her cheeks looked particularly cherubic as she
smiled at the camera. I'd grown up with photos of her all
around me, but I didn't remember this particular one.

"It was taken right before the party. You can't tell, but it's a
pink dress." Gram twisted her handkerchief around her hand.
"She was found wearing it."

I dropped the picture. No wonder my parents didn't hang that one anywhere.

The clippings shifted over time from pleas for everyone in town to keep a lookout to articles about the fruitless search dragging on. Several new reports described my parents as the lead suspects.

"At first we were grateful for the coverage," Gram said. "Hoped it would help find her. But then...." She trailed off and gestured to a newspaper photo of my dad snarling into the camera.

The new story beneath it reported that my dad swore at a television reporter. Which told me a lot. I almost never hear my parents swear. But sticking a microphone in your face and asking if you'd killed your daughter and where the body was would do that to a person.

An article toward the bottom of the stack covered the day a construction worker unearthed Q.C.'s body along with another little girl's. The state was widening a highway and rerouting part of it through the edge of a wooded area to accommodate more traffic. The second girl had been buried more recently. She wore the dress she'd been taken in, too, and her hair was blond and in pig tails. But her parents said they never styled her hair that way. Also, her hair was naturally light brown, not blond. The killer had bleached it into a yellowish, fake-looking copy of Q.C.'s.

Later articles said the medical examiner estimated Q.C. had been dead for at least a month before the second girl was taken.

"As if he was replacing Q.C.," I said. "Assuming it was a he."

Gram turned the article toward her. "I remember thinking that very thing at the time."

"When did they stop hounding Mom and Dad?"

"The local papers never did. Not until they moved here. And for a few years after that now and then a reporter called or knocked on our door. But the other body, the second girl, it was terrible. But also clear your parents had nothing to do with her, and the authorities stopped focusing on your parents. No one thought there were two separate killers." She pointed to a copy of a business card. "This is the local chief of police."

"Is he still around?"

"He was pretty new on the job. Around thirty. So he could be."

I did a few quick searches on my phone and found an article about his retirement. But no obituary. I felt sure I could find him through one of my subscription databases.

Gram looked at her watch. "Ten minutes to my train."

I put all the pages into the accordion folder and stowed it in my shoulder bag. "Do you have any ideas about who did it?"

Gram shook her head, put her purse over her shoulder, and stood. "A stranger, that's all. No one we knew could've done that."

42

———————

THE NEXT MORNING Tobias called me early from Kurt's office. Before anyone else arrived, he'd compared the keys Maria threw out to the ones on the University of Denver key ring. They were the same. Also, at my instructions, he'd scrolled through the display on Maria's desk phone. No calls to any criminal defense lawyers going out or coming in.

"All business related and junk calls," Tobias said.

He also told me that after throwing out the keys the day before, Maria had returned to the office, worked the rest of the afternoon, and gone home at her usual time. Tobias called her there later on her landline and she answered. He asked a question about the bookkeeping.

"She didn't seem upset or anything," Tobias said.

"Check the call log again tonight," I said.

Knowing Maria lied about having Kurt's house keys wasn't much. But it was something. Time to try E. Drake Draper.

I walked to his office without calling first. My paralegal's research had told me he needed to be at the Dirksen Federal Building for court at ten. I waited out of sight down the hall until he exited his suite at 9:35. My Response was saved on my laptop and ready to file this afternoon. But he didn't know that.

I stepped in front of him at the elevator bank. "I was just coming to see you. Talk for a minute?"

He reached around me and pressed the Down button. "For a minute. I'm on the way to court. Walk with me if you want."

"I'm hoping you'll give me an extra day for my Response. You're not filing a Reply, so how does it hurt?" I said as we stepped into the elevator.

He shook his head. "I need your Response by the end of the day to get ready for the hearing."

I frowned. "Fine. You heard about Bryan's arrest?"

"Guess being in jail is as good a reason as any to miss a meeting," E. Drake said.

"Do you think he killed Kurt?"

"He was mad at Kurt a lot. Or frustrated might be a better word."

We paused in the lobby to put on our hats and gloves. The scents of cinnamon, brown sugar, and coffee beans from the adjoining coffee bar filled the air.

"Why was Bryan frustrated?" I said.

"Kurt rarely let him do much in court."

"Isn't that your place to shine?" I said as we left through the revolving door.

"There's room for more than one," E. Drake said.

As we crossed Adams Street, a bike sped around the corner, nearly running into E. Drake. The rider wove around at the last second. I shivered just watching him. Though sunny, the wind from the north chilled all my exposed skin.

"I was thinking maybe Bryan figured he'd get to run the whole firm with Kurt out of the way," I said.

"If he looked closely at his partnership agreement, I doubt he thought that."

If E. Drake killed Kurt, I thought he might jump at the

chance to pin the blame on Bryan. But he wasn't exactly taking the bait.

We paused outside the courthouse. "You're probably right," I said. "Anyway, Bryan told me they opted not to charge him. Something about DNA ruling him out."

The wind blew my hair into my face. The ends stung my cheeks. I tucked them under my coat collar.

"DNA?" E. Drake said.

"Yes. On some sort of animal hair. White animal hair."

I studied E. Drake's expression, but it didn't change.

"Animal hair? Wonders never cease." He glanced at his phone. "Time to get inside. Good luck."

"With the murder?"

"With defending my motion next week. See you at the hearing."

I texted Ty, who was already sitting inside on a bench near the metal detectors pretending to wait for someone.

E. Drake on his way in.

I see him.

I hoped Ty could get close enough to overhear any calls E. Drake made.

———

AFTER I FILED the Response to E. Drake's motion, Joe and I drove together to Hyde Park. Joe had called Isabel Verde's office the day before pretending to be a new patient and asking about afternoon openings on her calendar. The receptionist helpfully told him Isabel was booked from two to five. He planned to work at the bookstore coffee shop across the street and keep an eye on her car in case my conversation with her prompted her to flee. She was the only one involved whom I knew had property in another country, and my research revealed that the authorities in Ecuador didn't always extradite people to the

U.S. That alone didn't make it more likely she killed Kurt. But if she did, she had the best means of escaping the consequences.

Joe dropped me off on 57th Street and Ellis. I walked four blocks in bright sunshine to the University of Chicago campus with its looming gothic buildings and expansive lawns. Isabel's private office was only half a mile away. In keeping with my plan to stay in public places, I'd suggested meeting in a large U of C building with plenty of open seating.

I got a blueberry flavored bottled water from a vending machine and sat at a round table in the center of the room. Ty texted that E. Drake, after a lengthy hearing, was meeting someone for lunch. I checked in with Tobias. He reported that he asked Maria for his dad's keys back. She returned the ones on his University of Denver keychain.

Isabel hurried in, her cheeks red from the cold, a sheaf of pages in her hand. She wore a gray pants suit with a navy turtleneck and carried her wool coat over one arm. She dropped in the chair across from me. "You said it was important. What happened?"

"The police arrested Bryan Stillwell."

She nodded. "Makes sense. I told Kurt he kept Bryan too much under his thumb. Bryan had over a decade of experience. It was time to step back, let Bryan take the lead more often. Second chair more hearings."

"Sounds like Kurt talked about his cases quite a bit with you."

"We talked about most things." She looked down at the table. "Other than his book. And Maria. I suppose it's more accurate to say we used to talk about most things. The last six months or so not so much. But Bryan – that was ongoing."

"When do you think Bryan became unhappy enough that you can see him doing something this drastic?"

"Around when he became a partner. He expected Kurt to

trust him more. Let him take on more. But the only thing Kurt did was hand over more of the business management."

I wondered if that was how Bryan justified inflating expenses. Maybe he decided if the money was all Kurt would let him handle, he might as well exploit it.

"Did Kurt ever tell you he regretted letting Bryan manage the firm finances? Or question Bryan's expenses?"

"No, never. Oh." She pressed one finger on the table. "Wait. Maybe that's what he meant."

"Kurt?"

"Yes." Her eyes turned upward, the way mine do when I'm on stage trying to recall the lyrics to a song. "He said something about a case, the one between him and that other firm, what's the name?"

"E. Drake Draper and Associates?"

"Yes. Kurt got mad when he was looking at some exhibits the Draper firm attached. He said Bryan did something wrong with the figures."

I scooted my chair closer to the table to let a group of students pass behind me. "Bryan, not the Draper firm?"

"Definitely Bryan. Because I was surprised. Usually, Kurt was so happy to have Bryan deal with the numbers."

"Did he say wrong as in Bryan mistyped the figures? Or wrong morally?"

"I took it as the first. But now that you asked about Bryan's expenses, I wonder. Because normally, if there was some sort of mistake, he told Bryan or Maria to fix it. But this time he said he needed to sort it out himself."

"And did he?" I said.

"No idea. He mentioned that the day before his party."

"Did you tell the police about that?"

"No. They didn't ask me much about Kurt's law firm or his work. Should I?"

"If you don't mind, I'd like a chance to ask Bryan about it first. Take him by surprise."

Isabel might be making up a story to throw suspicion onto Bryan, cleverly spinning based on my question. But if Kurt had confronted Bryan, it undercut my theory that Bryan had no reason to kill Kurt because doing so would be more apt to bring his embezzlement to light. And while he claimed to have an airtight alibi, I had only his word for that.

Isabel studied me. "Shouldn't I let the police know as soon as possible? Help build the case against Bryan."

"Except that's the other thing I came to tell you. There might not be a case," I said. "Bryan was set free almost as soon as he was arrested."

"You mean he's out on bail?"

"Yes, but Bryan told me DNA evidence will rule him out."

"Oh, no." She squared the papers in front of her. "I don't mean that. I don't want Bryan to be guilty. But I do want Kurt's killer, whoever it is, brought to justice. It's – it's worse somehow being in this limbo."

"According to Bryan, a white animal hair was found near Kurt's body. The thought is that it came from the killer and will have the killer's DNA on it. Also that the animal hair might be matched to an animal the killer owns or was near that day."

Isabel's eyes brightened. "So they'll have the killer in no time."

Nothing in her demeanor suggested worry or concern about herself or her recently-acquired white cat. But perhaps she had everything ready to flee the country.

"Maybe as soon as the DNA results are in." If there were DNA results, the police also would need someone to match them to. Which required DNA already on file, an arrest on other evidence that allowed police to take a suspect's DNA, or for the killer to volunteer for DNA testing. But I saw no reason to share that with Isabel.

"I hope that's soon. It won't bring Kurt back, but it might give Tobias some peace."

"What about you?" I said.

"I'm not sure I'll feel peace again," she said. The fluorescent lighting highlighted the dark circles under her eyes. "I knew before this that terrible things happen to people. I heard many of them from my clients. But somehow part of me still believed nothing that awful could happen to me or someone I loved. As if I were immune. But no one is, are they?"

"No," I said. "No one is."

43

———————

I TOOK the bus back downtown, watching the view of Lake Michigan, glassy blue and calm, out the window as we sped along DuSable Lake Shore Drive. My mind raced. Isabel struck me as the least likely suspect based on her demeanor, and E. Drake had little motive that I could see. Kurt's death seemed to do the most harm to Bryan, but Isabel's comments, if true, raised more questions about him. And he might have accepted my offer to help just to get me to focus on anyone other than him. I texted Lauren.

Up for a little reconnaissance?

Absolutely. Slow day today.

Early in the investigation, I'd pulled a lot of background information on the potential suspects. I'd sent Lauren Bryan's address yesterday. Now I texted his health club and the make, model, and license plate number for his car. I asked if she could figure out where he was now and keep an eye on him. Because she shows so many condos throughout the city, Lauren knows the ins and outs of most residential buildings and neigh-borhoods.

Twenty minutes later, back in my office, I called all three

273

named plaintiffs who belonged to the support group. I got voicemail for each and left the same message about who I was and that it was important they call me about their case. As I finished the last voicemail, Lauren called. She hadn't found Bryan, but she did have a great view of his condo.

"You're standing outside it?" I said.

"Better. I'm looking right into it from across the street. I searched all the listings for condos that have a view of his building. There's half a dozen. Then I figured out which ones actually face his windows and requested a showing for today. Only this one had an opening, and it's off at an angle. But Bryan's got floor-to-ceiling windows. With my binoculars, it's a perfect view of his bedroom and living room."

"When did you get binoculars?" I said. "Never mind. More important, are you going to get in trouble for this?"

"What? No. I've got a client in mind who will seriously love this place. I'll bring her over tomorrow night. Who knows, maybe she'll make an offer."

"And Bryan's blinds are open?"

"You'd be surprised how many people leave them open all the time. These condos are all small. Big windows are the only thing that gives them any sense of space."

She'd named the exact reason I bought in my neighborhood, which features a lot of old printing factories and paper warehouses converted into lofts. They have old building problems – mine was built in 1910 – but also open floor plans and lots of space. Six hundred square foot boxes didn't appeal to me.

"But he's not home?" I said.

"Nope. Not at his health club, either. I wheedled that out of the desk clerk. But I'll keep an eye out."

"I'm sorry if this is keeping you from other work."

"I can work remotely and keep watch, Quille," she said. "I'm an excellent multi-tasker. Though I can only stay until the owners get home, which is supposedly tonight at seven. Ish."

"Got it. Thank you. Let me know if Bryan shows up. I'm about to text him."

"You know I will."

I texted Bryan to tell him I'd gotten no reaction to my fake DNA evidence from anyone. I added that I'd keep trying, but that Isabel told me something that moved him up on the suspect list.

No response.

———

THIRTY MINUTES later I got an email from Ty. He said E. Drake seemed in command throughout the court hearing, which Ty watched. Ty got near enough in the hallway before and after to overhear E. Drake's phone calls. He'd even finagled his way into a booth behind E. Drake's in the restaurant. But E. Drake didn't say anything suspicious or sound worried about anything. After lunch, he headed back to his office.

I called Ty to thank him.

"I'm just leaving the building," he said. "Got a few calls to make at my office, but if you want me to hang around, see if I spot E. Drake heading anywhere, I can."

"No," I said. "He could leave out a different exit and you'd never know it. Plus he's got key court dates coming up, including my hearing and a five million dollar settlement, so I didn't expect him to leave the country the second I mentioned DNA evidence. I was more interested in how he reacted."

"Or didn't," Ty said.

"Right." I spun my office chair to one side and then the other. Files were stacked everywhere, reminding me uncomfortably of Kurt's office. But at least mine smelled of the vanilla candle on my window ledge, not dust and paper. "So far the only one who reacted at all is Maria when she got rid of the keys. But she's least likely to have the means to take off to evade prosecution."

"I could keep tabs on her," he said. "Drop by the firm, see if she'll talk to me. I hear I can be charming."

I laughed. "I hear that, too. But you've got your own work, and Tobias is at the firm. I'll check in with him toward the end of the day."

Lauren called me five minutes later. " Bryan's planning a trip. Looks like a long one."

44

"WHAT? HOW DO YOU KNOW?" I said.

"He's packing. Three large bags and a carryon. Oh, and seriously? I've never seen a guy pack so many shoes."

I rocked my chair forward and back. Someone out on bail can only leave the state with court permission, but if Bryan planned to flee to avoid conviction that wouldn't matter to him. It wasn't as if anyone was posted at state lines to stop him. I was less sure about leaving the country. No Fly lists include terrorist suspects. But I had no idea if they included anyone with pending charges.

I sent a quick text to Danielle to ask.

"How many exits to his condo building are there?" I said to Lauren.

"Two. Well, three with the parking garage, but the overhead doors are right next to the main entrance."

"Where's your car?"

"In our garage."

My desk phone rang as I shoved my iPad into my shoulder bag and groped inside it for my keys. I have one for Lauren's

Volvo on my key ring. The Caller ID showed an unfamiliar number. I let it go to voicemail.

"Once you see Bryan leave his place," I said, "go down to the street and watch the main exit and garage. I'll get your car and head your way. If we need to, I'll circle the block until he leaves."

"What if he gets on the L?" Lauren said.

My phone buzzed with a text from Danielle.

Wouldn't be on no fly list. Judge might have made him turn in passport.

"We'll park your car and follow," I said.

"You're paying the parking garage. Or the ticket."

Either would cost fifty dollars or more.

"Tobias is," I said.

I REMEMBERED the voicemail as I was unlocking Lauren's car. It turned out to be from Freya Watson, one of the plaintiffs I'd left a message for.

Lauren's car has Hands Free but I still don't like talking while driving. It's distracting, and I don't drive nearly often enough downtown to feel sure I'll avoid the cabs, pedestrians, and bicycles that dart out of nowhere. Or that I'll correctly navigate disappearing lanes or two-way streets that suddenly become one-ways.

Two blocks from Bryan's building I found a semi-legal spot. The nose of the Volvo ran afoul of the yellow paint line on the curb showing I was too close to the corner. But I liked being at the front of a line of cars. No maneuvering out of a tight spot needed.

After checking in with Lauren, who said Bryan was filling his last travel bag with polo shirts, I called the plaintiff, Freya, back. After apologizing in advance in case I had to cut the call short, I explained again who I was.

"I thought Mr. Draper was handling what's left of the case from now on," Freya said. "You're stepping in?"

"No. Just helping Kurt's firm through the transition, so I'm calling a number of clients about their cases. For yours, I need to know if Kurt told any of the other lawyers that you met him in the alien abduction experiencer support group."

I heard an intake of breath. "Who told you?"

"His son, Tobias, told me Kurt attended the group."

"What? And he knew my name?"

"No, no. His son doesn't know about you or the other plaintiffs. But part of my job is to go through all of Kurt's things. I was surprised when I learned you and the other two plaintiffs belong to the group. I know most members want to stay anonymous. So why would Kurt ask you to be plaintiffs?"

My other line beeped. I checked in case it was Lauren, but it was Ty. I declined and sent an automatic message that I'd call him back.

"He didn't ask us," Freya said. "I asked him. I feel so strongly about eating vegan. It's part of what I learned from the aliens, why we need to care for the planet. Preserve all our species. And it's so hard to find more than a couple restaurant options, and then the ones that claim to be vegan trick you. It's terrible."

I glanced at my notes on the iPad.

"You gave a deposition in the case, but I couldn't open the transcript file. Did the defense attorney ask how you knew Kurt?"

All the depositions had been taken over three years ago, and all were password protected. I was sure the firm must have copies somewhere but I hadn't found them.

"Oh, yes, yes he did. I said I met Kurt at the home of our mutual friend, an orthodontist, which was true."

"Art Feffor?"

"Right. Art."

Art was a dentist, not an orthodontist, but close enough.

"No follow up questions?"

I checked the side view mirror. A police car drove past, but didn't slow near me.

"He asked how long I knew Kurt. That kind of thing. Nothing where I needed to talk about the group. It went just like Kurt promised it would."

I didn't know how Kurt could promise that. But if he had enough cases with the same defense attorneys, he must have bet on them following a set outline of questions.

"So none of the attorneys know how you met Kurt?" I said.

"Well, his partner does."

"Really? You told him?"

"No, but turns out he knows. Which makes me so mad. Kurt promised me no one – no one – would know. And I can't give him a piece of my mind because there was that break-in and he got killed and how mad can I be at him? But I still am. Mad."

Her words raised so many questions I didn't know where to start. So of course that's when Lauren called.

45

I APOLOGIZED, promised to call back in a few minutes, and clicked over.

"Bryan pulled out of the parking garage. You still at the same spot?" Lauren said. Cars honking and the roaring of a truck came through the phone.

"Yes."

"Stay. I'm crossing the street in front of him now. He's turning left. He'll have to pass right by you."

She hung up. I got out and switched to the passenger side, keeping an eye on the intersection. Two seconds later a dark gray BMW sedan that looked like Bryan's drove past. After another moment, Lauren appeared, jogging. She was wearing flats for once. She darted into the car, which I'd left running.

"That was him." She shifted into Drive, pulled forward, and turned right on the red light to follow the route Bryan had taken. She nearly got us hit by a Honda Accord. The driver laid on the horn.

My heart hammered, but Lauren ignored it, eyes on the road. "He's not that far ahead. Looks like he's heading for the Kennedy. O'Hare?"

"Possible," I said.

The Kennedy expressway is the most direct route to O'Hare Airport from Chicago's River North neighborhood, though not necessarily the fastest depending on traffic. Today it was pretty bad.

Once we'd followed Bryan onto the Kennedy I called Freya back.

"When did you find out about Kurt's death?" I said.

"Uh, hmm. The weekend. Sunday. I remember because my husband was at church."

"Kurt was killed late on a Friday night or early Saturday morning. So you heard a little over a week after?"

"No, no. Right after. It had just happened."

"You're sure?"

Bryan had told me he hadn't contacted the clients. But maybe he meant he hadn't called everyone yet.

"Yes, I'm sure."

My iPad slid across my lap as Lauren made a quick lane change. I grabbed it with my free hand. "And Kurt's partner told you Kurt was killed during a break in?"

"Wasn't he?"

"Doesn't look like it. But Bryan might not have known that yet. Maybe he assumed."

"Bryan? That's his name?"

"That's Kurt's partner. Is that who called you?" I said.

"I guess it must have been. But it doesn't sound right. I don't think – it wasn't a B name I don't think."

I thought about what Calista had told me, and what I'd seen myself, of how little the plaintiffs knew about the cases. It probably wouldn't matter to them which firm the lawyers were with.

"Do you mean Mr. Draper called you?" I said. "E. Drake Draper?"

"Right, that's it. The initial. I remember that."

"What did he say to you exactly?"

It was possible E. Drake referred to a break in so the plaintiff would focus on the case, not on the idea of murder. Disturbing as it is, crime fascinates a lot of people. He might have wanted to keep Freya and the other plaintiffs, assuming he called them too, on track.

"Exactly? I'm not sure. But he said someone got into Kurt's house and Kurt was killed. And that he'd be handling the cases. He wanted to know, like you, if I told anyone that I knew Kurt from the support group. I told him no, and he said that was good and make sure I didn't because it could blow up the whole thing."

Lauren tapped my arm and gestured. Bryan's car had shifted into an Exit Only lane. I nodded to her to keep following him.

"Did he explain what that meant?" I said.

"Sort of. He said the judge might not be okay with the settlement. That I probably couldn't be a plaintiff anymore or he couldn't be the lawyer. I'm not sure which. But I got the idea someone else would take over the case and maybe nothing would change and none of us would get paid."

"Nothing would change meaning what?"

"The defendant wouldn't have to change their practices. I mean, they already changed some things. But they could change them back because they wouldn't have to follow the settlement anymore."

"Was E. Drake angry about any of that?"

"He wasn't happy," Freya said. "But mostly he said it was important not to say anything to anyone, and he wasn't sure if Kurt made that clear."

"Did he say how he found out?"

"Like you did. He was going through the case files after Kurt's death to make sure everything was okay. Which is why I'm mad, though I feel like I shouldn't be because Kurt's dead. But he promised there'd be nothing to connect us and obviously there was. And my husband's very upset about this. He's afraid after the hearing it'll all come out and be reported in the news or something."

But Kurt had kept his promise. No records I saw listed how he knew Freya or the other plaintiffs. Yet someone had told E. Drake. I was betting that someone was Kurt.

Concerned as I was about Bryan, who'd been able to put his hands on a million dollars so quickly, E. Drake was in a far better position to leave the country. Flush with cash from a recent settlement and he'd been practicing for decades. And hadn't Calista said something about plaintiff's class action attorneys being the ones who could afford private jets?

That might be the reason he was pushing our hearing forward. He wouldn't get paid right away if I filed an appeal, but the sooner the judge ruled the sooner E. Drake would know where he stood. A week later there was a hearing where he could be awarded five million dollars from Freya's case. That should keep him in town for a while, but five million might not be a lot of money to someone like him.

I hung up and told Lauren that maybe we ought to focus on E. Drake.

"But you said he didn't react to your pretend DNA evidence," Lauren said. "And that Ty told you the same."

"Ty – I forgot. He called."

I played his voicemail.

Hey, Quille. Just got an idea about E. Drake I want to run by you. Something I can talk to him about. Get a feel for him, how he's feeling after you dropped that info on him. You know, think I'll just head over to his office. Wish me luck.

I dialed Ty's number. It went direct to his voicemail. I scrolled through to the time of his call. "Over twenty minutes ago Ty said he was going to talk to E. Drake and now he's not answering his phone."

"Does he put it on Silent when he meets with people?"

"Usually. But I'm not liking what this client told me."

I texted Ty. *Got your VM. Tried calling. All OK? LMK.* I hoped the urgency came through. But not so much of it that E. Drake might wonder if he peered over Ty's shoulder.

"Which was?" Lauren said.

Gripping the phone in my lap, I filled Lauren in. As I talked, she stayed four cars behind Bryan. With the heavy traffic he couldn't drive very fast, and we were just one of many cars, making it easier to keep track of him without being noticed.

The phone hadn't vibrated or rung, but I opened the Recent Calls screen anyway to doublecheck. Nothing.

"Nothing's going to happen to Ty in E. Drake's office," Lauren said. "Didn't you say he shares a huge space with four or five firms?"

I nodded, but I dialed E. Drake's office line anyway. The receptionist must have stepped away. The call bounced to the firm voicemail. E. Drake's cell phone also went to voicemail.

"I don't think Bryan's going to O'Hare," Lauren said. "We're going too far north."

I looked up from the phone, which I'd been staring at as if I could make it ring. The area had become less populated.

I redialed Ty's number. The phone rang twice. Three times.

Lauren slowed the car. "We're going to start looking obvious."

"I bet he's going to his parents' house," I said. They lived in Lincolnwood, which was one suburb north. "And I'm more worried about Ty."

Ty's voicemail kicked in again.

"You're sure?" Lauren said.

"No. But the worst that happens if Bryan runs is he's gone.

But if E. Drake's the killer and Ty's alone with him somewhere–"

"Got it." Lauren pulled a U-Turn. Five minutes later we were back on the expressway.

———

THE RECEPTIONIST DESK behind the glass double doors stood empty. But when I hit the buzzer, E. Drake's assistant appeared. Today he wore red-framed glasses rather than black.

"Oh, hey, Quille. Crazy day today. Receptionist is out. Can I help you?"

"I was hoping to see E. Drake."

"Just missed him. Want to leave a message?"

At least he'd been here recently.

"No. Thank you. But can you tell me – my friend Ty stopped up to see him and I'm having trouble reaching him. I'm wondering if he left with E. Drake."

"Someone was with him. A tall, uh, dark-haired man, in a sport coat."

The assistant was white. I guessed he felt self-conscious about describing Ty by pinpointing how he was different. I'd noticed the more homogenous a firm or company was the more everyone there wanted to pretend they didn't notice differences of race or ethnicity.

"Tall good-looking Black man?" I said.

"Yep. Probably him. He's a broker?"

"Yes, why?"

"They were talking about a West Loop development. Something about a rehab and less expensive office space."

"Were they going to see it?" I said.

I could imagine Ty thinking that was a perfect way to spend a long time talking to E. Drake. But I didn't know why he wouldn't answer his phone or return my texts if that's all it was.

The assistant shrugged. "Could've been."

"Is your lease here up soon?" Lauren said.

"Uh...two years? I think two years."

We thanked him. Outside the suite's doors, Lauren gripped my arm as I hit redial for Ty's number.

"I bet I know what Ty was talking about. And it's not one of those shiny new buildings busy with tenants."

Ty's voicemail came on again.

"How could you know that?" I said.

"Well, first, obviously, if they're filled with tenants they're already done, not rehabbing. Ty's brokerage handles warehouse to office conversions. E. Drake can get a good deal if he signs on now for two years down the road when it's all done. It's one of the sagging old buildings in the West Loop that's set to be rehabbed. Got to be. Where you swear you haven't seen a soul in miles."

"Quille?" The assistant pushed through the doors, holding out an iPhone. "Found this on the floor in E. Drake's office. Under the desk. Maybe it's your friend's?"

I hit redial. The phone vibrated.

"He must've dropped it and it got kicked under," the assistant said.

Or someone purposely kicked it under.

He handed it to me.

"Thank you," I said, straining to keep my voice even as I thought about multi-million-dollar fees and private jets. "You know, I do need to talk to E. Drake about the fee lawsuit. Can I get an appointment with him tomorrow?"

"He's pretty booked. He's heading out of town for a long trip three weeks from now and it's crazy until then. I can try to fit you in Friday."

I squeezed Ty's phone. "Great. Any time."

"I'll text you."

"Thanks again for your help," I said.

We hurried down the hall to the elevator.

"What's the deal with three weeks?" Lauren said. "You looked worried."

"E. Drake's expecting five million dollars more from another settlement. And that long trip might be one way." I hit the elevator button. "How many of these developments are there?"

46

"HE'S GOT no reason to hurt Ty, right?" Lauren popped her credit card into the parking machine to pay the thirty dollars for our half hour of parking.

"None I can think of," I said.

"Maybe they just walked out together."

"I don't buy that Ty left his phone behind by accident. No way he wouldn't notice it was missing." I blinked and put on my sunglasses as the Volvo drove up the ramp and emerged into the bright, sunny day.

"If he was talking away when they left, he might not," Lauren said.

"Or E. Drake convinced him he lost it somewhere else and hurried him out," I said.

It was too late, but I wished I'd thought to go down to the coffee shop and ask if two men came by looking for a lost phone.

Lauren took Michigan to Madison and headed west. "Ty probably convinced him to look at the space to see if he could get information out of him while sowing the seeds for a future sale. If, you know, E. Drake's not a murderer."

"But he knows he might be. Why would Ty take a chance like that?"

"Have you not been listening to him? He's still kicking himself over not being there for you at the end of the Santiago investigation. We all are. Me, Joe, Ty. You could have died, and it would have been our fault."

I stared at my friend. "What? No. Not your fault. I choose to do these investigations. And you're not the ones who tried to kill me."

"But each of us said we'd be your back up. I literally still wake up at night and think about what could have happened. Believe me, none of us are ever taking that chance again."

She had both hands firmly on the wheel. I squeezed her shoulder. "I appreciate that. But it's okay. Really."

Lauren cleared her throat, then took a breath so deep her shoulders rose and fell. "It's not. But let's focus on now. The two most likely buildings are only three blocks apart."

The light turned green, but the sedan in front of us didn't move. Lauren laid on the horn.

I dialed Beckwell's number and put him on speaker. When he answered he said, "Make it fast. At a crime scene."

I gave him the shortest version possible.

"Any chance of police help?" I said.

"It's not an easy sell. Your boyfriend's showing a building, but you're not sure which one, to a lawyer you think is a possible murderer. But who's not the man the police just arrested for that same murder."

"You have made mistakes. Not you personally. The police."

"We have. Also me personally. And I trust your instincts. But I'm telling you how it will sound to a 911 dispatcher."

We were now several blocks past the United Center. Trendy restaurants and glass and steel corporate centers gave way to low-rise brick warehouses and cracked asphalt.

"There must be something you can do," I said.

"Text me the addresses Lauren thinks are possibilities. I'll see if anyone I know is in the area. Or can make themselves be in the area. But you see something really wrong – 911."

By the time I texted the addresses, Lauren had turned off Madison Street and headed north. "You think he'll be able to send someone?"

"Not counting on it. Whole department's short staffed."

There had been double the yearly number of retirements in the Chicago police department over the last year, and a drop off in applicants. Working in Chicago is more dangerous and pays less than quite a few nearby suburbs. Plus the police are convinced the current mayor is against them.

Lauren slowed. I saw no pedestrians. All the same, cars and SUVs were parked on both sides of the road. Unlike downtown, though, there were empty spaces. I scanned the vehicles, looking for a silver Mercedes SUV with E DRAPER on the license plate. Thank God for vanity plates and E. Drake's penchant for advertising.

"There." It stood in the middle of a row of cars on the east side of the street.

Lauren groaned. "Great. Exactly in between the two build-ings. What do we do? Split up?"

"Too risky. Exactly in between?" I said.

"Just about."

To the west, there were fewer parked cars. To the east there were more. If he were heading to the building farther west there was no reason E. Drake would have parked in this block.

"Back the way we came."

The road was too narrow for a U-turn. Lauren drove to the intersection, which was deserted, and did one there, then stepped on the gas. Two blocks later she screeched into a parking spot across the street from a barricade. The road beyond it was all gravel and gaping holes.

Lauren pointed. "End of the block. With the scaffolding."

We ran on the narrow stretch of sidewalk on one side of the broken street.

My ex-police academy trainer's insistence on including jogging and some sprints in my workouts paid off. I outpaced Lauren, slowing only when I reached the scaffolding. The building had heavy glass double doors, large windows, a few of which were cracked, and quite a few crumbling bricks. The front doors were locked. There was no buzzer or intercom.

Toward the west corner a second-floor window was broken out. I was already climbing up the ladder-like bars on the side of the scaffolding by the time Lauren reached me.

The soles of my low-heeled boots gripped the metal bars well enough, but the structure shuddered as I climbed. Lauren grabbed it to steady it.

I pressed my hand against the building as I crossed the wooden platform.

"Careful," Lauren said.

After I tossed my crossbody bag through the open window, I gripped the window sill with both gloved hands, pushed off my feet, and swung my legs sideways and over as if going over a vaulting horse. I stumbled and pitched forward when I landed. My hands smacked the floor. They stung even through my gloves, reminding me there was concrete under the cracked tile. The air tasted gritty with dirt. But I didn't see any broken glass or concrete chunks.

I motioned out the window to Lauren that I'd let her in the front. As I ran down a flight of stairs, I listened hard for voices but heard none. I hoped we hadn't chosen the wrong building.

The unfinished lobby featured off-white worn tile. Scuff marks marred the bottom third of the grayish-green walls. I eased the left front door open but still it creaked. Lauren stepped in, typing into her phone as she did.

"Where would they be?" I said, keeping my voice low.

Lauren glanced up from the phone and around the lobby

area as if it would give her a clue. "I don't show this type of property. But Ty would want him to see whatever he'd like best for office space. What's his current suite look like?"

"Not like this. Floor to ceiling glass. View of Lake Michigan. Modern."

"Is his office big? Crowded? Cozy?"

"Not cozy. Or crowded. Good size. Sparsely furnished."

Lauren scrolled pages of dense type on her phone. "Probably one of the upper floors then. Lower are going to be chopped into smaller offices. Also upper are pricier. I always start with the most expensive, work my way down."

Lights on the two elevators showed they worked, but I wasn't about to get in either in a building this old. I took the concrete stairs two at a time. By the fifth floor, Lauren's breath was ragged. We stopped and listened on each landing. By the eighth, my thighs burned. There were ten floors. But I thought I heard voices on this one.

Lauren was a flight down. I motioned her to stop and she did. I pressed my ear to the heavy door to the hallway and held my breath. Definitely voices. I inched the door open and peered through the crack.

There were no dividing walls. Only wooden studs, concrete pillars, and the outer brick walls. Debris piled in the corners. The double elevator bank took up the center of the floor. Ty and E. Drake stood about forty feet from me looking toward the east windows, several paces apart.

"Construction won't start for how long?" E. Drake asked.

Ty shifted to look more directly at E. Drake rather than out the windows. "Between weather and financing, late March at the earliest."

I pushed the door open a little more. Lauren must have taken off her shoes because I didn't hear her until she was right behind me. She leaned close, her breath on my neck.

"So why the construction scaffolding?" E. Drake said.

I clicked the record function on my phone and signaled Lauren to stay out of sight. Someone needed to call the police if things went bad. For now, I meant to stay out of sight. If there was no danger, I didn't want E. Drake to know I worried so much about him being alone with Ty that I followed them here.

"City requirement," Ty said. "Façade's in bad shape. Can't risk falling bricks hitting anyone below."

"Many people coming to see this?"

"There will be, but probably not until after the holidays," Ty said.

"Good to know." E. Drake nodded and glanced at his watch. "I'm heading out of town tonight, but I can talk to you when I'm back."

"Fantastic. I'll get in touch next week."

"No, I'll contact you. I'm not sure how long I'll be gone."

"Don't you have a hearing with Quille coming up? You'll be back for that."

"Oh, right. Yes." E. Drake shifted from one foot to the other. "Quille. She's quite impressive. Must impress the police, too, the way they share information with her."

Ty smiled. "Oh, yeah. She's good friends with a detective sergeant. Gives her an inside line."

No no no no. I held my breath. It was one thing to bait E. Drake in public and follow him from afar. Another to tweak him alone in a deserted warehouse. I put all my weight on my front foot, ready to charge if I needed to.

"And if she calls him, he acts quickly on what she tells him?"

"Oh, yeah," Ty said. "He really trusts her."

"That's unfortunate." E. Drake glanced away as he spoke, almost as if talking to himself, and his hand rose to his hip. "For you."

Ty's head cocked to one side. "What?"

E. Drake's hand darted under his sport coat. I shoved the door open. "Ty. Down."

E. Drake pulled a gun, and Ty froze. I ran toward them, yelling again. E. Drake's head twisted my way as his mouth dropped open. He didn't turn his body, so he looked almost comically contorted, but the gun stayed trained on Ty.

Ty dove toward E. Drake's feet. Instinctively, E. Drake stepped back. But then he spun and fired at me. The sound boomed through the open space, making me squeal in fear. I kept moving, veering behind a concrete pillar. I had no idea where the bullet went.

Lauren raced out of the stairwell. As E. Drake rotated toward her, she ducked behind a pillar opposite me and yelled the building address at the top of her lungs into her phone. I had no idea if she'd called 911 or just wanted to give the impression she had. I ran for E. Drake as Lauren kept hollering. "Old white man. Old white man shooting at young Black man and two women. Old white man has the gun."

I felt grateful for her quick thinking. We couldn't afford the police misinterpreting the scene.

Ty, on his hands and knees, lunged and grabbed E. Drake's legs from the side. I slammed into E. Drake's upper body from behind. He screamed as his entire body twisted in different directions. The gun flew from his hands, hit the floor, and skidded toward Lauren. She kicked it farther away and dove on top of us like a football player piling on, her body flat over the three of us.

For what felt like forever E. Drake groaned in pain and I held my position, arms out, hands on the floor, body half over E. Drake, half under Ty, and crushed beneath Lauren, barely able to breathe. At last, sirens sounded nearby. A few minutes later the stairwell door burst open. A young LatinX woman and an older Black man, both in blue police uniforms, burst in.

47

LAUREN and I were bruised but could walk and move our limbs and speak clearly. E. Drake could barely stand. Paramedics took him down the elevator on a stretcher. Ty's wrist and ankle were injured. The paramedics ignored him when he insisted he was fine and whisked him away, too.

After answering the male officer's questions, and then Beckwell's when he got to the scene, Lauren and I drove to the emergency room. Ty was in an emergency room bay, his wrist splinted and his ankle bandaged.

"Lucky it was a quiet day." He waved toward the door to the waiting area. He spoke more slowly than usual because of the pain meds. "If it weren't, my injuries are so minor I might still be out there."

"Uh-huh," I said, breathing in the smells of alcohol and peroxide.

Monitors beeping in the bay next to us and an intern in scrubs rushing past reminded me this could have been so much worse.

"I think the paramedics bringing you in might make you a priority," Lauren said.

I dropped my crossbody bag on a chair and stood in front of Ty, hands on my hips. "What were you thinking?"

"Uh-oh." Lauren sank into the other hard vinyl chair against the wall.

"That I could help you," Ty said.

"By almost getting yourself killed?"

Ty ran his good hand through his hair. "By getting him to talk. Figured if he didn't do it, he still might share something, some sort of clue. Something he didn't know he knew that might come out if he was thinking about something else, like his lease or the building."

"And if he did do it, you'd be in a deserted spot with no one around."

"Seriously. Not smart," Lauren said.

Ty glanced at her. "He's a guy. Old guy. Older. Out of shape. I wasn't worried."

"Because everyone knows you've got to be in great shape to pull a trigger," I said.

"Didn't think he had a gun on him. Who carries a gun to work in a law firm?"

"A criminal. A killer. Someone determined to get out of the country before he gets arrested," I said.

"I wasn't thinking, all right?" Ty said. "Wasn't. Thinking. Except that I wanted to make up for last time. You get people to talk. And it's kind of my job. Relating to people. Talking. So why couldn't I do it?"

"You entertain people for your job." I took a few steps back and forth between him and Lauren's chair. "I get information from them. Those are different kinds of talking."

"Obviously." He let his body fall back against the raised gurney. "Sorry. Really. Stupid."

I took a breath, stopped at Ty's side, and took his hand. "I'm sorry, too. I shouldn't have yelled. I just – you just – I was scared. Any idea why he suddenly started asking about me and the police?"

Ty frowned. "Besides you telling him about DNA on an animal hair?"

"If the fake animal hair evidence worried him," Lauren said, "he'd be infinitely more likely to quietly flee the country. Not take a ride to a warehouse with you to kill you."

"Huh. Oh." Ty blinked a few times. "In his office. He said it was odd Tobias trusted a woman business lawyer to look into murder. That if it was his dad, he'd hire a professional investigator."

"And what did you say?" I said.

He shut his eyes. "Ah. I'm an idiot. Let him piss me off. Said you were a professional. That you solved four murders in the last two years."

"Which made him think Quille's a major threat," Lauren said.

"He must have guessed I had some experience before," I said, "or why would Tobias hire me?"

On the other hand, it was far from the first time an older male lawyer looked at me and assumed I knew nothing. Sometimes being underestimated was an advantage. Other times, apparently, it nearly got your boyfriend killed.

"Oh, and he said he didn't see why anyone committed murders. And I said you told me love, sex, or money. And joked that as long as he didn't just get a lot of money, he was good."

"But he absolutely just got a lot of money." Lauren glanced at me. "That settlement Maria told you about?"

I nodded.

"Didn't know," Ty said. "I was trying to lower the tension. And that's when he sent off a few texts and agreed to go see the office space. Before that he told me he had too much to do that day."

"So you asked him to go there because you wanted to get

information from him, and he must have accepted to get more info from you," I said. "Then he panicked when he slipped and told you he was leaving town tonight."

"But why try to question Ty?" Lauren said. "Why not just leave the country?"

"E. Drake had more money coming soon," I said. "He was probably trying to see if he needed to leave right now or could risk waiting another three weeks. Beckwell told me he owns a private jet. He arranged via text for a flight crew to be on standby tonight."

"And when I bragged about how close you were with Beckwell–" Ty said.

"He was convinced the animal hair evidence was real. And worried if he let you go, you'd get to me fast enough that the cops would be waiting for him at Midway."

"I'm sorry. I just wanted to help."

"Help?" I pressed my lips together and counted to five. Suddenly I had sympathy for all the times he and Joe reacted with anger when I got hurt. "What did you think happened to your phone? Didn't you wonder?"

"Thought I left it in the coffee shop. I called you from there earlier. But they didn't have it. Then I figured I dropped it on the way out or in the elevator. Didn't realize it might be at Drake's."

An Emergency Room nurse gave Ty a prescription and discharge instructions. Ten minutes later, Ty and I waited in the circle drive outside while Lauren went to get the car.

The temperature had dropped, turning a cool November day into one that threatened snow. I stuffed my hands into my pockets. Somewhere between the parking garage and the hospital, I'd lost my gloves. Probably when I got out of Lauren's car. I imagined them lying on the concrete floor until another car drove over them and flattened them.

But Ty, though he stood with all his weight on his uninjured side, looked more alert. Maybe the cold air was good for him.

"Tell me you won't do anything like this again," I said.

He put his arm around my shoulders. "I promise. But how mad you are now? How worried you were? Sound familiar?"

I sighed. "It's how you feel every time I talk to a witness or a suspect?"

"Yep. So can you keep that in mind next time you want me to be chill?"

I kissed his cheek, but carefully so as not to throw him off balance. "I will."

"We'll both be more careful next time," Ty said.

"Yes," I said, though I had been careful, and he hadn't.

48

———————

MARIA REFUSED to tell Tobias anything about Kurt's keys on the advice of her lawyer. She'd hired one this time. Beckwell told me there was no thought of charging her with murder, but I couldn't blame her for being cautious with her past experience.

"It's the second place she worked where there were embezzlement charges," her attorney told me. We sat in my office suite's conference room. "The prosecutor keeps questioning her. Nothing you found implicated her?"

He had a rather forgettable look. Medium height, brownish-blond hair, a face that was neither attractive nor off-putting. Danielle told me his trial record was good and he'd do solid work for Maria. Her opinion of E. Drake Draper's lawyer was much lower, which didn't bother me a bit.

"Nothing," I said. "But I turned the books over to a forensic accountant and I don't know what he found."

"My next meeting." He shook my hand and left. The door to the suite shut with a bang, as it always did, and the wattle on the tissue paper turkey on the door shook. Ty arrived fifteen minutes later to take me out for my birthday. He still wore his wrist splint, but his ankle had healed.

Given E. Drake's ability to flee, the judge refused to set a bond, so he'd be spending the winter holiday season in the Cook County Jail. Danielle told me that was rare, especially now that electronic monitoring was an option. His assets must be vast. So vast that no amount of cash bail was likely to keep him in the country.

Two weeks later, in mid-December, Bryan entered a plea deal. The forensic accountant said the total embezzled was just over $100,000. Not a small amount, but I couldn't imagine he thought it worth it now that he'd lost his law license and pled guilty to a felony.

But he didn't need to worry about murder charges. No one did, other than E. Drake. When the DNA results came in, they were less of a mess than anticipated. Kurt's cleaning service had cleaned his house and the coach house thoroughly the day of the party. Most of the DNA collected was from the main house and the downstairs of the coach house, not the loft where Kurt's body was found.

Bryan's DNA didn't appear there. The court excluded the gun found in his office because Tobias had no power to consent to the search. Bryan's girlfriend, now fairly certain she'd never need to testify, voluntarily came in and gave a statement. Along with statements from two bed and breakfast guests, and receipts from Bryan's visit there, he was in the clear.

No DNA from Maria or Isabel was found in the coach house loft. But E. Drake's was. The gun found in Bryan's file cabinet was wiped clean of prints and unregistered, so it couldn't be traced to E. Drake. But whether he was convicted of Kurt's murder or not, he'd attempted to kill Ty, Lauren, and me. His attorney made self defense rumblings, but Danielle felt reasonably sure between the two crimes he'd serve twelve to fourteen years in prison.

"Hopefully more," Beckwell said. He sipped a candy cane martini. Our office suite's receptionist made pitchers of them every year for our holiday party, which we held the week before Christmas. Behind Beckwell fat snowflakes, the first of the season, fell outside the windows.

All the tenants, and there were over a dozen, chipped in for the soda and alcohol and invited friends and business acquaintances. The landlord, an annoying but occasionally helpful red-headed attorney known as Mensa Sam, surprised us by popping for dinner this year. He ordered from Maggiano's, one of Chicago's best known Italian restaurants. Aluminum pans held classic tomato bruschetta, stuffed mushrooms, tossed salad, and Taylor Street baked ziti, a specialty.

"I've got more good news," Ty said. He was splint-free now, though still in physical therapy for his wrist.

Beckwell raised his eyebrows. "You recovered from your bout of–"

"Misplaced helpfulness," I said, before Beckwell could go on.

Ty grinned. "That and I sold my boat."

"That's not good news," Lauren said. She and Joe sat opposite us in a corner of the conference room, a plate of crescent shaped lemon cookies between them. "I love the boat."

"I love it too," Ty said. "But I don't love living in a tiny apartment so I can afford it. You'll like this part, though. We're not closing until February. And with the weather so warm this year it's just possible we can take a New Year's Eve cruise."

Average temperatures in November and December had been nearly twenty degrees above normal. Even today, the snowflakes were melting as they hit the streets and sidewalks.

Lauren clapped her hands. "Seriously? And watch the fireworks from the lake? I will love you forever."

"Hey," Joe said.

Lauren rolled her eyes. "Figure of speech."

"Just hope the lake doesn't freeze between now and then," Ty said.

Beckwell left a few minutes later. I walked him to the elevator bank. He hit the down button. "The police chief get in touch with you?"

I shook my head.

"Sorry. That's the latest email address I could find for him."

My efforts to trace the Edwardsville Chief of Police had gotten me nowhere. But Beckwell knew a detective sergeant in central Illinois who started his career in Belleville, a town about twenty-five miles from Edwardsville. He knew the Chief of Police, who he said was still living. Though he hadn't talked to him in some time, he'd passed on the last contact information he had.

The phone number, though, belonged to someone else, as did the house where the police chief had once lived. I hadn't gotten a bounce back message from my email, but I also hadn't gotten an answer. It might well be like the Yahoo address I used as a teenager. Still active but long ignored.

"Once the holidays are over, I'll see what else I can do," I said. "Mom and Dad are coming for Christmas. First time in forever. It's just as well we won't spend it talking about Q.C."

"Looks like Ty will have a boatload New Year's Eve." Beckwell stepped into the elevator. "Literally."

I laughed.

———

THE DAY after my office holiday party, Bryan pled guilty, agreed to restitution, and got probation. The remorse he expressed weighed in his favor. So did his ability to pay back the money, not only to the firm but to class members where those expenses came out of settlements. He was also on the hook for the costs to find and send small checks to each of those class members, something Calista Zopp told me could cost more than a hundred thousand dollars all on its own.

"I made a terrible mistake," Bryan said at his sentencing hearing, his voice quiet but clear, his head bowed slightly. "I believed I should be paid more. But I couldn't convince my partner of that. Or of the greater role I thought I was entitled to. I told myself I was only taking what I was owed. But that was wrong. I knew it then and I know it now. And I'll do my best to make up for it."

Maria's lawyer told me that right after sentencing Bryan signed up for courses in public speaking and coaching. He planned to speak to and advise lawyers and law firms on ethics, using his story as an example.

"Just shows you," Ty said as we walked out of the criminal court building. "No matter the crime, you can't keep a white man with lots of family money down."

"Scratch a felon find an inspirational coach," Lauren said.

At least Maria was in the clear. The evening of Bryan's plea, Tobias invited her and me for drinks at the Train Car. Gold and silver garlands draped the bar and tiny white lights twinkled around the windows.

Maria told us she'd been seeing Kurt closer to three months rather than three weeks, but he'd given her the keys long before that. She often watered his plants for him when he traveled. She'd been afraid with her past it would be used against her. Tobias promised to help her find a new job. With Kurt dead and Bryan a felon, there was no King and Stillwell to salvage. He was farming out the cases to other class action attorneys.

————

THE SKY WAS clear on New Year's Eve. The temperature soared to forty-nine with no wind.

"Perfect for boating. At least, for boating in winter," Ty said.

Following tradition, my niece and nephew took the train in to stay overnight with me. We played games until around nine, then all bundled in our coats. I carried hats, scarves, and gloves in a duffel bag in case it got windy, which it did around eleven when Ty anchored the boat. The city was shooting fireworks from Navy Pier starting in about half an hour. A few other boats whose owners had opted not to winterize yet gathered in the area.

Lauren had made dark hot chocolate – one thermos for my niece and nephew and the second, for the adults, laced with amaretto.

She and I sat on the bow of the boat. Ty stayed in the cockpit and Joe sat in the stern with the kids. They weren't kids anymore, they were teenagers, but I couldn't quite get used to that.

The boat felt chilly beneath my thighs despite my blue jeans and long coat. Lauren and I leaned close together as the first red sparks shot into the air.

"It's been a good year," she said. "Your mom's better, Joe and I got together, you and Ty seem stronger than ever. Hey, that almost rhymes. Must be the amaretto."

"And we didn't get shot. Also in the plus column." I linked my hand with hers. "Thanks for all the fast driving, fast talking, always-there-for-me help."

"You kidding? I loved it. I like being a real estate agent, but it's not a thrill a minute."

"In that case," I said, "You ought to be thanking me."

"Seriously, though," Lauren said. "You know I'm there for you. Including if you need help with the Q.C. investigation."

"I'll let you know," I said.

A canon boomed and green and red sparks formed into the shapes of bells against the night sky.

"Still nothing from that police chief?" Lauren said.

I didn't want to lie, but I also didn't want to spoil the night. Fortunately, three more booms in quick succession sent bursts of poppy red flowers with gold edges into the sky.

"Amazing," I said. The smell of sulfur filled the air.

"Gorgeous," Lauren said.

The email had come that afternoon, one so formal in tone it was clear it came from someone over sixty-five.

Dear Miss Davis,

My apologies for not responding sooner. I felt unsure whether I ought to. But after asking around about you (of friends of friends in Chicago), I'm told if I don't answer eventually you'll appear at my door anyway. Or you'll track down another investigator on the case. There were quite a few over the years, and surely somebody's still around. I'd rather you hear from me.

Based on your email, there's something important that I don't believe you know. And I'm sorry to have to tell you. But whatever your grandmother or anyone else says, it's not only that the case remains open and your parents were never conclusively cleared. They were – and still are – the main suspects.

In light of that, I don't know if you want to go forward. I personally believe no good can come of it. But if you're determined to look into this crime and you want to talk to me, I'll answer your questions as fully and honestly as I can. I can't promise my memory is perfect. But I'll do my best. My current phone number is below.

Yours,

Donald P. Highbottom

Ret. Chief of Police

Edwardsville, Illinois

Fireworks exploded over our heads as Lauren and I made

our way to the stern for the finale. She grabbed the plastic champagne glasses and filled them.

My niece threw her arms around my waist, "Happy New Year, Auntie Q!"

The fireworks started forming into numbers.

10, 9, 8.

"Thanks for taking us out," my nephew said to Ty.

7, 6, 5, 4.

"My pleasure," Ty said. He leaned close and whispered in my ear. "Happy New Year."

3, 2, 1.

Dozens of fireworks burst at once.

"To a wonderful new year," Joe said.

"And many successful investigations by Quille," Lauren said and drank down her champagne.

"To success," I said. But I didn't drink.

LOOKING FOR MORE QUILLE?

Read *No Good Plays*, a Q.C. Davis Mystery Novella. Find it at your favorite retailers.

Or download the ebook edition free by joining the author's Readers Group at LisaLilly.com/QuilleStories. You'll also get an enewsletter and notice of new releases.

ABOUT THE AUTHOR

In addition to the Q.C. Davis Mystery series, which includes *The Worried Man*, *The Charming Man*, *The Fractured Man*, *The Troubled Man*, *The Hidden Man*, and the novella *No Good Plays*, Lisa M. Lilly is also the author of the *Awakening* supernatural thriller series.

A resident of Chicago, Lilly is currently working on the next Q.C. Davis mystery. In addition, she hosts the podcast *Buffy and the Art of Story,* and her stories and poems have appeared in numerous publications.

Join Lisa M. Lilly's Reader's Group to receive *No Good Plays (A Q.C. Davis Mystery novella)*, short stories, an author e-newsletter, and updates on sales and new releases.

ALSO BY LISA M. LILLY

Q.C. Davis Mysteries

The Worried Man

The Charming Man

The Fractured Man

The Troubled Man

The Hidden Man

No Good Deeds (Short Story for Readers Group members)

No New Beginnings (Short Story for Readers Group members)

No Good Plays (A Q.C. Davis Mystery Novella)

The Awakening Series

The Awakening (Book 1)

The Unbelievers (Book 2)

The Conflagration (Book 3)

The Illumination (Book 4)

The Awakening Series Complete Supernatural Thriller Series Box Set/Omnibus

Other Fiction

When Darkness Falls (a standalone supernatural suspense novel)

The Tower Formerly Known As Sears And Two Other Tales Of Urban Horror

As L.M. Lilly:

Happiness, Anxiety, and Writing: Using Your Creativity To Live A Calmer, Happier Life

Super Simple Story Structure: A Quick Guide to Plotting and Writing Your Novel

Creating Compelling Characters From The Inside Out.

The One-Year Novelist: A Week-By-Week Guide To Writing Your Novel In One Year

How To Write A Novel, Grade 6-8

Write On: How To Overcome Writer's Block So You Can Write Your Novel

9 781950 061358